BURDENED WITH MORALITY

BOOK SIX OF THE CLOVIS ACADEMY LEGACY

ROSS HARRINGWAY

Omega Press
El Paso, TX

CLOVIS ACADEMY LEGACY:

BURDENED WITH MORALITY

OMEGA PRESS

An imprint of Omega Communications Group, Inc.

For information contact:

Omega Press
5823 N. Mesa, #839
El Paso, Texas 79912

FIRST EDITION

Printed in the United States of America

CHAPTER ONE

It was supposed to be a friendly competition between four prestigious military academies in which the cadets would attempt to capture their opponents by use of non-lethal force. But something had gone wrong and the cadets from three of the academies had unwittingly become the prey of the fourth. It was a long standing blood feud between members of the Gorski Gang from Clovis Academy against the powerful Rosenburg family.

The final conflict between them was about to end on the surface of the lunar body known as the Blood Moon. Unbeknownst to the cadets of Clovis Academy, Caine Rosenburg and his followers of cutthroats had already killed the judges of the tournament and the cadets from one of the four academies. Within moments, Cadet Yuri Gorski and his comrades would learn that they will be in the fight of their lives.

As Lomax was annihilating the Tyr cadets, Eamon O'Grady had his team from Clovis Academy assembled at the exit ramp of their Raumschiff. Mary Lincoln was landing the ship onto the surface about one hundred feet from their designated headquarters. None of them had heard or seen anything regarding the attacks on the Judge Towers. Mary Lincoln had cut the news reports so that her three view screens in the pilot command section could be used to see the lunar surface and the surrounding terrain. She slowly guided the Raumschiff to the surface and began to shut down the engines.

"Landing complete," Lincoln reported over the Raumschiff communication system.

"Okay, let's get a move out!" O'Grady ordered as their ship touched the ground. "Secure the HQ. Cardenas, you Doernitz, Zerbe and Andolini get the small fighter ships up and running."

Each of the ten cadets was wearing their enviro-suits. They had done their safety checks and all systems on their individual suits were operational. Their oxygen tanks were full and working properly. Julia Steiner and Drew Harrison had checked their enviro-suit communication functions and found them to be in working order.

The rear Raumschiff loading bay door opened and the exit ramp lowered to the surface. Yuri Gorski marveled at the green hue of the poisonous gas before him. He was honored to be the first to jump onto the surface. He did not hesitate and began running toward the doors of their headquarters. O'Grady was soon by his side.

The pilots, Cardenas, Zerbe, Doernitz and Marco, were walking toward the four purple Allen Corporation Fighter Type

CC76A3 ships to the west of the headquarters. Their duty was to get their ships airborne and keep a lookout for the cadets on the opposing teams and thwart any attempt at an ambush.

Harrison brought up the rear, following Steiner and Les Gillis. Harrison stopped and looked up at the two story safe house. There were windows on the upper level that were supposed to be one way viewing glass. Harrison believed that one of the larger windows was broken, which could not be so since the judges had inspected all of the cadet headquarters and cleared them for use. He blinked his eyes and shook his head as he thought he saw something moving inside the premises through the broken window.

"Eamon, Yuri!" Harrison said, speaking into the teardrop microphone inside his clear enviro-suit helmet. "I think I saw activity inside the building."

Gorski and O'Grady stopped in their tracks and inspected the front of the two floor building before them. To their mutual chagrin, Harrison's admonishment came too late. The front doors of the Clovis Headquarters flew open as if someone had kicked the doors down. Glass and metal flew from the entrance from the force of several of the Saharakaree breaking out. They landed on the patio of the headquarter building and then let out some high pitched cries. They saw the humans in their space suits in the distance. Gorski and O'Grady both cursed when they saw the aliens. Their long sharp pointed tails were waiving in the air, the black liquid venom was dripping from the points and they were slashing their sharp claws at the air and chlorine gas around them, expecting that there would be some prey to kill in their reach.

Unknown to the cadets, each of the aliens were being controlled by micro-chips in the base of their brains. They were responding to a single command that was being sent to them by David Rosenburg, lying on his bed in his safe location of his Raumschiff. David spoke into his holo-com device and gave the Saharakaree one order, which was to kill the ten Clovis Academy cadets.

These were the Saharakaree that had been planted by Dell Ragnarsson days earlier. Upon receiving the command from David Rosenburg, they leaped from the ground and into the air. With each jump, they would soar as high as fifteen feet high.

One of the Saharakaree landed on Gorski and rolled him to the ground. Gorski felt the Saharakaree pin his arms with its' legs. He saw the poison tipped tail of his adversary aiming at his face plate. He moved his head to the right and the razor sharp point of the tail narrowly missed, stabbing the lunar surface. Gorski wriggled one arm free and punched the Saharakaree in the face. The creature screamed and rolled off of him.

The other creatures were targeting the other team members, leaping at them.

"Saharakaree!" Julia Steiner yelled as she recognized the alien species.

Les Gillis had given her a few of the magnesium ribbons

he had prepared during their flight to the Blood Moon. Steiner ignited one of the ribbons and held it the face of a Saharakaree that was charging at her. The creature grabbed its' eyes and screamed as the bright light blinded the alien permanently. The Saharakaree were cave dwelling creatures and had a high sensitivity to lights. Steiner knew that their major weakness was bright lights and intense heat.

"Blind them!" Gillis was yelling to his team mates. "Use your lasers and fire into their eyes!"

Gillis had pulled out his leather pouch of magnesium ribbons just as a Saharakaree pounced on him. The deadly point of the alien tail slashed the shoulder strap of Gillis' leather pouch and his magnesium strips fell to the ground and bounced out of his reach. The Saharakaree ducked underneath Gillis swing of his left fist. The creature watched as Gillis was turned due to his missed punch. It jumped, wrapped its' arms around Gillis' torso, tearing his enviro-suit with its' sharp claws and forced Gillis face first onto the lunar surface.

Porfirio Cardenas heard over his headphones in his enviro-suit that their fellow cadets were under attack. The four cadet pilots were only a few feet away from their one man small space ships fighters.

"Jurgen, Pierre, Marco! Draw your lasers. We need to get back and help!"

The four men turned away from their space craft to run and assist their friends. Cardenas pulled out his hand laser from his enviro-suit utility belt as did Marco. Doernitz and Zerbe followed their example and drew their weapons.

"Did they say Saharakaree?" Zerbe asked with a nervous tone of voice. "They aren't indigenous to this solar system!"

"Yes, they did. How in the name of all that is holy did Saharakaree get on this moon?" Cardenas asked as he ran toward their Raumschiff

"The fact is that they are here!" Marco yelled as he heard the screams of their team mates over his helmet communication system.

Unseen by the cadet pilots, the four canopies of their small fighter ships began to raise open. Inside of each ship's cockpit was a Saharakaree, waiting to ambush them. Since the four humans turned away, the aliens determined that they would have the advantage of a sneak attack from behind. The four Saharakaree walked onto the front hood of each ship and leaped into the air. Zerbe thought he saw a shadow over his shoulder and turned his head back. He saw the four aliens descending upon them.

"Behind us!" Zerbe yelled and wildly fired his laser at the Saharakaree that was closest to him. He hit the creature in the chest with the stun blast. The creature cried out and landed harmlessly on top of Zerbe, unconscious. Zerbe pushed the alien off of him and rolled over on his side. He aimed his laser pistol at the next creature, trying to get an open shot at it.

The other three Saharakaree were able to land on or near

their targets. Marco grunted as a larger than average Saharakaree knocked him to the rocky lunar surface. Marco was able to hold onto his laser pistol and rolled with the fall. The creature was running on all fours, pursuing him. Marco was able to fire two shots from the prone position, both missing, as the creature closed the distance between them. Marco cursed himself and wished his brother were by his side. Dominic never missed when he fired. Marco was not as talented a marksman as his brother.

Doernitz was able to roll free of his opposing Saharakaree and fired his laser pistol three times at the alien, hitting it twice. The alien made a loud sound that caused Doernitz to wince. The Saharakaree collapsed onto the lunar surface. Doernitz turned and saw that Cardenas was in trouble. The fourth Saharakaree had Cardenas pinned down on his stomach. Doernitz could see the deadly tail waiving in the air, the sharp tip pointing at the prone Cardenas. Doernitz yelled and ran to his brother-in-law's aid. As the tail began to shoot downward, Doernitz grabbed it and pulled as hard as he could. The Saharakaree screeched in anger as Doernitz pulled it off of its' intended prey. The creature turned its' attention on Doernitz, making a hissing noise and charged at the young cadet.

Marco was tackled to the ground by his opponent. Marco wrapped his arms around the Saharakaree and used his body weight to hold the Saharakaree down. He used his right knee and trapped the tail of his competitor on the moon surface. The creature desperately clawed at Marco's uniform and tore it in several locations. Marco heard the hissing of escaping oxygen from his enviro-suit. The Italian cadet pilot placed the muzzled of his hand laser in the face of the Saharakaree and pulled the trigger. The laser beam blinded the alien and it cried out in pain. Marco quickly rolled off of it and looked to the others to determine if he needed to come to their aid.

Doernitz kept pulling on the last Saharakee's tail and was dodging the sharp claws of the alien as it slashed at him time and time again. The creature kept slashing its' claws at Doernitz until Zerbe was able to get a good aim.

"Let it go!" Zerbe yelled at Doernitz.

Doernitz let go of the tail and Zerbe fired his laser pistol. The Saharakaree made a piercing cry and went limp. The stun blast sent an energy current through the alien and knocked it out. For how long, Zerbe was unsure.

Cardenas was back up on his feet and judged the distance left between him and the others. "Let's go! We're needed!"

Marco followed behind the other three as his enviro-suit computer began cautioning him, "Warning, oxygen levels at fifty percent."

In the distance, the four cadets could see the peril that their team mates were in. Drew Harrison was dodging the tail of a Saharakaree. He was trying desperately to grab the tail each time it slashed at him. At one point, he was able to do so as he caught the tail in his left hand.

Harrison began rolling the large tail around his left arm,

similar to a man rolling up a water hose. The Saharakaree was showing its' displeasure by the tone of it's' voice and slashing at Harrison with its' upper claws. Harrison used his own body weight to twist the face of the alien to the surface. Harrison used his shoulder and drove it into the Saharakaree as they both fell, a move Harrison learned in a wrestling class.

He stood and placed both of his feet into the back of the Saharakaree. Harrison began pulling on the tail with both of his hands. He was grunting and straining his muscles to their limit. The Saharakaree screamed, pounding its arms and legs on the lunar surface as Harrison ripped its' tail from its body. The brown colored blood spattered all over Harrison's enviro-suit. Harrison threw the tail to the side and pounced on the alien. He then grasped it by the chin and skull with both of his hands. Harrison twisted the creatures head to the left. The Saharakaree cried and Harrison could hear the crunching of the alien's bones. The creature screamed one last time as Harrison ripped the head off of its' neck.

Steiner had dodged another of the aliens as it landed to her left. The creature made a cackling noise as it stood on its hind legs and towered over her. Steiner immediately stepped into the creature and kicked its legs out from under it with her left leg. The Saharakaree cried out in surprise as it fell backwards onto the lunar surface. Steiner had pulled out one of her six inch double bladed knives and pressed her advantage by jumping onto the chest of her attacker. She buried the knife into the abdominal area of the Saharakaree which was the location of the heart. The creature let out a pitiful cry as Steiner twisted the knife to the right and then upward, slicing through several vital organs. The Saharakaree spit out blood from its mouth and shuddered for a few seconds before it died. Steiner rolled off of the corpse and recovered her knife. She felt guilty about having to kill the alien.

Mary Lincoln had heard the screams of her team mates and could see the attacking Saharakaree on the pilot command view screens. She unbuckled her safety harness and leaped out of her pilot's seat, slid down the ladder and was running for the rear of the ship the second her boots hit the metal floor. As she ran, she pulled her laser pistol from her utility belt.

Gorski was rolling on the surface with the Saharakaree that had pounced on him. Gorski knew from his studies on the species that the tail was poisonous. He grabbed the tail as it swung at his torso. The tail lifted Gorski into the air, swinging him back and forth. Gorski held on to the tail for dear life, refusing to let go. The Saharakaree realized it would not shake Gorski so it decided to use a different tactic. Using the tail, the Saharakaree slammed Gorski back down onto the planet surface. Gorski struggled to hold onto the appendage of the alien. Gorski knew it gave him an advantage in the battle if he held it. The Saharakaree continued to lift Gorski in the air and slam him back to the ground. Each time Gorski was slammed onto the surface he felt the sting of pain in his arms and shoulders from the impact.

Gillis was still fighting his alien, rolling on the rocky surface as the creature slashed at him with its' sharp claws. Gillis was also moving evasively to avoid the strikes of the sharp tail by his opponent. Eamon O'Grady, seeing that a second Saharakaree was closing in on Gillis, charged to assist.

O'Grady called out to Gillis, "Les! There's another one coming at you!"

Gillis struggled on the surface with the first Saharakaree. He could see to his right that another was leaping toward him, its' tail extended for the kill. Gillis cursed. He could not avoid the new Saharakaree. He braced himself for the tail to stab into him.

Fortunately, O'Grady was there first. He slammed his body into the leaping alien and sent it veering off course. It missed Gillis by several feet. O'Grady ran at the prone alien. It rose to its' feet and jumped at him. O'Grady and the alien began grappling. They were soon rolling on the lunar surface. In the fight, O'Grady lost sight of the alien's tail. O'Grady felt a sharp pain in his left shoulder as the alien had been able to stab its' tail into him. The point of the tail had been sharp enough to rip through the light fabric and metal of the enviro-suit. O'Grady screamed in pain as the sharp tip went through his shoulder. The Saharakaree began making a joyous chirping noise to the others, signaling that one of the humans would soon be dead.

O'Grady screamed again as the alien pulled its' tail out of his torn shoulder. His blood was spilling out of his enviro-suit and onto the rocky covered moon. O'Grady could feel sharp pain all over the side of his body and found he could not move his injured arm. The Saharakaree whipped its' tail around again and was going to finish him off. Gillis, seeing his friend in mortal danger, used his upper body strength to throw his own opponent into the Saharakaree standing over O'Grady. Both to the Saharakaree fell to the surface and tumbled for a few feet before they both regained their footing.

O'Grady was crawling, holding his bleeding shoulder with his uninjured hand. His enviro-suit was losing oxygen and the poison was causing his upper body to become numb. Gillis knew that O'Grady would have less than fifteen minutes before the Saharakaree poison would kill him. He needed to be injected with the anti-venom quickly.

The two Saharakaree regained their footing and charged Gillis in unison. Gillis could not avoid both. He started to move to his left when a third Saharakaree jumped on his back. Gillis went sprawling face first into the lunar surface. Gillis spun so that he would be facing his new adversary. The other two creatures were closing in on him.

Pierre Zerbe, seeing that Gillis was in danger, fired his hand laser at one of the two leaping Saharakaree. Zerbe had grown to consider Gillis a good friend and wanted to protect him. The alien gave out a guttural scream as it fell, stunned by Zerbe's laser. The other turned and looked in Zerbe' direction.

The Saharakaree leaped in the air at the direction of

Zerbe. Zerbe fired at the Saharakaree twice and missed. He misjudged the angle in which the alien was coming at him. The creature aimed its' tail at the cadet pilot. Zerbe attempted to move out of the path of the creature but was not fast enough. The sharp tail slashed into his abdomen and ripped all the way through and came out of his back. Zerbe screamed as the creature lifted him in the air on its' tail. It was waiving Zerbe back and forth, showing the other human combatants. The Saharakaree then threw Zerbe into the air. The alien was making the same guttural noise that the other had made when it had stabbed O'Grady. The others watched helplessly as Zerbe sailed about twenty feet up into the sky and then landed on the surface with a thud.

"Pierre! No!" Lincoln bellowed. She was assisting O'Grady to his feet when she saw Zerbe get injured.

Cardenas and Doernitz began firing on the other Saharakaree. Cardenas stunned the alien that had impaled Zerbe. Marco was still losing his oxygen levels and was struggling to keep up as he stopped running and was walking toward the ship.

Gorski finally was able to pin his opponent to the lunar surface. He had his knees on the arms of the Saharakaree. Gorski pulled out one of Gillis' homemade magnesium strip weapons and placed it on the eyes of the alien. He ignited the weapon and closed his eyes as Gillis had instructed. The Saharakaree screamed as its' eyes were burned by the hot, bright flash. Gorski released the sightless alien and ran to assist the others. Blinded, the Saharakaree was harmless.

Steiner and Lincoln were helping O'Grady back onto the Raumschiff. Gorski saw the blood on O'Grady's left shoulder and the pale look on his face.

Cardenas and Doernitz located Zerbe on the lunar surface and did their best to give him medical attention. Despite their best efforts, they could not stop the bleeding. Cardenas warned the other team members that they needed emergency medical attention for Zerbe and lifted him up over his shoulder. Doernitz helped carry Zerbe on the other side as they began to rapidly carry him toward the ship.

Marco was grateful when Harrison found him crawling on the surface, struggling to breathe. Harrison was able to lift Marco up with one arm and carried him back to the ship, urging Marco to hold on.

Gorski and Gillis were in a kneeling position, firing their laser pistols at the few remaining aliens, stunning them all.

"Get back to the ship!" Gorski ordered.

Gillis nodded and retreated, running backwards in case any other Saharakaree were hiding in the headquarters. Gillis paused to retrieve the head of the Saharakaree that Harrison had decapitated. He had formulated at theory that he wanted to test out.

Gillis had recalled reading in some manual that the Saharakaree would only attack if they felt cornered. The humans had done nothing to provoke them. Further, the Saharakaree were not indigenous to the moon or the planet Semiramis. They should not have been here at all. The ambush made no sense.

As soon as all of the team was on board, Gorski saw one last Saharakaree charging at them. Gorski aimed his laser pistol and fired, hitting the creature in the chest and it crumpled to the ground.

The Raumschiff walk way was covered with blood. Gorski ordered the ship's computer to retract the landing plank and seal the bay doors. He watched as it retracted and the bay doors closed. Gorski waited until they were secure before he rushed to the medical area. Three or more of their number had been hurt. He needed to see how bad the damage was and to formulate a plan of action to determine why the attack on them had occurred. The idea of winning the tournament was the furthest thing from Gorski's mind.

Gillis and Harrison ran inside to find Pierre Zerbe lying on the floor of the Raumschiff. He was struggling to breathe, blood was filling his lungs. Gorski rushed over to the group.

"Yuri!" Julia Steiner held out a hyper-dermic needle filled with a red fluid. "This is the anti-venom. You need to inject it in Eamon's neck."

"But," Gorski began to protest.

"He won't let me do it!" Steiner's voice sounded rushed. "He wants to speak with you first. Go!"

Gorski took the needle from Steiner and rushed over to where O'Grady was lying on the floor. He saw that Steiner was running toward the other injured cadet.

Cardenas and Doernitz were able to get Zerbe's helmet off. He was looking up at them, blood oozing out of his mouth and down the sides of his chin. The wound in his stomach and back looked bleak. Steiner was pushing through the men and quickly injected Zerbe in his arm with a powerful pain killer drug. Steiner looked over the wounds and knew immediately that Zerbe was terminal. She gave him the drugs because she had wanted to relieve him of the intense agony and to make him comfortable for his last moments.

"Help me get him to the medical area," Steiner instructed the other cadets.

Gillis, Cardenas and Harrison lifter Zerbe up and they rushed upstairs as his blood dripped on their enviro-suits. They laid Zerbe gently onto the first operating table after they rushed into the medical section.

Steiner had taken out a medical scanner from one of the drawers and was taking quick x-rays of his internal organs.

Zerbe reached out his hand toward Gillis and the two men grasped hands.

"Les, are you okay?" Zerbe asked, his voice was weak and blood was running from his lips down his cheek and chin.

"I'm fine, Pierre. Just relax," Gillis told him softly.

Gillis felt sick to his stomach as he observed the gaping wound in Zerbe's stomach. He looked over to Steiner who was shaking her head. Gillis knew it was only a matter of time.

"Good, my friend. Tell Cara," Zerbe gasped. He was spitting out more blood. His eyes staring at the ceiling as he grimaced to get the words out. "I love her. Tell her." His voice was growing weaker with each statement.

"Hold on! Pierre!" Gillis looked into Zerbe's eyes and he could see the life leaving them. Zerbe took one last gasp of air and his head slumped to the side.

"I am so sorry," Steiner told the others. She reached over Zerbe's face and closed his eyes. Steiner was not a doctor; she had only taken some medical courses that were required for her studies to earn a science degree. But she felt as if she had been kicked in the stomach. She lost a patient and a friend. Steiner began to cry. Harrison put his arm around her to comfort her. She did not pull away.

Elsewhere, in the loading area of the bottom of the ship, Gorski leaned over O'Grady. "Eamon. I have to inject you with the anti-venom or you will die."

O'Grady had beads of perspiration on his upper lip and forehead, his face was losing color and his eyes looked tired. The poison of the Saharakaree was working its' deadly magic. "Take charge, Yuri. This was a set up."

"I got it Eamon," Gorski told him softly. "I promise, I will get us all out of here."

"Okay," O'Grady nodded, his breathing sounded labored. "Look at the other cadet teams. Who would put Saharakaree in our safe house? Find out. This attack makes no sense, Yuri. Someone ambushed us. We need to know why."

"I told you that I can handle it Eamon! Now let me inject you before the venom kills you!"

"Inject me. But I am still going to kick your ass when I wake up."

Gorski stuck the needle in O'Grady's neck and injected the fluid into him. Gorski watched as O'Grady passed out from the pain and the effects of the anti-venom fluid.

Gorski looked to his left and saw Marco lying on the metal floor, breathing deeply, his enviro-suit helmet on the floor. Marco's uniform was torn in numerous places. Doernitz and Lincoln were helping remove the torn enviro-suit from Marco. Gorski noted that the tears in the space suit were claw marks. Gorski stood to see if Marco also needed an anti-venom injection. Marco sensed Gorski was worried for him and gave him a thumbs up.

"Don't worry about me; I just need to catch my breath. I didn't get stabbed by one of their tails. I will be fine in a few minutes," Marco assured Gorski.

Gorski gave Marco a pat on the shoulder and rushed up the ladder to see how Zerbe was doing. Gorski made it to the medical area and saw Steiner covering Zerbe's body. Steiner made eye contact with Gorski and walked past him, saying nothing. She ran down to the lower level to begin treating O'Grady and his shoulder injury. Harrison was following her with a bag of medical supplies in his hand. Gorski looked into the eyes of the other team members. He saw despair, anguish, pain and anger in their stares. Gorski grinded his teeth together after he learned that Pierre Zerbe had died due to the attack. O'Grady only had a fifty percent chance of surviving from his wounds. It was up to the rest of the team to make their unknown assailants answer for the cowardly attack.

Steiner put her feelings aside as she worked on saving the life of Eamon O'Grady. Today had been a first for her on several levels. She helplessly watched a friend die and she killed an alien. Steiner had never killed before and never watched a friend die. She hoped that she would complete another milestone in her life which was ensuring that her friend O'Grady survived his wounds.

CHAPTER TWO

Secretary General Alexander Lyss was livid. He stormed into the office of Colonel Nikolai Gorski, shouting expletives for all to hear. He noted that the Colonel was in the middle of discussions with Major Sigebert Evart. Lyss did not care. The entire planet of New Edinburgh was just portrayed, to all of the eight solar systems, as a community of lawless thugs.

"I knew your damn son was nothing but trouble!" Lyss pointed his finger in Gorski's direction. "How many more innocent people does he plan on murdering?"

Evart responded in defense of his commanding officer, "Mister Secretary, I can assure you that Yuri and the other cadets from Clovis Academy did not commit the acts you saw on the view screens. This is a set up."

"Set up? Like hell!" Lyss was screaming so loud that his face was red and his blood veins were bulging out, his composure long lost as he had given in to anger. "I just saw eight retired officers, all decorated men and women, wiped out in a split second by Clovis Academy ships and cadets. The Tyr Academy cadets were brutally murdered by another of our ships!

How the hell did they sneak weapons past the security checks?"

Lyss was raising his voice so that it was so loud that it had attracted the attention of Sean Collins. The lawyer walked calmly into the office and he leaned against the far wall. Standing behind him was Sergeant First Class Mark Lund from Military Intelligence. Lund crossed his arms across his chest as he listened to the out of control Lyss.

"Mister Secretary, please, your voice is carrying and upsetting the staff," Collins told him. "You cannot believe what you saw."

"It was our colors!" Lyss yelled. "Our ships!"

"No sir, I think not." Lund told the emotional Secretary General. "My staff and I have examined the last few broadcasts from the moon of Semiramis. The killers made a fatal error in the attempt to frame our cadets."

"Which was what?" Lyss' voice was still loud, but not as before.

"One of the pilots referred to himself as 'Evart'." Lund told everyone. "Michel Evart is here, in Clovis City. He had been replaced on the team by Zerbe. The real killers did not do their homework. Had they paid attention, they would have known Major Evart's nephew never left New Edinburgh."

"The killers, whoever they are, got reckless," Collins told Lyss.

"So, then, our cadets are probably innocent?" Lyss said calmly.

"Probably? No." Colonel Gorski finally spoke up. "They are absolutely innocent. My son and his friends did nothing wrong."

"So what are you going to do about it?" Lyss demanded.

"We were going to send out a few crews on some Raumschiff's to assist the survivors," Gorski answered. "That is, until our Glorious Leader sent out a general quarantine order for the planet Semiramis and her moon."

"So then no one is allowed to go there?" Lyss was curious. "I wonder why?"

"So do we," Major Evart said.

"Perhaps we should ignore the quarantine order and send out the rescue mission anyway," Lund suggested.

"And if we did disobey a direct order from the Glorious Leader, which officer and enlisted soldiers would be willing to suffer the punishment?"

Gorski stood up and faced the window overlooking the city.

"I would go myself, but I am not a skilled pilot and need a few astronauts to get me there. Even though the life of my son is in jeopardy, I cannot order any officer to risk their careers and their lives to assist me."

"I would gladly go, sir." Lund volunteered.

"Can you fly a Raumschiff?" Evart asked him.

"No sir. I cannot."

"Then you see our dilemma. Without qualified pilots to

get us there, we are stuck, which leaves my son and his friends to fight on their own without help from anyone." Gorski told them.

"What if we contact Mary Lincoln's father on the Cortez?" Evart suggested. "A Battle Cruiser could get to the moon faster than we could from here in a Raumschiff. With his daughter in danger, he might be receptive to lend a hand."

Gorski nodded, "That's why I keep you around, Sigebert. Great idea. I will contact him myself."

"Even a contact like that, no matter how innocent, might be construed as an act of treason. We need an emissary, someone neutral, that can contact the Royal Family and ask for permission to violate the quarantine," Collins told the men. "I know a lawyer on Sikorsky's Planet that is good friends with Admiral Sikorsky. She might be able to convince him to let the Cortez or one of our ships enter the restricted moon for the purpose of extraction of the surviving cadets. If she agrees to do this for me, then there would be a plausible denial for us and we could all escape any charges of treason that might come later."

"We do both," Gorski instructed them. "My son is in danger and I do not give a damn if my actions to protect him get me indicted. Sean, contact your friend and see if she will help us. I am contacting the Admiral immediately. Every second we waste is more time my son goes without a rescue mission heading his way."

Lyss cleared his throat, "I know this might not be a popular idea with any of you. But if you were to release Rebecca from jail, she has some connections with the Royals on Sikorsky's Planet. If we release her and offer her a pardon, she might help us."

Collins shook his head, "No, Alex. She cannot be trusted. Rebecca Rosenburg remains in jail until I can prosecute her."

"Just an idea," Lyss responded weakly.

"Forget her," Collins told him as he stood up. "This frame up is a masterful plan. That means that those behind it are better than average intelligence and have considered the probable outcomes of their actions. They discredit our cadets, our Academy, our city and our people, all at the same time. We never found Alfred Rosenburg in any of our raids. I wager he is on that moon and a major player in this."

"If that is so, what can we do about it now?" Evart barked. "We failed those kids by not apprehending the biggest catch, Alf Rosenburg. We should have ignored the order from the Judge that delayed our arrest warrants. He must have escaped during that window of opportunity."

"We followed the law," Collins reminded him. "But your point is well taken. I am going to get some more Intel from my hidden witness about that Rosenburg family tree. There very well may be more at play here than any of us can imagine. My hope is that we can find a way to assist the cadets before it is too late. Nikolai, I suggest that you find two pilots from the Planetary Defense that you can trust. Make certain that they are loyal to you. Assign them a Raumschiff, give them Sergeant Lund here and send them at best speed to the Blood Moon."

"You just said we should follow the law," Evart blurted out. "The Glorious Leader issued a quarantine of the moon. We would be committing treason if we send a rescue team out there."

Gorski smashed his right fist on the nearest table top, "To hell with the quarantine. My son is in danger. Mark, contact pilots Aura Lynda Glenn and Natazia Essex. Tell them that this mission is strictly voluntary and that they might be on a one way trip. Tell them that I will not think anything less of them if they refuse."

"Who else should I take with me, sir?" Lund asked.

Gorski paced around the room, "Get Preston, Lewis, Zhao and Stewart to go. Arm the ship to the teeth and take enough medical equipment to help any injured once you arrive on the Blood Moon. Above all, tell them to be careful. After you make all of the arrangements, report back to me in person. We need to maintain silence on the satellite system because the Royal Family will be listening. They have spies everywhere."

Lund walked toward the door, "We'll bring your son back, sir. I promise that."

CHAPTER THREE

Elsewhere on campus one of the cadets refused to adhere to the quarantine order of the Glorious Leader and made plans to take his personal Raumschiff on a trip. He would have to miss over two weeks' worth of class and run the risk of expulsion from the Academy, but Dirk Fenster cared more about the lives of his friends than his collegiate performance. The large space craft had been a birthday gift from his mother and father and delivered to him as a surprise gift. Fenster had hopes of using his ship as a great way to seduce women as opposed to flying into the middle of a combat situation.

He had confided in his best friend that he planned on flying out to the Blood Moon, alone, in an attempt to rescue Yuri, Les, Drew and the others. What Fenster had not anticipated was that Arch Frazier had no intention of allowing him to fly into harm's way alone.

Frazier rounded up a small band of cadets that might prove useful in such a rescue attempt. Frazier appreciated that Fenster was a skilled pilot, but the travel time to the moon from planet New Edinburgh was over one week. Fenster would need some other pilots to allow him time to sleep.

Frazier recruited cadet pilots Rolf Rhinehard, Dino Black and Lupita Calderon to join the illegal mission. Frazier did not end his mission building with them. He found the best cadet military tactician in the sophomore class, Katarina Strahovski, and was elated that she was willing to risk her entire future to go help the cadets on the Blood Moon. Frazier also found a few engineering students that were willing to assist.

His last area to recruit was the most logical and that was for medical assistance. Frazier recalled that pre-medical school students William Windfohr and Clark Blundell had been more than willing to lend a hand when the assassins attacked during the dust storm. Frazier led his small band of cadets to the main landing strip in the center of Clovis City and waited for Fenster to show up. It was before dawn and the sun was barely rising, turning the dark sky into a red orange hue.

Dirk Fenster saw the gathering of fifteen cadets waiting for him at the rear of his parked gold and black Fenster Model Super Raumschiff. He dropped his oversized dark blue duffel bag onto the transparent metal runway and looked at the purple sands beneath it. He slowly looked up at his friends and regarded Frazier first.

"Arch, I told you not to tell anyone."

"You risk your life and tell me to stay home? You really think I would not be at your side at a time like this?" Frazier motioned to the ship with his left arm. "These cadets feel as strongly about what is going on at the Blood Moon as you and I do. Our friends are in danger and we need to go get them."

Fenster shook his head, "Rolf, did you tell Klaus that you were going to do this?"

Rolf was leaning against the side of the massive ship with his arms crossed. He was wearing a black turtle neck sweater, khaki pants and black leather boots. His duffle bag was lying at his feet filled with hygiene products and enough clothes for the trip.

He shook his head side to side, "Nein, I told him nothing. I am still a member of the Gorski Gang, ja? So we go, that is what we are supposed to do. We stand together. You will need me out there."

Fenster looked over the faces of the other cadets, "The rest of you are not Gorski Gang members so this does not concern you. Go back to the dorms and get ready for your classes. We are not going out for a picnic. You all know that moon is infested with killers. Go home."

"That is a hell of a way to tell us that you appreciate our being here," engineering cadet Fara Kiesbye said as she pointed her finger at him. "We all know the score here so, speaking for myself, I would rather you thank me for being here and give me permission to board your ship."

"I will go as far to say that today we are all Gorski Gang members," Strahovski told Fenster. "I can work your weapons system and take on a Battle Cruiser if I must. Based on what I saw on the satellite broadcast we are going against some mean bastard's that love to kill. You will need someone like me with you if we run into any action. Remember the old motto of the cadet corps? An attack on one of us is an attack on us all. I am ready to go over there and teach those people that they cannot go around framing our fellow students."

Lupita Calderon walked over to Fenster and stood a few inches from him and smiled, "I know you paid for my surgery. You showed me a kindness that I will never forget and I can never repay you for. I would gladly die for you for what you did for me. I know how hard it is to find good friends in this world and I would gladly die for your friends as I would for you. Those people out there that killed all of those judges and the other cadets are nothing but malditos and we should go over there and give them a bloody nose."

"We all feel the same way," Dino Black added.

"We are wasting time debating this," Blundell pointed to the sky line. "The sun is rising and every second we waste is time that we could be using to get to Yuri and the others and help them. What do you say, Dirk? It is your ship and your call as to whether or not we all go with you. But we can really help. If there is any of our team injured, we can help render aid. What do you say?"

Fenster tried his best to suppress his smile but was unsuccessful. He nodded and pulled out a four inch long and three inch wide razor thin computer from his breast pocket and ordered it to open the rear loading entrance of his ship. "We are all now traitors to the Glorious Leader because we are about to violate his quarantine. I welcome all of you aboard and, yes Fara, I thank each and every one of you."

Frazier smiled and slapped Fenster on the shoulder, "Let's roll people! Board the ship!"

"Arch, you aren't planning on going are you?" Fenster asked as the others began to rush toward the rear loading ramp that was lowering onto the transparent landing strip.

"I already told Elektra where we were going and she will be watching Theodora for us while we are way. Where ever you go, I go. You should know that about me by now."

Fenster shook his head and looked at the others and was frowning at them.

"What is wrong?" Strahovski asked him.

"I was planning on going alone," Fenster began. "I did not stock enough freeze dried food and water for so many passengers. Arch, I already know that you are thinking that I am only saying that to get rid of all of you. But it is the truth. If all of you come with me, there will not be enough food on board to feed our friends on the moon and to feed us for the return trip. The reality is that I must go it alone."

Frazier chuckled and slapped Fenster on the shoulder, "Give me some credit, Dirk. I thought of that problem already. Before we all arrived here, I had Supreet, Ristina, Bao and Gleaia stock the ship's freezer units full of food and water. We also have a fully stocked medical section to treat any wounded we find and I was able to get some illegal weaponry on board. Dirk, we are wasting time."

Fenster frowned at his friend, "How did you get past all of my ship security protocols?"

As if to answer his question, the rear entrance of the ship began to slide open. The rear loading ramp lowered to the ground and Fenster watched in stunned silence as Cadets Supreet Patel, Bao Mingjuan, Ristina Bedrosian and Gleaia Chin walked down the ramp from the inside of his space craft.

"Arch did not get past your security system," Mingjuan announced proudly. "We did. We also brought along enough food, medical supplies, clothing, linens and water to last several months in space. The ship is fully stocked for a long mission. We should lift off."

Fenster grunted and smiled when the Kotek, Ristina Bedrosian, meowed at him. She had a coat of white fur with black dots scattered sparingly over her body. Her long tail was waiving free out the back of her light blue cadet uniform.

"I suppose you all are volunteering to go along?" Fenster asked the four women that had stowed away inside his ship.

"That is why we are here," Gleaia Chin responded.

She was human with raccoon DNA that had been spliced into her parents, making her a second generation of that hybrid race. She was furry, like the Koteks and Osos that Fenster had met over the years. But she had a black stripe over her eyes, with a dark nose, short fangs and a thick, bushy, multi-striped tail. Fenster was aware that Chin was one of the engineering cadets and that her talents could prove to be useful in the event they ran into any difficulty.

Fenster pursed his lips, "All right. My ship, my rules. I am in command. Katarina, you will be my XO. Rolf, Lupita, Dino, Ristina and I will take eight hour shifts flying the ship. Bill, Clark and Supreet, you three will need to get the medical area ready to receive wounded. Fara and Gleaia, make sure there are no malfunctions. Bao and Arch monitor everything from the computer section and learn everything you can about the weaponry of the ship from Katarina. Any questions?"

Patel motioned with her head, "So I take it we all have permission to come aboard?"

Fenster laughed, "Let's move out. We lift off in ten minutes. I am glad about one thing."

"What's that?" Black wanted to know.

"I am glad that I am not committing treason alone," Fenster told them as he walked rapidly up the ramp of his ship.

Rolf met Patel at the top of the docking bay and smiled at her, "This could be a long trip."

Patel took hold of his hand, "No worries, Rolf. I am here to help the gang. But on the way there, I will gladly be your personal sex toy."

"What if I get bored with just being with one woman?" Rolf asked her.

Patel motioned to Bedrosian, Chin, Kiesbye and Mingjuan as if to answer his question. "Why do you think I brought them along? They are my reinforcements if you want to get really kinky. I cannot promise you much, but I can promise that you will not get bored on this flight."

"You are a very bad girl," Rolf whispered in her ear.

CHAPTER FOUR

Cadet Alan Anderson and his team from Newton Academy witnessed the deaths of the judges and the Tyr Academy cadets on their computer view monitors.

They were settled in at their headquarters when the attacks commenced. Anderson looked to his nine teammates and thought about their options. Anderson was the highest ranking and oldest among them. He was twenty-two years old when the next oldest was twenty-one. Anderson was watching the events on the screens and the reactions of his friends. He recalled his time during the summer on old Earth when he had attended the Spetsnaz training and his first encounter with Yuri Gorski. Anderson found Gorski to be a man that cherished life and lived each second to the fullest. He was also one that was serious about his studies and his career. Anderson did not need any evidence to prove to him that Gorski was not a cold blooded killer. He knew that Gorski was being set up by someone else.

Finally, Anderson came to some decisions, "Angelique, turn off the receptions for now."

Cadet Angelique LeClair complied and shut down the

monitors.

Anderson motioned for the Team to sit around the large kitchen table. He regarded them all. "Ellen, our one man fighters are armed with pulsar blasts. In your opinion, if we were attacked as the judges were, can a pulsar blast bring down an opposing ship?"

Cadet Ellen Benson nodded, "Yes sir. A direct pulsar blast hit will cause the vessel to lose power. It would force the craft to land. We can work with it."

Anderson looked to his computer genius, Cadet Laurence Thompson. "Larry, where are you on hacking into the Achilles and Clovis communications systems?"

"I need more time," Thompson regretted saying. "They both put some major security precautions on their systems. It could be a while."

"Then get to it," Anderson told him. "Ellen, take Hal, Torch and June to the fighter ships. Get airborne and be ready. Patrol our area within a few kilometers. I don't want our ships on the ground if these bastard's attack us. I have a sinking feeling that the killers out there will be targeting us very soon."

"Yes sir," Benson stood up and motioned to cadets Palmer, Woods and Carter to follow her to their ships.

"Nick, prepare some defenses on the roof of our HQ," Anderson told Nicolas Curtis.

"Angelique, start scanning the surface of the moon. See if there is anything out of the ordinary. I am specifically looking for any means or possible way that the unknown attackers could have brought weapons to this place. Understand?"

Le Clair nodded, "Yes, Alan. I will get right on it."

The others looked at Anderson expectantly. They all respected him as their leader. His resume as a cadet was extensive to include the fact that he had graduated from Spetsnaz. He would soon be a doctor in search and rescue. If anyone could lead them to safety, Alan Anderson could. He observed that some of his team had fear in their eyes.

"Look, I know that none of us expected this to happen. But it has happened. I need all of you to be ready to fight if necessary. If we are set upon by the enemy, we must be willing to fight back and kill them. We cannot hesitate. I want each of you to keep knives on you and the stun lasers. These people showed the others no mercy. Their attack was cowardly. Make no mistake, if they can kill you they will. Picture in your minds your families, your lovers and your friends. You will each have to come to terms with the fact that if you ever want to see them again, you will have to fight. Can I count on all of you to do your part?"

"Yes sir!" Benson yelled out.

"How about the rest of you?" Anderson asked.

In unison, the other nine yelled: "Yes sir!"

"Good, everyone get to work. The rest of you are with me."

Anderson walked to the communications area,

"Computer. Send out a general SOS signal to the cadets at Achilles Academy and to the entirety of the Space Command. Let them all know that there has been an attack on the Moon of Semiramis and we request immediate assistance."

"And then what do we do?" Curtis asked.

"We prepare to dust off and evacuate. The attacks were unprovoked and cowardly. That means that we are in the middle of a dynamic that we should avoid at all costs. Once we determine that we can leave this moon safely, that is what we will do."

The computer began to broadcast the SOS as requested.

The cadets at the Achilles Academy building received it.

Caine Rosenburg began laughing as he heard the request for help from the Newton Academy cadets being repeated, "They are begging for assistance that will never come for them. Pathetic."

Dell Ragnarsson listened for a few moments and then turned to the others, "We should go finish the Newton cadets right now. I read Anderson's file, he is a Spetsnaz graduate, trained in search and rescue, a skilled pilot and a good marksman. He is not one to be toyed with."

Alfred Rosenburg, II, patted Ragnarsson on the shoulder. "Dell, please. You worry all the time. Relax and enjoy what we have accomplished so far. The Glorious Leader issued a general quarantine for the moon and the planet. Even if the closest Battle Cruiser were to begin traveling this direction in contradiction of the quarantine, they would need over seven days to get here."

David Rosenburg rarely disagreed with his father, but this time he had to side with Ragnarsson.

"Father, the ship you refer to is the U.N.S.C. Cortez, a fully operational military Battle Cruiser. She has a crew of well-trained fighter pilots, Military Intelligence soldiers and Marines. Her commander is Colonel Lincoln. His daughter is one of the Clovis cadets. I would be willing to bet Lincoln disobeys the quarantine and makes best speed over here. So, I have to agree with Mister Ragnarsson. We need to finish these other cadets off now and then leave this place. Now, father. Right now."

Peter Lomax shrugged, "With the slave Akarzdamedians and my extra ships, we can go finish them at any time. I have real lasers and armor piercing missiles. The cadets are all dead and they don't even know it. Let them suffer from not knowing when the attack comes. Let their fear build. Then we kill them."

Cleon Alexander grunted, "I just want to cut some people. Wipe out Anderson's group with the ships or in whatever manner you wish. But please let Avery and I kill the Gorski people by hand. We have traveled a long distance to get our revenge on them."

Avery Jackson growled and pointed the tip of his twelve inch blade at all of the assembled in the room.

"Gorski is mine. I kill him when I say so. And, I say we eat a good meal tonight and begin the hunt in the morning."

"I agree," Caine hit his hand on the table. "Steaks, ale,

bourbon and good wine for everyone!"

The other cadets began clapping at that suggestion. Kai Chin walked next to David Rosenburg and Dell Ragnarsson.

"For what it is worth, I agree with you two." Chin whispered the words so that Caine and Alfred would not overhear him. "We should not become complacent based on our successes of today. All we are doing is giving the enemy time to prepare."

"The rest of them are fools," Dell whispered to himself.

He looked at Alfred Rosenburg, II, with contempt. He had grown to despise his employer. Due to the infamous hubris of the Rosenburg family, Dell had lost three of his sons. Junior, who was dead, and Ellis and Ivar, who were both in jail. Two of his daughters were also gone, Ella and Emma. He had heard rumors that both girls were in jail. Other reports he received indicated that Emma had died. He had also lost touch with his other daughters. He hoped that they fled for their own safety and to avoid the warrants that had been issued. Although Dell blamed Yuri Gorski and his pack of cadets for some of his family losses, the ultimate blame rested on the shoulders of Caine and Alfred Rosenburg, II. Dell had been ordered by Alfred Rosenburg to bring in his remaining children to assist in this mission.

Dell had refused that demand as he was not willing to risk any more of his offspring to help out the anti-social behaviors of Caine Rosenburg. He made excuses that his other children were doing other missions for the Glorious Leader.

Dell considered the group he was allied with now. Only Chin and Austin seemed to be competent. The rest were narcissistic, prideful, and sadistic. Some had personality disorders and others were clearly manic. One of the men seemed to exhibit signs of a bi-polar disorder. These men were not the professional assassins that Dell was accustomed to working with. They were amateurs which made them dangerous for any person that was allied with them. He grimaced as he overheard Jackson and Alexander bragging to the others how they had beaten and raped a defenseless woman. Professional killers never bragged about their past acts as the cadets were doing.

As the braggarts continued to drink and stuff their faces with the junk food provided by the Rosenburg's, Dell quietly hoped that the other plans that he had launched were coming to fruition. It took every ounce of his patience to keep from drawing his laser weapon and shooting the entire lot of the team in the back.

Lila Zapata had finished disassembling and assembling an atomic engine for a Raumschiff. The engine weighed a ton and the largest portions were suspended from the engineering hangar by tough metal cables. She was wearing an engineering technician uniform which was covered in soot and oil stains. Her face had patches of black oil. Her hair was under a baseball cap. She had goggles on to protect her eyes.

"Done!" Zapata called out to the engineering professor.

The other fifty cadets in her class looked over at her

direction. Most were amazed she worked as quickly as she had. She was the first to finish the assignment. The professor walked to her work table and began inspecting her effort.

Sophia DuBravac smiled from her work bench. She was also covered with stains from the engine work. She was still assembling parts. DuBravac wondered if the professors were assigning some of these surprise tests, such as seeing how fast one could take apart an engine and then put it back together, to keep all of the students pre-occupied. It worked for most of the cadets.

DuBravac continued putting the pieces of her engine together. She worried for Les Gillis and the others. She took a deep breath. She hoped to see him soon, as a free and exonerated man. She pulled a solar powered screw driver out from the bottom of her work bench and began to work on her engine. She had hoped that the busy work would take her mind off the fact that the man she loved was in danger. DuBravac could not focus because of that fact and her studies were the last thing that she wanted to be doing.

CHAPTER FIVE

Using the latest in laser medical technology, Julia Steiner was successful in stopping the bleeding in Eamon O'Grady's shoulder wound. He had lost too much blood and required more. Steiner used the pints of blood on board the medical section of the Raumschiff and began an IV to replenish O'Grady's body. He was unconscious due to the anti-venom injection given to him. Steiner was reasonably hopeful that O'Grady would recover. She believed that his chances of surviving the poison from the Saharakaree were about fifty percent.

Steiner instructed the medical computers to monitor Eamon O'Grady's heart rate, breathing, body temperature and brain waves. She walked out of the medical section and saw that Les Gillis had brought one of the Saharakaree heads on board. It was from the one that Drew Harrison had killed.

Gillis was scanning the alien head with a hand held computer. He stopped and looked at the scan results.

"Just as I thought," Gillis reported. "The Saharakaree

that Drew killed had an implant in his brain. He was being controlled. This attack was planned and someone was directing this from another location."

Steiner retrieved a cutting utensil and a medical instrument that resembled a pair of pliers. She cut into the Saharakaree skull and used the pliers like medical instrument to pull out the computer microchip. She held it up for all to see.

"It looks like the computer chips found in human slaves," Harrison recalled from one of his criminal investigation courses that concentrated on the illegal slave trade. The chips could be used to implant memories, erase memories, or just overwhelm the host brain to be compliant.

"I will have the computer scan it and see if we can determine where it originated from," Steiner told the others.

"This means those aliens were not attacking of their own free will," Harrison concluded. "They were being controlled by someone or something. They were forced to attack us."

"Then whoever put that chip in those Saharakaree are responsible for Pierre and Eamon," Cardenas concluded.

Gorski was pacing back and forth as he took in the comments from the others. "Okay, someone wants us all dead."

Mary Lincoln nodded, "Or, at least one or more of us. The rest would be collateral damage."

"But who?" Doernitz blurted out.

"Let me be blunt. Any of us that have been in the gang could have pissed off the wrong person or persons. I would say that the Ragnarsson family has plenty of reason to want a few of us dead."

Steiner pointed at Gorski, Gillis and Harrison as she spoke. "Then there are all of those old bar fights we used to get into with all of those pilots and drifters. Any number of those rogues would have wanted to kill us."

Gorski looked into the eyes of his seven class mates. They were all looking to him for direction. Steiner had apprehension in her eyes, Cardenas had a silent bravery about him, and perhaps the strength Gorski saw in Cardenas came from his faith in God. Doernitz had a look that indicated the youngest cadet would walk through fire if Gorski asked him to do so. Gorski took a deep breath. His decisions could have the effect of life and death for each of the remaining team members.

"Julia, I need you to scan the entire lunar surface for life signs," Gorski began. "Our unknown enemy seems to like to use aliens to do their dirty work for them, so I want you to differentiate between human and alien life forms. I want to know their exact locations and how many of the life forms are on the moon.

Les, I need you to monitor for any weapons residue and I also need you to contact Admiral Seward and find out what is going on out there. The rest of the eight solar systems had to see us get attacked. Ask for them to send in immediate assistance. Drew, I want you to go over the recordings of the other three Academies for the last hour. See if any of them were attacked as we were."

Gorski turned and faced the four cadet pilots, "We are sitting ducks here so I need you to get those four small fighter ships airborne. The Saharakaree should still be unconscious, but be cautious out there in case there are more of them. Check your craft for booby traps before you board them. I don't want any of you sitting on a bomb. Once you clear the ships, get airborne. I want you four to scan the area around us for anything abnormal. Understand?"

Cardenas nodded, "Marco will need to take one of the replacement enviro-suits. Yuri, if the rest of the empire saw what happened, why aren't the Judges contacting us?"

"Good point," Gorski agreed. "After I return I will check on that issue."

"Return from where?" Lincoln asked.

"I am going into our headquarters," Gorski told them. "I am going to see how much damage those Saharakaree did to our supplies."

"Shouldn't we say some words for Pierre?" Cardenas asked. "He deserves a decent burial."

Gillis and Doernitz nodded in agreement with Cardenas' suggestion. They seemed to have been the closest to Zerbe and most effected by his death.

Gorski paused and considered their fallen comrade for a few seconds. "He will get one when we all leave this rock and return home alive. And I mean all of us. Let's move out."

Steiner nodded in agreement. The cadets all began to work on their assigned tasks.

Gorski packed several flares on his utility belt and wrapped the belt around his waist. He took his hand laser in his right hand and ordered the Raumschiff computer to open the bay door. He waited and secured his enviro-suit helmet.

The door was open in twenty seconds and the exit ramp slid down to the surface in less time than that. Gorski noticed that there were still blood stains on the ramp from Zerbe and O'Grady. He had his enviro-suit computer scan the surface to the headquarters. The Saharakaree were either dead or blinded and would pose no further threat.

"Computer," Gorski directed, "scan the headquarters for life signs."

"No life signs detected on the lower level," his computer responded. "Detecting faint signs of alien life on the upper level."

"More Saharakaree?" Gorski braced himself.

"Perhaps," the computer responded. "But not fully grown."

Gorski looked to the sky and took in a deep breath. He began to jog toward the building. He was able to cross the distance in under two minutes. The front sliding doors were lying on the ground and broken from when the Saharakaree had knocked them down. Gorski asked the headquarters computer to turn on the inside lights. No lights came on.

Gorski pulled out a flare and popped the top of the hand held flare and a flame shot out, about a foot high. Gorski knew that the life of the flare was only an hour. Gorski stepped into the hallway entrance and slowly walked into what should have been their safe house.

Gorski saw that the Saharakaree had demolished the interior of the building. Lights were busted, tables crushed, walls were ripped apart and chairs and computers were demolished. Gorski slowly moved in a circular motion and held the flare above his head. Once he was confident there were no surprises such as traps, trip wires or other aliens, Gorski moved quickly inside. He saw that all of the computers and technical machinery crushed and broken. All of the scanners and communication devices were damaged to the point of being inoperable.

Gorski found his way to the medical section. He noted that the medical supply cabinets had been ripped out of the walls. The medicine was scattered all over the trashed floor. He walked to the storage lockers and saw that all of the medical operational tools had been thrown about. Gorski found some scalpels and other sharp supplies. He gathered them up, for potential use as offensive weapons against their unknown assailants.

Gorski turned and went to the kitchen and found it in a similar state of disarray. The freezers were opened and the frozen foods were strewn all over the floor. Many of the food packets had been ripped open, the food devoured by the Saharakaree. Gorski cursed. If they were to survive, then they needed to find food. The Raumschiff might sustain them for a few more days, but they were relying on the food supplies to be at the headquarters.

Gorski climbed the winding stair case to the second floor. He saw that the beds were shredded and the remains of the mattresses had been tossed about. The other technical devices were destroyed. He concluded that their headquarters would not be suitable. The Saharakaree did not kill them all, but they left the team survivors homeless.

Gorski was prepared to leave when he heard a rustling noise behind him. Gorski turned around and saw about seven or eight baby Saharakaree hiding behind the damaged beds.

Amazing he thought to himself. One of the Saharakaree attackers had given birth to a litter of children. They were all about a foot tall and crying. They had to be starving, Gorski thought to himself. He pondered his next move.

The Saharakaree children would be helpless if left alone. He could not leave them to die. The humane thing to do would be to take them with him. Gorski put the metallic lid on his hand flare to avoid blinding the offspring. He knelt down to them and began talking to them in a soft tone of voice. One by one, the baby Saharakaree came to him. He counted eight. Gorski found a small box and began loading the eight baby Saharakaree into it. He hoped that he would be able to protect them from the dangers that were to come.

Gillis sat down in the computer section of the

Raumschiff to follow Gorski's orders. He sent message request after message request to anyone he thought of that might be able to lend assistance. He requested information from retired Admiral Seward, Dean Harvard, Professor Kirby and Professor Rand. He sent out similar broadcasts to Colonel Nikolai Gorski, Colonel Jamal Lincoln, Rear Admiral Cardenas, attorney Sean Collins, Dominic Andolini, Jen Staszko and Sophia DuBravac. He even sent messages to members of the O'Malley family.

He received no direct responses.

Gillis was perturbed. He was receiving messages from numerous sources demanding to know why he and Yuri had murdered the judges. Other messages were requesting an explanation for why they had massacred the Tyr Academy cadets. But there were no requests for information regarding the attack by the Saharakaree. Gillis asked the computer to explain if there was a malfunction to the Raumschiff communication systems. The computer indicated that the on board communication system was operating at one hundred percent capability.

Gillis leaned back in his chair and scratched his head. The responses from the others made no sense. They were non-responsive to the questions he was forwarding. Gillis began mulling over the possibilities. He knew the answer before he asked the question.

"Computer, are our communications being blocked by an external source?"

There was a long uncomfortable pause. Finally, the computer responded. "That is correct, Mr. Gillis. Scans of the lunar surface indicate that there are twelve Jammers on the lunar satellite towers."

"Computer, download the exact coordinates of the jamming devices," Gillis ordered. "And, in addition, download the instructions as to how to disarm them." Gillis sighed.

He thought of Zerbe and how he died. Gillis had grown to like his fellow cadet. Zerbe had become a friend. Gillis felt even worse of Perez Guerrero. The United Nations social workers would take her child from her after she gave birth due to the cruel and unfair orphanage laws of the Glorious Leader. He wondered whether or not his killing of the assassin named Prescott had anything to do with the ambush by the Saharakaree.

Harrison had pulled up the recordings of the events over the last hour on the moon. He asked the computer to display all of the other cadet teams on separate screens. Harrison watched three screens appear side by side and he watched them simultaneously as the Newton and Achilles Academy cadets seemed to arrive safely. Harrison watched the gruesome events of the slaughter at the Tyr Academy headquarters. Harrison took in a deep breath and saw that the attack at the Tyr building was from a small purple, one man operated Allen type space craft. The attacker identified himself as Andolini.

Someone was framing them, Harrison thought to himself. But who? And for what gain?

Harrison asked the computer to show the last hour for the judges. If the judges believed that the Clovis team had killed the other cadets, they would have made efforts to arrest them by now. But no judges had come calling.

Harrison saw why when he viewed the past events of the Judge's Towers being destroyed, again by one man fighter space ships, bearing the colors of Clovis Academy. Harrison stood up, watching the two main judges being gunned down by men wearing enviro-suit uniforms with the names Gorski and Gillis adorned on the chests.

"Computer, were there any conversations between the Gillis or Gorski cadets and the three fighter ships?" Harrison played a hunch.

"Yes," the computer answered.

"Play me the audio," Harrison instructed.

Harrison listened intently to the muffled voices. They were using the names of Gorski and Gillis. The three ships were using the names of Cardenas, Lincoln and Evart.

Harrison smiled to himself. The people that were producing the false evidence against us did not do their homework, Harrison thought to himself. They were careless. Michel Evart had been injured and removed from the team. Harrison hoped that others in the United Nations realized the glaring mistake. The incriminating evidence that was being orchestrated could now easily be challenged. Any decent criminologist would be able to see that the Clovis Academy cadets were not the ones that killed all of those people.

"Computer, please download all of this evidence to my holo-com," Harrison requested.

Steiner had set up Eamon O'Grady in the medical area with IV fluids being pumped into his veins. She was hopeful that the anti-venom would save his life. Steiner calculated that his chances of survival were about fifty percent.

She had not been able to save Pierre and felt guilty for that. The Saharakaree tail had penetrated Zerbe through and through, slicing his stomach and intestines. He had lost too much blood by the time she had gotten him back on the Raumschiff.

Her feelings of guilt were multiplied by the personal feelings for Zerbe. The whole team had grown close during their training. Zerbe was a good man. Steiner thought of Cara Perez Guerrero, Zerbe's pregnant girlfriend wondered how she would be able to cope with being a single mother. That is, if the draconian orphanage laws did not cause the seizure of the child after birth. Steiner did not want to dwell on those thoughts as there was no time. Whoever put together the ambush would most likely strike again once they realized that the majority of the team survived.

Steiner completed her scans of the lunar surface. She found nine life forms for the Clovis Academy and eight faint alien life signs with Gorski. She contacted Gorski to warn him, but he told her it was nothing to be concerned about. Steiner found that all ten of the Newton cadets were alive and well. She detected two life forms at the Tyr Academy headquarters. Both were in distress and the computer indicated they needed medical attention.

The Achilles cadets had been a different issue. Steiner picked up thirteen human life forms, twenty Akarzdamedians and another ten Saharakaree.

"Computer," Steiner said calmly. "Can you scan the alien life forms at the Achilles headquarters?"

"Yes," the computer replied.

"Do the Akarzdamedians and the Saharakaree have computer chips in their brains?"

"I cannot tell," came the answer.

"I would be willing to bet that they do," Steiner said to herself.

"I have detected another fifty faint life signs on board one of the Raumschiff's at the Achilles Headquarters," the computer reported.

Steiner slid her swivel chair across the room to another computer panel and began typing on the keyboard. As she worked on that task she looked to the ceiling. "Computer, the fifty faint life signs, could they be an alien life form?"

"It is like nothing I have ever scanned before," the computer answered.

Steiner spun her chair in circles as she was thinking of what it might be, "Cryo-sleep?"

"Undetermined," the computer replied. "I have detected a large mass approaching planet Semiramis."

"What kind of mass?"

"Scanning. It is large enough to be a Battle Cruiser. Confirmed, it is a Battle Cruiser."

"From what direction did the ship come from?"

"From the flight trajectory it would seem that it came from nearby Sikorsky's Planet."

"Can you identify her?" Steiner pressed. "Is it sending out the required security pulse signal so that we can identify her?"

"My scans indicated that it is emitting a computerized identification pulse and I conclude that she is the Battle Cruiser Lysander," the computer reported.

"Are they coming here for a rescue mission?" Steiner asked hopefully.

"Negative. I am receiving a message from the Lysander that indicates she is not on a rescue mission."

"Play the message," Steiner directed.

She waited for a few seconds as the computer downloaded the broadcast and routed through the communication system of the Raumschiff. She grinded her teeth as she heard the warning:

"This is General Kimberly Sikorsky of the Battle Cruiser Lysander. The Glorious Leader has ordered a quarantine of the moon over planet Semiramis. Our scientists indicate that there is a viral outbreak on the moon that must be contained. I have been ordered to destroy any space craft that attempts to escape the moon. I have been further ordered to destroy any space craft that attempts to approach the moon. Make no mistakes, I will shoot down any ship that attempts to violate the decree of our Glorious Leader. This is General Sikorsky, signing out."

Steiner heard the message begin to replay, "Computer, shut off the download. I have heard enough."

The voice of General Sikorsky ceased as the computer followed Steiner's order.

"I am sorry Miss Julia," the computer said abruptly.

Steiner frowned, "Sorry? That is an emotion that computers are not programmed for."

"I realize that," the computer responded. "It is just that you were always polite to me. I hope that you find a way to continue your life line and escape from here."

Steiner pursed her lips, "So do I."

Since leaving the moon behind would be suicide, Steiner thought about the sentiments of the computer and had an idea. She looked back to her keyboard and continued typing. She finished typing in her command for a scan and saw the screen report that the other Academy Headquarters for the Tyr Academy had plenty of food and water. She smiled to herself. The enemy, whoever that was, had left behind the basic necessities for survival at the Tyr building. Food, water and shelter had been left behind by those that murdered the Tyr cadets.

"So our enemy is not that bright," Steiner whispered to herself.

Marco Andolini and Jurgen Doernitz scanned the four Allen Corporation one man Fighter Type CC76A3 model space ships. No traps, no bombs or explosives of any nature were detected.

"Looks like we are clear," Marco reported to Cardenas.

Cardenas walked to his ship and looked back at the others. "Let me fly mine up first, see what happens. If I make it up about fifty feet without incident, then the rest of you follow me up."

"Maybe one of us should be the test pilot," Lincoln said.

"No, Mary. I will do it. I am in charge and it is my responsibility," Cardenas replied as he climbed the side of his space craft. He sat down in the pilot's seat, strapped on his safety harness and started up his engines.

"There might be something that our scanners could not detect," Doernitz said to Cardenas. "Perhaps I should check first."

"No," Cardenas said while he was doing his systems check simultaneously. "There are other people in danger. We have to help them. And I have faith that the Saharakaree trap was the only one set for us here."

The others watched as Cardenas flew his ship up into the sky.

Marco began to board his small vessel, "You have to

have faith."

Cardenas' religious views, his nature, his positive outlook and amiable personality were beginning to grow on Marco.

Lincoln and Doernitz began climbing on board their own personal ships. It was time to fly and do the job they were trained to do.

Gorski returned to the Raumschiff with the eight Saharakaree children. He ordered the ship computer to dim all of the lights and then carried them up the steps to the command section to find Gillis, Harrison and Steiner waiting for him.

"Porfirio reports that the four ships are airborne," Gillis told Gorski. He looked at the metal container. "What have you got there?"

"Eight Saharakaree children," Gorski set the sibling group on the metal floor. The children crawled out, making chirping noises as they began crawling around and inspecting the ship. "I couldn't leave them to starve to death."

Steiner picked one of the babies in her hands and looked it over. "They are so cute. Hard to believe they will grow up to be lethal killers."

"They will be killers if that is what they are taught," Harrison had one of the babies Saharakaree in his lap. He was stroking the young alien behind it's' ears. It was making a soothing cooing sound and looking up at Harrison with wonder. "They are kind of cute."

"I need reports," Gorski told the others.

"Well, we have come up with some issues," Gillis told Gorski. Gillis pulled out his holo-com and activated it. A large schematic of the lunar surface appeared and there were twelve red blinking lights on the moon.

"Our communications are being blocked, Yuri. There are twelve satellite towers on the lunar surface located where you see the blinking lights. All communications and live broadcasts go through those towers. From there the signal is uploaded to the satellites orbiting the moon and planet Semiramis. Those satellites then send the signals out into space to the other numerous satellites throughout the multiple solar systems occupied by humanity. Each of the lunar satellite towers all have advanced Jammers magnetized to their base. If we are to communicate with Seward and the others, we need to remove those Jammers. I have downloaded the locations and the procedure for deactivating them."

"Good," Gorski was petting one of the Saharakaree behind the ears. It was rubbing against his leg. "What else?"

Harrison cleared his throat, "Well this should come as no surprise. We are being framed. Someone is using our colors to make the rest of the universe believe we are the aggressors. They murdered the eight judges, Yuri. The world believes that you and Les killed them.

"The Tyr Academy cadets were ambushed the same time we were under attack. They were blown to pieces by a one man fighter ship, painted in our colors. The pilot identified himself as Marco."

Gorski's mood seemed to darken. He was pacing back and forth as he thought. "Have we any information or clues as to who is doing this? Whoever it is would have to be well financed."

Steiner asked the computer to display her life form findings. "I think, based on this scan, the Achillies Academy is to blame. Newton has ten human life forms. Achilles has thirteen humans, as well as more Saharakaree and some Akarzdamedians. The cadets from Achilles must be the aggressors."

"But why? Why go through all this trouble to frame us and kill everyone? Anyone here have any enemies at Achilles?"

All of the cadets shook their head in the negative.

Gorski stroked his chin in thought, "What else?"

"I found two human life forms at the Tyr Headquarters," Steiner told him. "According to the scan, their heart rates are weak. Both are in distress. We need to go help them. In addition, the food and water reserves at that location are still intact."

Gorski leaned against a floor to ceiling computer panel, "Drew, contact Porfirio and instruct him to follow us to the Tyr Academy headquarters."

"It could be a trap," Gillis observed.

"Could be," Gorski agreed. "But our training is all geared toward helping our fellow man and woman. If there are two cadets that need our help, then we will do the right thing. We may be in the middle of a war, but we can still keep our humanity and dignity. We are going to help those two cadets. Get ready to take off."

"And these little ones?" Harrison pointed to the baby Saharakaree.

"Feed them something," Gorski shrugged and began climbing up the ladder to the pilot section. "We should have a lot of milk and cheeses in the refrigeration compartments. That's what they normally like, isn't it?"

Gorski sat in the pilot seat and ordered the computer to start the nuclear engines. He took the half circle steering column in his hands and flew the large ship up into the sky. He had the computer navigation system display the most direct route to the Tyr Academy headquarters. He began guiding the Raumschiff toward that location.

The flight to the Tyr headquarters took about twenty minutes. Except for Cardenas, the cadets flew their ships low and close to the lunar surface. Cardenas flew his single person fighter space craft about a thousand feet up, watching for any incoming attacks.

While in route, Cardenas observed the four large transport containers on the lunar surface that had been deposited by Flynn, Ilyasova, Griffin and Hahn. He reported to the others what he saw. Gorski ordered Gillis and Harrison to scan the four containers.

As Gorski landed the Raumschiff near the Tyr Academy

building, he and the others could see the devastation left from the carnage of Lomax's attack. There were numerous pieces of metal, in varying sizes, all with scorch marks from the explosions, lying all over the surface. Steiner reported that one of the life signs she had detected was actually on the lunar surface.

Gorski ordered the ship's computer to open the rear bay doors and lower the walk ramp to the surface. Steiner and Harrison were rushing out to get to the injured person on the surface.

Gillis followed them out, a hand laser at the ready. He watched the roof top of the building and the windows and detected no movement.

Edmund Ross Koch was near death when Steiner located him. He had been exposed to the deadly chlorine gas for almost an hour. Harrison lifted the man up into his arms and carried him inside the Tyr Academy building. Once inside, Steiner was grateful to discover the lights were working. The interior had not been demolished as the Clovis headquarters had been.

Harrison rushed to the medical area and set Koch down on one of the beds. Harrison looked Koch over closely. His skin was burned from exposure to the gas. Harrison observed redness and blisters all over Koch's body. Koch had vomit residue on his cheeks and chest. His eyes had been tearing up. Koch was having difficulty breathing.

"Drew!" Steiner called out. "Help me over here!"

Harrison ran to her and found Steiner kneeling over a

naked woman. The nude stranger had bruises all over her body. Her lower lip was busted, her left eye was bruised shut and she had dried blood on her chin and neck. Harrison had seen enough photographs in his studies for criminal investigations to conclude that the woman had been beaten and raped.

Harrison fought the urge to vomit at the sight of the lady. He reached down to lift her up in his arms. Steiner cautioned Harrison to be careful since the victim was so badly beaten. Harrison gently placed the woman on the bed that was next to Koch. He covered the woman with a bed sheet.

Steiner was already pulling out a syringe and locating some pain killer for the beaten woman. She quickly injected the female with the medication.

"Computer, scan the male victim for evidence of edema," Steiner instructed. "Drew, search the building for clues on who did this. DNA samples, anything."

She injected the female victim, Barnes, with another shot of some vitamins and minerals to give her body energy to survive the wounds.

"I am going to personally punish whoever did this to her."

Gillis and Gorski surveyed the damage outside. They both agreed that it had been an attack with explosives and lasers. They located a few body parts, but no other survivors could be found. Gillis was pulling out his hand held one foot long solar powered Allen Corporation Magnetizer device and directing it at some of the larger metallic pieces and lifting them in the air and moving them aside. The Magnetizer allowed a person to be able to lift up extremely heavy or bulky pieces of metal with ease. The user or operator of a Magnetizer could lift up a thousand pound piece of metal and it would only feel like they were lifting ten pounds.

Harrison reported to Gorski that the Tyr building was not damaged.

"I guess this is our new outpost by default," Gorski said. "Porfirio, land here. We have to formulate our strategy."

Gorski and Gillis returned to their Raumschiff and helped each other carry Eamon O'Grady on a stretcher to the building. He would be the third patient of the unofficial doctor of the team, Julia Steiner.

After delivering their injured team leader to Steiner, Gillis and Gorski went back onto the lunar surface. Steiner reported to the two men that the Lysander was in orbit over planet Semiramis and would shoot down any ship that attempted to leave the moon.

"So we are trapped on this moon," Gorski concluded.

Steiner nodded, "Yes, but Jurgen might be able to fly his fighter ship past the Battle Cruiser. He is very talented. He could get to the Robert Andrews moon or Space Station Cy-5 which are a few days flight from here. He could attempt to get some help to us, or even use the satellites out in space to let the rest of the eight solar systems know what is happening here."

"We might need Jurgen here with us," Gorski responded. "Although I agree that Jurgen is talented, a Battle Cruiser could launch a thousand magnetic R-5 rockets at him simultaneously. Jurgen might be able to out maneuver two or three of them. But he would not make it."

Gillis continued collecting sheets of metal from the destroyed fighter ships and the larger Raumschiff.

"What are you going to do with those?" Gorski pointed at the long pieces of metal that had been part of the demolished Raumschiff.

"Rorke's Drift," Gillis said, thinking out loud.

"Excuse me?" Gorski responded.

"The Zulu War," Gillis responded. "One of the greatest rear defense battles in military history. About one hundred thirty men stood against an estimated four thousand."

"And that helps us here how?" Gorski prodded.

"We create protective barriers," Gillis was picking up big pieces and small pieces of metal with his small magnetizer device. "We make it so the attackers, when they do come, have to enter where our defenses lead them. We make a redoubt and lead them to it."

"Les, you are smarter than any of us. I do not have any concerns about your military history and what not," Gorski told him. "But, they have real weapons. They have space ships with lasers and rockets. We cannot hope to fight behind slivers of metal."

Gillis picked up a piece of a metal pipe. It had been blown off of the Raumschiff and was sharp at one end. The other end was still rounded. The pipe was about six feet long.

"Yuri, if I get a man close enough to me, this piece of metal pipe becomes a sword. Yes, they have superior weaponry, but we are the scrappiest."

Gorski laughed at the quote from Sophia DuBravac. "So then we convince them to fight us hand to hand?"

"Absolutely," Gillis handed Gorski the pipe and picked up another piece of metal, about seven feet long. "They want to fight us face to face. They are framing us so this is personal, Yuri. We clearly pissed off someone that has some money or power or both. They don't want to blow us up like they did to the judges and the Tyr cadets. They want to go mano a mano with us, then we give it to them. Only, they will be walking into my little fun house."

Gillis swung the new found piece of metal like a sword. "We decide how the fight occurs. Even though they have the superiority of weaponry and more fighter space ships, that is not what they want. They want to look us in the eyes as they kill us. But, our biggest dilemma is that if we bloody their noses, they may change their mind set and decide to blast us from the sky. If they do, we are all dead. But to lure them here, we have no choice but to hit them. I need to determine how we do that."

After the small fighter ships landed, the eight Clovis Academy cadets met at the main dining table. The subject of the discussion was how to survive. After several options were tossed around, Yuri Gorski had made some decisions.

"Porfirio, I want you to go with Marco, Mary and Jurgen to those four large canisters you saw on the surface," Gorski instructed. "Find out what is in them. If there is anything useful for your fighters, install it immediately. Use your tow cables to bring the rest back to us. Les, you and Drew stay here, keep building the defenses we spoke of. Julia, how are your three patients?"

Steiner sighed and looked over at the medical area. "Eamon is out. He won't be able to move for at least a week, if he survives. The poison may still take him. Koch, the Tyr cadet commander, he has pulmonary edema. I have put an artificial respirator on him, but it is only stalling the inevitable. The girl, her name is Barnes; she was beaten badly and raped repeatedly. I have her sedated. She should live, but she needs therapeutic help. The prognosis for all three is not good."

"Stay with them," Gorski ordered. "If Koch or Barnes wake up, see if you can get a description of their attackers. It might help us."

Gorski stood up and he paced around the room for a few seconds, "Les, I want you to remove the safety filters on our communications system."

"But then the Newton team will be able to hack us!" Harrison protested.

"Exactly," Gorski smiled at his friend. "I want Anderson

to know we are not behind this. I want our attackers to hear as well. But we only speak about the things we want them to hear. Les, I will give you a green light when I have removed the twelve Jammers from the surface tower satellites. I need you to deliver a speech to the rest of humanity. You draft it. You were always better at speeches than the rest of us."

"What do you want me to say?" Gillis crossed his arms.

"Tell the United Nations and the rest of humanity that we are fighting for our lives," Gorski suggested. "Lie to our competitors, tell them we suffered numerous casualties. Beg for intervention from any source. Tell them that we can only hold out for so long. Plead for the rest of the space command and civilians to show us mercy."

Harrison was checking his holo-com. "Yuri, bad news."

"What is it Drew?"

"As you are aware, the Glorious Leader put quarantine on the moon and planet Semiramis. He just confirmed his order." Harrison up loaded the news report from his small metallic device into a three dimensional broadcast. A male news reporter was arguing with a female reporter that the Glorious Leader was only trying to protect the rest of humanity from horrors on the Blood Moon. The female began to question the Glorious Leader and his decisions regarding the quarantine orders. She asked what evidence Sikorsky had to prove that there were extraordinary dangers on the lunar surface of the moon over Semiramis. The reporter urged that a rescue mission be sent to save the remaining cadets on the moon and ignore the rules of the Glorious Leader.

The expression on Vladimir Sikorsky's face was one of controlled rage. One rule in the United Nations was to never question the Glorious Leader. It was a matter of law on all of the solar systems under the control of the United Nations. The laws and the orders of Secretary General Sikorsky were not subject to debate. Dissent and be prosecuted or even disappear without a trace. If arrested and fully prosecuted the punishment for treason was death.

"She just committed an act of treason," Cardenas observed.

"Maybe she is right to question the Glorious Leader," Lincoln spoke up. "Why can't we demand explanations from our government? Sikorsky is supposed to work for us, not the other way around. Quarantine? Based on what? We eight are here and none of us have been attacked by some strain of bacteria. I say to hell with the Glorious Leader. We need help here and we need it quick. Why is he not allowing it?"

"What if they are watching us right now?" Harrison responded. "They will come and arrest you for that."

"Good! Get down here and take me away. Arrest me you cowards!" Lincoln shouted, pointed her finger at the ceiling. "I hope they are listening. There are so many unjust laws in our Empire! We need a new direction. Come on! You killed these cadets without provocation! Come and arrest me! I am a traitor!

Come on down here and take me away!"

Harrison shook his head, "Come on, Mary. You are being a little dramatic here."

Lincoln glared at Harrison, "Drew you of all people should agree with me that there are some laws that need to be abolished. You were ostracized by one of the more influential families on New Edinburgh because of some of those laws."

"What laws are you referring to?" Gillis folded his arms across his chest.

"Look at Julia and me. We are told, by force of law and under threat of imprisonment, that we cannot use contraception or birth control. We are not allowed to have an abortion. And when we give birth, our children are subject to seizure by the government of our Glorious Leader to be placed in an orphanage. Maybe some talk of treason is warranted."

Lincoln had long told other women of her desire to change the laws on reproductive rights. She decided why not express them now since they would all be dead soon from another ambush.

Gorski shook his head, "Mary, really? Just speaking like that could get you thrown in jail. You should be careful with what you say."

"To hell with caution," Steiner chimed in. "We may all be dead within the next few hours anyway. If they attack us with their ships, we all die. So we all may as well say what we need to say. Mary is right. Unless we are lucky enough to have money or have a husband, our children get taken. No due process rights are afforded the accused. No court to protect our interests. Each of us has met the product of the current orphan system. Look at the sociopaths like Johann LeSkaysner and Angus McWilliams. We women have our children taken from us so they can grow up to be like those two, or even turn out worse? How is that fair?"

"I have to agree with the girls," Gillis spoke up. "We all know what will happen to Cara when she has her child. Pierre is now dead and the government will seize their child. That is completely unfair. And remember Yesenia? She had to marry that pig, Bragg, to keep her child with her. The laws are not just and need to be changed. Frankly, this 'quarantine' of this moon, is proof to me that the Glorious Leader is involved in our situation. Some way, somehow he is involved."

"You all know that I was raised in an orphanage," Doernitz told them. "I would like to think that my sister and I turned out okay."

"I was not referring to you, Jurgen." Steiner touched his shoulder. "But you and your sister escaped and were eventually adopted by Admiral Yamamoto. You have to admit that he was a good father to you and being a member of his family had a huge impact on the man that you grew up to be."

Doernitz stood and walked away from the table. He was not comfortable speaking out against the Glorious Leader. Perhaps because he was younger than the others or the subject matter of the orphan issue had struck a series of bad memories for him. He recalled his older brother that had been beaten senseless several times when they were together at the orphan home. He ordered him and Freya to leave him behind. Jurgen never learned the final fate of his long lost brother and it was not a set of memories he wanted to relate to others.

Cardenas cleared his throat, "The Apostle Paul did write that we are all subject to man's law while in this level of existence. Change in the law must always be done peacefully. We have to have faith that God will place the right leaders in the positions to give us just laws."

"And if the wrong leaders are placed in power?" Lincoln challenged. "We just all have to take it? Look at us right now. Pierre was murdered! Eamon might die! Les is right. There is no reason for any quarantine here. There is no biological outbreak on this moon. No unknown bacteria or alien life form attacking. This is simply humans out to kill each other."

"You all do realize that the Glorious Leader has several hundred thousand children, grandchildren, great grandchildren, great great grandchildren and so on and so on?" Harrison pointed out.

"I think it is well known that Secretary General Sikorsky family has a huge amount of offspring. Why bring that up?" Steiner asked.

"Because one of us could be a Sikorsky," Harrison said. "Think of it. The Welker name belongs to offspring of the Glorious Leader. How many Welker's are in high positions of power? Dozens of them."

"And the Murdock's." Gillis added. "The Tsukifuji's, the Urbanczyk's and the...Rosenburg's." Gillis stood up abruptly. "Yuri, that computer chip we took from the dead Saharakaree. You know who was accused a few years ago of manufacturing such chips?"

"The Rosenburg Corporation," Gorski concluded. "My father's commanding officer was investigating the link, just before, just before he was killed during Darktober."

The group was silent for a moment.

"As you all know I have been spending most of my evenings at the Collins mansion. I overheard Collins speaking with one of his other prosecutors, Goldsmith was his name, and there were several Rosenburg's that had escaped. Among them were Alfred, Matthew, David and a few others. It would be plausible that one or more of the escapees arranged this situation."

Steiner hated telling the others about confidential communications between the prosecutors that she heard. But the information might be vital to help Gillis and Gorski in their war plans.

"The implication being made here is treason," Cardenas finally spoke up. "We are cadets, students. We are not even officers yet. We could be arrested for such talk."

"What about freedom of speech?" Lincoln challenged. "On old Earth, many countries held that the freedom to speak out, to debate, was paramount in their culture. Now, all of humanity trembles in fear to dare to think of things we just talked about. It is wrong."

"If they have listening devices in this building, we will all be indicted." Harrison pointed out to the others.

"We are all going to be dead soon anyway," Steiner said.

"Enough debate," Gorski waived his hands. "We have work to do, or Julia will be right. We will all be dead very soon. If we go on a working theory that the Rosenburg's are involved in this then we could be wiped out with one smart bomb. These people play for keeps. Perhaps they are involved to get back at my father for arresting so many of them." Gorski paused for a moment. "My friends, if we are going to survive, then we must get prepared. I have given you your assignments. Let's move out."

Marco Andolini and Jurgen Doernitz were the first to leave the room. Both men did not want to speak at all regarding the subject matter of the debate.

Lincoln rushed to catch up with Marco, "You sure were quiet back there."

"I have a huge sibling group. Several sisters and brothers." Marco reminded Lincoln. "I know that when people speak out against the Glorious Leader they disappear. Their families also disappear. Remember General Tan back on Lynott's Land? She didn't just enforce the laws, she loved to execute people. Years back I watched her shoot seven people in the back of the head for protesting some of the farming taxes that were levied by the Glorious Leader. I am no coward, Mary. I would fight for you and for freedom any day. But to say something that would get my other siblings in danger? Count me out."

"Marco, you are being extreme," Lincoln said. "It was just us talking, blowing off some steam. We are all friends here and I did not mean to challenge your courage. You are one of the bravest men I have ever known."

Marco stopped walking and turned to face her, "Mary, I love you. I never want to see you harmed. One thing I have kept secret from everyone is that my aunt was a political leader on the Martian Colonies. She once spoke out against the Glorious Leader. Some assassins killed her, and then killed her husband and finally their children. The Sikorsky family does not play games. People die when they challenge Sikorsky. They would not think twice at killing all of us for saying the things we just said. I do not want to be a part of such discussions against the Sikorsky's."

Marco turned from Lincoln and began walking toward the exit of the building again. Lincoln just watched him in silence. She understood his hesitance to be verbal about the two hundred year rule of the Glorious Leader. Lincoln also knew that he was correct. Several ranking military officers had been killed without any arrests or indictments for the murder. Politicians as well. The Glorious Leader would allow some formerly illegal drugs to be legalized, alternative lifestyles were acceptable and local elections were allowed for small positions such as Mayor or City Council. All of these small offerings were to give the people the illusion of freedom.

Lincoln followed Marco to their ships. Such ideas or thoughts could wait. There was work to do.

Cardenas stopped walking and placed his hand on Doernitz's shoulder. "Jurgen, you do realize that you could try and fly off this moon and get past that Battle Cruiser out there?"

Doernitz nodded, "My chances would be less than twenty percent. I thought about it for a split second and then dismissed the thought. My place is by your side. I will not leave you or the others. I was not raised to do such a thing."

"Jurgen, do not take to heart what Mary and Julia said back there about the orphan homes. Freya and I often talk at night about how proud we are of you. You have grown into a good man. I know that the Yamamoto clan is proud of you as well." Cardenas paused for a moment. "Your life is just beginning. I have faith that we were all placed here for a reason. We will most likely have to fight to survive. I need for you to be brave, Jurgen. When the time comes for you to have to kill, don't hesitate."

"I won't let you down, Porfirio."

Gillis and Harrison placed their helmets on and attached them to their enviro-suits. They both walked to their Raumschiff and climbed the walk ramp to the rear entrance. Gillis led Harrison to one of the supply storage rooms. In the room was several tool kit boxes, two blow torches and a large drill, standing seven feet tall with a metal spiral drill tip. Harrison recognized the large drill as one of the tools that was normally used for geological or archeological excavations, to assist the scientists in digging deeper under planetary surfaces.

"Let's get all of these out of here," Gillis said to Harrison.

They both knew that they had to hurry as Gorski was going to be taking the Raumschiff to disarm the Jammers that had been placed on the land based satellite towers. The large drill was on wheels, so Harrison was able to easily pull it out of the storage closet and then push it down the exit ramp. Gillis was right behind him, with a tool box kit in each hand and the two blow torches balanced on top of the tool kit boxes. As the two men descended the steps, Gorski met them.

"Yuri, we are certain that the Achilles cadets are the perpetrators?" Gillis asked.

"No doubt," Gorski answered. "You heard Julia. They have aliens, some Saharakaree, and they have extra fighter ships and an extra Raumschiff. Make sure they regret their actions, Les."

"Pierre was our friend," Gillis began walking away from him. "They won't live to regret it. I plan on killing them all."

"I can go along with that," Harrison kept pushing the large drill.

"Les, remember the underground rail system we talked

about?" Gorski asked.

"Way ahead of you on that Yuri." Gillis pointed to the large drill. "I think we can take the offensive to them. Remember what I said about giving them a bloody nose? I have a plan."

"Do it," Gorski ordered as he boarded the Raumschiff. "And Les? Kill them all for Pierre and Eamon. It would be nice if we could net us a survivor or two. The people will want to prosecute someone for all of the murders and I for one would like to beat the reason for the attacks out of them."

"We all feel that way," Gillis assured him. "You give me the word and I will give them a counter attack that will rock them to their knees."

CHAPTER SIX

The cadets at all of the Academies would gather at local bars, recreation centers and other locations to see if there were any updates on the events on the Moon of Semiramis. The four large student bodies were understandably curious at least and personally involved at best to learn the fate of the forty cadets on the Blood Moon.

One of the Clovis Academy students, Dominic Andolini, was arrested for assaulting a news reporter for calling Marco Andolini a multiple murderer. The reporter realized as he was being beaten that perhaps he should have used different terminology when speaking of Dominic's twin brother. Harumi Shigeta and Jen Staszko paid the bail amount to have Dominic released from the jail.

The staff at O'Malley's kept their doors open twenty-four hours every day so that all of the cadets could come and wait for the blockage in the broadcast to end. Of the over fourteen thousand cadets at Clovis Academy, there were several hundred that spent most of their spare time at O'Malley's. Each of them waited for news of their colleagues, friends, siblings, lovers, or husbands.

Ginger Collins O'Grady had staked out a table on the fifth floor of O'Malley's and took personal leave from her job at the United Nations so she could wait for any updates. She intended to remain at her table for as long as it took. Occasionally, she would be joined by the other effected cadets and civilians. Piotr Gorski, Yuri's younger brother, would come and go to see if there was any news about his brother. Cormac Collins, one of Ginger's brothers also would come and go, asking if any updates had been released.

Jen Staszko would check in between her classes and stay for several hours each night, desperate for news regarding her lover. Lila Zapata and Sophia DuBravac were also regular visitors, both having huge interests in the men Gillis and Doernitz. Zapata was very quiet, which was not in her bubbly character. She seemed to be handling the situation internally, not expressing her fears to the others.

Cara Perez Guerrero was the one that would show the most emotion, sometimes unable to stop crying. Several of the other women wondered if Perez Guerrero's hormones were affecting her due to the pregnancy. The entire Andolini family would also join them on occasion. Ginger had never realized that the twins, Marco and Dominic, had such a massive sibling group. The Andolini parents took the Glorious Leader's orders to breed seriously. All of the Andolini children were well behaved, other than Dominic beating the one rude reporter for insulting Marco.

Ginger would attempt to contact her husband every hour on the hour using her personal holo-com. She would leave a message each time, telling him she loved him. But he never responded. Her computer would indicate that her messages were being sent. She was certain that her husband could hear her. For some unexplained reason, he could not respond to her. She pondered that for a moment and then she came up with a theory. She looked up at the women sitting around her. They were all gossiping about some professor at the Academy.

"Girls," Ginger stated to get their attention. She saw Staskzo, DuBravac, Zapata, Perez Guerrero and Ann Harcourt, who had joined the group that evening stop their discussion and look at her expectantly.

"You have some news?" Staszko asked hopefully.

"No, but I think I know why we cannot get information from our men." Ginger told them, holding her holo-com in the air. "They can hear us, but they cannot reply. That means they are being blocked on the lunar surface. Communications go in, but cannot go out."

"Who would do that?" Perez Guerrero demanded.

"The real killers would do that. The real question is who could do that? Who has the money and or the influence to do it?" DuBravac stood up, understanding what Ginger was getting at.

"We can help clear the names of our men by finding out who would have that technology. I think we need to get to the main library and hit the computers and start researching."

"Sit down, Sophia," Staszko said suddenly.

"Jen, we have to..."

"I said, sit down," Staszko repeated to DuBravac. "I already know where such technology exists."

"Well, Jen? Are you going to just keep us in suspense or enlighten the rest of us?" Perez Guerrero demanded.

"Do you all remember when Yuri and Michel were on the Ragnarsson's Raumschiff, the Blitzkrieg?" Staszko asked them. "I went on board after it had crashed. I was there when the military intelligence officers began their inventory. Of the items they found, there were dozens of devices called 'Jammers.' I overheard the MI investigators sent by General Tan discussing them. They were newly manufactured by the Rosenburg Corporation and considered untested for use. They said they were to block out going transmissions from a ship, or a space station, or even a planet."

"So the Ragnarsson assassins are involved in what is happening," DuBravac concluded.

"Ginger, tell your father I wish to speak with him," Staszko stood up. "I want to interview one of his prisoners. I want to see Ella Ragnarsson. I think I can make that bitch talk."

As the women were discussing the issue of the Ragnarsson's, Elektra Papanikolaou was relieving her stress at the Academy gymnasium. She was concentrating her efforts on learning how to control the new strength of her mechanical arm. Assisting her in that endeavor were two licensed physical trainers, Flora Evart, Zarnella Bedrosian and Hua Thon Ye. All of them were wearing Academy issued sweats and tennis shoes. The physical trainers would hand Elektra a metallic object and instruct her to squeeze slowly until the object would begin to buckle under the stress of the force. After several hours, Elektra felt as if she had a better control over the power of her Allen Corporation mechanical arm.

"You know that the pigmentation of the skin really blends in with your natural color," Hua Thon Ye complimented her.

Elektra wiped some sweat from her brow with a purple towel, "Thanks. It feels just like my real arm. It has all of the sensations of touch just like before. The only difference is that I can crush metal as if it were a paper cup."

Zarnella was hanging upside down from the air vents, her tail wrapped around one of the thinner pipes. She could hear everything around her with her sensitive ears and her whiskers twitched when she overheard members of the Bragg Gang down the hall discussing the murders on the Blood Moon. She glanced in the direction of the other group and noted that it consisted of four of the Lipinski sisters and two of the Calderon brothers. Deciding that whatever the Lipinski's or Calderon's had to say was a waste of her time, Zarnella loosened her tail grip around the pipe and flipped head over heels three times as she fell the fifteen feet to the floor. She landed on all fours and meowed at Flora and Elektra.

"What's up Zarnella?" Flora inquired of her new friend. After their sexual foursome with Supreet and Rolf, they were fined by the University Dormitory accountants for the shredded carpet courtesy of Zarnella. Flora did not hold it against the half feline woman. She actually had found Zarnella's sexual performance with Rolf quite entertaining.

"Bragg members at three o'clock," Zarnella warned.

Elektra glanced down the hall and shrugged, "It's alright, and we were planning on leaving anyway. I want to get a shower and then meet the others at O'Malley's; hopefully, there is some good news of our friends."

The three girls said good bye to the trainers and Hua Thon Ye before departing for the showers. Unknown to the girls, they had been spied on from a distance.

Being a niece of the infamous Dell Ragnarsson was a curse and a privilege at the same time. Savara Ragnarsson had to follow the orders of her uncle just as she would have followed orders from her father, Felix. Savara was twenty and easily passed herself off as an Academy student. Her mission was to kill Elektra and then move on to Jen Staszko and kill her as well. Savara waited in the lobby of the busy gymnasium for her prey to depart the building. Savara learned from the mistakes of Junior, Ella and Emma: never try and kill a target in a crowded location. A good kill required patience. Savara had all the time in the world to stalk the cadets and stick them with a flame dart when the time was right.

Savara did not have long to wait. She kept her reaction to herself as she observed Elektra, Flora and the Kotek woman walking down the long stair case toward the lower lobby. The women were all carrying purple gym bags with the Clovis Academy logo on the side emblazoned in white. Elektra led the other two women out the large glass sliding doors at the front entrance. Savara followed them at a distance, looking for her opportunity to kill them all.

Elektra, Flora and Zarnella walked from the gymnasium and in the direction of some of the taller buildings in Clovis City which were located in the business district. Past those buildings they would find O'Malley's and some of the restaurants that the cadets frequented.

Savara watched the passing crowd like a hawk and calculated in her mind the possible areas where there might be a lull in the number of witnesses so that she could dispatch the cadet named Elektra and then slip away into the night. After the three cadets passed the large skyscraper buildings, they were in the large Academy court yard that was flat, open, paved with transparent metal and the only cover for about a kilometer radius were the few trees, a flag pole and statutes of the Glorious Leader and other past heroes of humanity. Savara decided the time to act was upon her. There were a few dozen cadets walking around, here and there. The risk was negligible in Savara's mind.

She pulled out her stun darts and prepared to inject the women with them. She paused when she noticed that the Kotek woman hugged Elektra and Flora near the large flag pole that had the colors of the Academy waving in the sky. The Kotek departed the other two women, which made Savara Ragnarsson's job easier. She waited for the Kotek to walk in the opposite direction of Elektra and Flora before continuing to follow.

Zarnella Bedrosian was tired and wanted to take what she referred to as a "cat nap." She bid Flora and Elektra a good night and began walking off in the direction of the women's dormitories. Although she would have loved to spend her spare time with the other girls at O'Malley's, Zarnella was exhausted. As she walked away, Savara Ragnarsson's scent was blown in her direction. Zarnella took in the smell and her feline instincts recognized the odor of a predator. Her fur stood up on her back and her tail enlarged as her fur stood up in alarm. She looked over her shoulder and observed a strange woman moving quickly in the direction of Elektra and Flora. Zarnella crouched down on all fours as her double jointed body collapsed low to the ground. Her claws on her hands and feet expanded outward from her finger and toe tips as she began to charge the strange woman like a leopard charging in to kill her next meal.

Savara Ragnarsson raised her right hand up and moved up behind Flora Evart, ready to deliver a stun dart into her neck. Before the assassin could deliver the blow, she felt her back tear open as the claws of Zarnella ripped into her. Savara screamed out loud as Zarnella's jaws opened and closed over her right wrist. The sharp teeth of the Kotek woman tore the flesh and tendons in the would-be assassin's arm.

Elektra and Flora turned around to see their friend Zarnella mauling a strange woman. They ran in their direction in time to see Zarnella slash the strange woman across the throat, ripping it open and spilling several pints of blood on the court yard. The stranger fell backwards, gasping for air as she began to twitch spastically on the ground. Her abdomen had been ripped open by Zarnella's claws, exposing her internal organs. Elektra noticed the dropped stun darts near the dying woman and quickly realized that Zarnella had quite possible saved her life.

As the assassin was bleeding out, Flora pulled Zarnella off of her while Elektra searched the woman. Naturally, the stranger had no identification on her person. But she was armed with several flame darts, knives, a laser pistol and stun darts.

Flora was shaking with obvious fear from what she observed. "Zarnella? Why did you kill this woman?"

Zarnella let out a deep meow, "She was stalking you two. I could smell her. She intended to kill both of you."

Elektra showed the weapons to Flora, "She's right. Look at these weapons. She was going to kill us."

Several other cadets were crowding around them as Savara Ragnarsson died. Some of the cadets stared at Zarnella with concern in their eyes.

Flora whispered to her friend, "You need to take another shower, Zarnella."

"Why?" Zarnella asked.

"You have blood all over you," Flora explained to her.

"You saved our lives," Elektra told her. "Thank you."

"You are welcome," Zarnella said. She had never killed before and the ease in which she had done so scared her. She had always thought of herself as human, even though she resembled a feline in so many ways. She had heard some of the feline/human hybrids ended up going feral and shunned humanity for the animal kingdom. She feared that she was losing control of her animal instincts based on what she had just done. By the way some of the other cadets were looking at her she concluded that they had the same thoughts about her as well.

CHAPTER SEVEN

The surface of the moon had grown dark as she orbited behind her host planet, Semiramis. The planet stood in the path of the sunlight and it would remain dark for the next several hours. The temperature dropped as well.

Jurgen Doernitz led the small pack of fighter space craft to the four large red storage containers on the surface of the moon. He landed his ship and saw that, to his left, Porfirio Cardenas was doing the same. Mary Lincoln and Marco Andolini landed their ships on the other side of the four large storage containers.

Doernitz asked his computer to conduct one last scan of the four containers. No life signs were detected which gave Doernitz some peace of mind. He did not want a repeat of the ambush they had suffered at the hands of the slave Saharakaree. He opened his canopy and disconnected his safety harnesses. Doernitz drew his hand laser and climbed down the side of his space craft. He began to walk toward the nearest storage unit.

Yuri Gorski flew the Clovis Academy Raumschiff at full

speed to the first of twelve large communication towers on the lunar surface. Gorski intentionally chose the tower that was the furthest in location from the Tyr Academy cadet headquarters, hoping that by doing so he would throw off their adversaries as to their real location. He landed the large Raumschiff, secured his enviro-suit helmet, and picked up some tools that had been given to him by Les Gillis.

Gorski ordered the computer to lower the exit ramp and open the rear bay doors. He climbed down the ladders, made his way to the rear of the ship and ran down the ramp. Gorski was certain that once he began deactivating the Jammer's, the attackers would react. Most likely, they would come for him to try and stop him from releasing all of the large free standing communication stations.

Gorski found the one foot tall magnetized Jammer at the base of the first tower. Using a small pen shaped instrument, called the de-magnetizer, was able to remove the Jammer from the base of the tower. Gorski opened the side of the Jammer with a solar battery operated drill. He took out a pair of cutting pliers and sliced through the wiring inside of the Jammer. The first tower was now able to send messages and images to the rest of the galaxy.

Gorski quickly ran back to his Raumschiff. He had no doubt those that meant them harm would soon know what had happened. He boarded his craft, tossed the Jammer to the rocky ground and climbed up the ladders to his pilot seat. He guided the Raumschiff back up into the sky and flew at full speed to the location of the next closest satellite communication tower. Gorski knew that he was now racing against time.

Les Gillis checked and rechecked the grid on the computer generated map. He and Harrison were out on the lunar surface and they had the large drill in place. One of the tool boxes was set a few dozen yards away with some rope and a blow torch. Gillis ordered Harrison to stand back as he maneuvered the point of the drill on the lunar surface. Gillis activated the machine and stood back.

The drill began spinning and cutting through the dust and rock. Gillis and Harrison hid behind some of the large sheets of metal from the doomed Tyr Academy Raumschiff that the two cadets had anchored to the lunar surface to shield them from flying debris. The drill made a loud grinding noise as the surface rock gave way to the stronger metal. After less than fifteen minutes, the drilling stopped.

Gillis beckoned Harrison to follow him. The two men moved the drill backwards. It had created a round hole of approximately a four feet wide radius.

"Thank the Stars Arch Frazier was right about the surface rock," Gillis remarked as he looked down into the hole. He was shining a solar battery powered flashlight into the hole as Harrison joined him. Below he could see the long rail system that had been constructed many years ago. As the scans had predicted there was a computer control pad on the wall near the hole. Gillis grinned and looked over at Harrison. "Get the rope and lower me to the Catacomb of Despair. I am going to hack into the computer controls and see if I can get one of the rail cars to travel over here by remote control."

"And then what?" Harrison said as he walked over to the long rope.

"And then I send our enemies a present," Gillis took the rope and tied it around his waist.

Harrison had the rope in both hands, his legs spread open so he could handle Gillis weight. He watched as Gillis dropped his tool box down the hole and secured the blow torch to his harness. Gillis tossed the other end of the rope down the newly dug hole and began to climb downward. He landed on the bottom of the rail tunnel and pulled out of his enviro-suit breast pocket a handful of Illuminators. They were each about a foot long and a quarter of an inch thick. Gillis twisted each one of the Illuminators and they began to glow. He threw each one of the shining objects in different directions, lighting up the tunnel for about fifty feet in each direction.

"What do you hope to accomplish down there?" Harrison yelled down at Gillis.

"My uncle Andrew, back in Ireland, taught me how to hot wire engines to space ships and other machines," Gillis said as he scanned the area around him. "I plan on wiring a train engine so that I can detonate it with a radio transmission. It will make a hell of a weapon."

"You aren't going to blow us up? Are you?" Harrison swallowed. Gillis had mentioned his uncle Andrew a few times in the past. According to Gillis, Uncle Andrew was a master of producing weaponry. Gillis learned many things from his uncle that the Academy Professors would never consider teaching. Harrison was relieved that Gillis was on his side.

Gillis laughed at Harrison's questions.

Jurgen Doernitz opened the large doors of the first storage container. It was a double door held together by two latches. Whoever had deposited the containers on the lunar surface did not seem concerned about security. There were no locks, no traps and no cameras that were visible to Doernitz. Mary Lincoln was behind him, shining a flashlight into the large storage unit.

"Am I dreaming this?" Lincoln spoke out loud.

Cardenas walked in first. He took in a deep breath at what he saw.

From floor to ceiling were racks of weapons. All kinds. There was a locker with dozens of laser rifles lined on the floor. Above the laser rifles in that locker were at least fifty hand lasers. There were rocket launchers, rockets, stun darts, flame darts, knives of all shapes and sizes, thermite grenades, concussion grenades, explosives, engineering tools, and other items.

"Marco, inventory this stuff. Check to see if the laser rifles and hand lasers are for combat use." Cardenas ordered. "If so, we need to each arm ourselves. We should each take a few of the items so we can fight back."

"Why would they leave all of this stuff out here, unguarded and unprotected?" Doernitz was wide eyed at the treasure trove they had stumbled upon.

"Because they are over confident?" Marco speculated as he began scanning the lasers. "Perhaps they thought we would not scan the surface as Yuri ordered. Maybe they thought we would panic and not try to fight back. Maybe they thought that the Saharakaree would kill all of us. Who knows?" He inspected his scanner. "Porfirio, these lasers have full range of attack, stun, kill and vaporize."

"Everyone grab a hand laser and a laser rifle," Cardenas instructed as picked up a laser rifle and checked the charge level. "Get a knife or two, some stun darts and flame darts. Now we can take the fight to them. Let's see what is in the other three lockers. We need to hurry because Les will be sending in our response to what they did to us at our HQ. We need to be ready to fight."

Yuri Gorski made a quick landing at the second tower. He deactivated and damaged the Jammer he found there, ran back to the Raumschiff and leaped up onto the landing ramp. Only ten towers left and no sign of any opposition. Gorski began to wonder why. He did not bother closing the back loading dock or retracting the landing ramp before he lifted off. He decided to leave both open so he could save a few seconds on each trip.

Les Gillis removed the metal plate guard from the computer control on the wall of the underground rail system. He looked over the controls and found what he was seeking. The red letters "AUTO-CONTROLS" stood out like a lone bright star shining in the deep reaches of space. Gillis took out his pocket computer, connected his splicing wires from his computer to the rail system control panel. He ordered his small computer to display his holographic keypad. He began to type rapidly and was glad that he was able to hack the system easily.

"Drew!" Gillis reported. "I'm in! I am going to get a light rail over here. Let Julia know so she won't panic when she feels the tremors from under the ground."

Harrison ran back to the headquarters and rushed inside and removed his safety helmet. "Julia! Where are you?"

"In the medical area," Steiner announced. Her voice sounded sad.

Harrison ran to her and stopped when he saw that she was covering the body of Koch with a white sheet. She had tears in her eyes. Several of the baby Saharakaree were watching, making a sad cooing sound, as if they understood the concept of mourning.

"Oh no," Harrison walked to Steiner and hugged her.

"I tried to save him," Steiner said softly. "We just got to him too late."

"I am so sorry, Julia."

"The woman, Barnes, she is sedated. She might live. But, you have to swear something to me Drew." Steiner looked up at his eyes. "Swear that you will not let what they did to her happen to me. Swear that you will kill me before those animals get near me."

"Julia, it won't come to that," Harrison told her.

"Drew, swear that you will kill me when the time comes," Steiner was glaring at him. "The men that did that to her are immoral beasts. If they start to take over our position, kill me. Please Drew. Please. Swear that you will not let me go through that. I would rather be dead."

"I swear, Julia. I will protect you with my last breath," Harrison promised. He held her and felt it was now or never, to tell her how he still felt for her. "You know I still love you, Julia. I never stopped. I just hope that if, I mean, when we get out of this, you can find it within you to give us another chance."

Steiner looked up at Harrison for a moment. She gently pushed herself out of his embrace. "I am so sorry, Drew. But I do not feel the same for you. I am with another man now."

Harrison looked down at the floor, his heart broken. He had hoped that one day she would change her mind about him. "Cormac is a good man. If you love each other, then I am happy for you."

One of the baby Saharakaree jumped onto Harrison's shoulder and rubbed its small face against his. It was cooing to Harrison. Harrison patted the top of the little alien's head. He found the presence of the child Saharakaree soothing. It was as if the alien child understood Harrison's pain and sought to console him.

Steiner shook her head and thought hard about a different subject. "Drew, do you remember the pictures I showed you of my home in Switzerland?"

Harrison smiled, "Yes, of course I remember. The mountains and the snow. It was all so beautiful."

"If we survive I want to go back and ski at Kleine Scheidegg one last time. I want to climb the Eiger again. I miss my home and family so much."

"Then we need to fight like hell, Julia. We need to survive this and the only way that will happen is if you dig down deep and bring out that instinct to survive. When you get the opportunity to kill one of the enemy, take it. Do not hesitate." Harrison put his hands on her shoulders. "You did well with the Saharakaree. Do the same against the humans."

Steiner recalled how she had stabbed one of the Saharakaree to death. "I wanted to study the sciences so I would not have to involve myself in military operations. I hate what I did to that alien."

"Be ready to do it again," Harrison advised her.

Porfirio Cardenas and Jurgen Doernitz entered the second storage locker. They shined their lights inside and both men smiled as they viewed the rows of weaponry inside.

"I don't believe it!" Cardenas said as he walked into the

large storage locker and surveyed the contents.

Doernitz was immediately scanning the larger objects. "And they are operational."

"What is operational?" Lincoln asked them as she approached the entrance.

"Laser batteries," Doernitz reported excitedly. "We can replace our worthless pulsar weapons with the lasers. Then our ships can fight theirs and the armor piercing rockets in the back are battle ready. I can mount up to four rockets on each of our ships."

"Is this for real?" Marco was looking at the laser batteries and rockets. "How could they just leave all of this out in the middle of nowhere?"

"Like you said, they were over confident," Cardenas answered. "Each of you grab a laser battery. We need to mount them on our ships so we can fight back. Once we get that done, we mount the rockets."

"That will take some time," Lincoln warned. She was also feeling tired as they had gone without sleep for longer than recommended.

"Have faith, Mary," Cardenas told her. "The Lord has a reason for everything. I believe that we were destined to find these weapons. Jesus is watching over us and has blessed us with the means to fight for ourselves. Nothing ever happens by chance. Now we need to use them to fight back. The Newton Academy cadets and Yuri will need for us to be able go face to face with our adversaries. Let's get to work. We need to be ready to take the fight to them."

Yuri Gorski landed and deactivated the third of the Jammer's. He met no opposition just as he had experienced at the previous two towers. He continued to ponder why their attackers had not come after him yet. Gorski was certain that the Jammer's had some form of security device inside. His actions had to be detected by the enemy. Once the devices were disconnected, the other side had to know. Gorski opened the third Jammer and cut the circuitry.

"Where are you bastards?" Gorski whispered to himself as he ran back on board his Raumschiff. "Did they leave the moon? Are they still here?"

By now, Gorski speculated, the rest of the eight solar systems should be receiving images from the moon. One fourth of the Jammer's were destroyed.

CHAPTER EIGHT

At the Achilles Academy Headquarters, Caine Rosenburg and his friends were drinking wine, whiskey and ale. They were eating steaks that they had cooked on the oven grill. Almost everyone was drunk, except for Kai Chin and Dell Ragnarsson. Chin had gone upstairs to sleep, which was difficult to do due to the cacophony below. Alexander had ordered the computer to play some death heavy metal music at the highest volume. Dell retired to his personal Raumschiff to sleep.

David Rosenburg had left his black leather jacket on one of the kitchen chairs. Inside his breast pocket was his small hand sized computer. The red alarm light had been blinking ever since Yuri Gorski disconnected the first Jammer device. David Rosenburg never saw the red light as he was drinking with his sibling, Caine, and watching pornographic movies on one of the computer screens.

Alfred Rosenburg, II, was in the cadet Raumschiff with one of the female Akarzdamedian slaves. Using the computer microchip implanted in the alien Akarzdamedian, Alfred forced her to perform numerous sex acts on him.

As they celebrated and continued with their party, Yuri Gorski was able to go from tower to tower, diffusing Jammer after Jammer.

The Newton Academy Cadets had assembled in their headquarters. Alan Anderson stood before them, pacing back and forth.

"I have conferred with Nic and Angelique," Anderson began. "We are cut off from the rest of the Empire. The moon has been quarantined by order of the Glorious Leader. So we have to believe that no help will be coming for us. We have decided to make best efforts to leave and get to the nearest space station for safety. I am not one to run from a conflict, mates. But we have no weapons to fight back. Hell, we don't even know who our enemies are."

"So we run?" Ellen Benson asked. "What if they give chase? Wouldn't we be sitting ducks? They would just blast us out of the skies before we made ten kilometers. That General from the Lysander was quite clear that any of us attempting to leave would be blown up."

Nicolas Curtis shook his head, "For God's sake, Ellen. We already are sitting ducks. We have no choice. We must get off of this moon. Maybe some of us can make it to Cy-5 and ask for asylum."

"I have never run away from a fight," Benson told him. "We should stand up to these people."

Curtis shook his head, "We have to survive, Ellen. Fighting an adversary that outnumbers us and possess the weapons they have would be suicide."

"Suicide is trying to outrun a Battle Cruiser firing hundreds of R-5 rockets at you," Benson pointed her index finger at Curtis. "You know that what I say is true."

Laurence Thompson was working diligently, sitting at the main computer board and was monitoring several different programs simultaneously. He cleared his throat to get everyone else to be quiet. "Alan, I think the satellites are sending signals again."

Anderson turned his attention toward Thompson and approached him. "How can you tell, mate?"

Thompson had eight different fifteen by twenty inch holographic screens around him. He pointed to one that had waves of power fluctuations. "These waves are monitoring outgoing messages. It just started going wild during the last few seconds. It seems that we are back up to twenty-five percent broadcasting ability. What do you think is going on?"

Anderson paced back and forth behind where Thompson was seated. "I think another attack might be coming. Or it could be that someone else figured out where the blockage was coming from. Keep monitoring it, Larry."

CHAPTER NINE

The cadets slowly gathered around the oval shaped metal conference table that was part of the second floor of the gold and black Fenster Raumschiff. They had just learned of the fact that a Battle Cruiser was sent to patrol planet Semiramis to shoot down any and all space craft that attempted to enter the area. Dirk Fenster called his fellow cadets to the meeting to give them a last chance to opt out of the rescue attempt.

"We can never get past a Battle Cruiser," Katarina Strahovski concluded. She looked into the eyes of each of her ship mates on the Fenster ship as she spoke. "The Lysander has an entire level dedicated to unleashing weapons of death. We are talking about unlimited R-5 rockets, laser canons, laser batteries, drone attack ships, a minimum of fifteen hundred fighter ships and at least fifty battle ready Raumschiff's. We would not stand a chance."

"I never said it would be easy," Dirk Fenster responded calmly. "None of us suspected that the Glorious Leader would send out one of his best ships to enforce the quarantine. If anyone wants off the ship, now would be the time to speak up."

"You mean you intend to try and get past a Battle Cruiser? Are you nuts?" Ristina Bedrosian hissed, her white fur was bristled as she glared at Fenster.

"This is one of the reasons that I wanted to go alone," Fenster told them. "Look, when we enter the edge of the solar system we will be in range of the outpost space station called Cy-5. I can dock there and let everybody off before I continue on. I respect all of you for volunteering to come with me, but the presence of the Lysander changes things. We will make C-5 in two more days and I expect to leave everyone there."

Arch Frazier cleared his throat, "Dirk, I am not going anywhere. I stand with you til the end."

"As do I," Lupita Calderon told them.

"I am not leaving," Rolf Rhinehard stated boldly. "If you think that you can get past that Battle Cruiser then I am with you."

"I never said I thought I could get by that ship," Fenster corrected him. "I said I was going to try."

"You are going to die," Bedrosian growled. "I am getting off on Cy-5. My older sister died in a transport ship explosion. I don't want to go out that way. We should turn the ship around and go home."

"I agree with Ristina," Fara Kiesbye added. "This is suicide, just like Kat said. I'm out."

"Well, I am staying. I did not come this far to run away at the first sign of trouble," Supreet Patel spoke up.

"We are not cowards," Kiesbye felt the need to defend herself from Patel's statement.

"Nobody is suggesting that you are," Fenster spoke up to diffuse what he sensed to be a tense situation. He noted that Blundell, Windfohr, Mingjuan, Chin and Black were silent on the issue. Fenster silently hoped that all five of them would join Bedrosian and Kiesbye and leave the ship at Space Station Cy-5. "Look, this is a difficult decision for anyone to make. Everyone go sleep on it. I am going to take over the flight duties for now while you each consider whether to stay or leave."

"But it is my shift," Calderon reminded him.

"Then come with me," Fenster told her.

Windfohr and Blundell stood up from the conference table and walked down the ramp to get back the third floor of the ship. The two men said nothing as they left. Fenster climbed up the metal ladder at the north of the conference table, followed by Calderon. Strahovski silently walked toward the computer and weapons sections at the east of the conference table.

Frazier's first instinct was to follow Fenster to the pilot section to discuss the issue of the Battle Cruiser and the threat of death issued by the General. He thought better of it and walked down the ramp to spend some time alone in his quarters.

Hand in hand, Mingjuan and Black followed behind Frazier. The cadets slowly made their way to their room.

"Would you like for me to stay with you?" Black offered Mingjuan as they approached her quarters.

She smiled and kissed him gently on the lips. They had been sleeping together for the past week and both enjoyed each other's companionship. "You know I would like nothing better."

Black followed her into her room and was elated that she was pressed against him, kissing him passionately, before the sliding doors had shut. She frantically unzipped the front of his cadet uniform as he ran his hands over her body. They led each other toward the queen sized bed at the far end of the room and were soon on top of the dark satin sheets kissing as if it were their last day of life. Mingjuan pulled off her sweater dress and quickly removed her undergarments, giggling as Black kissed her neck, shoulders and breasts. Black laid her down and climbed on top of her, kissing her all over before they consummated the act through intercourse.

Her moans of pleasure could be heard by Frazier in the next room. Frazier smiled to himself and thought of Elektra and how much he missed her. He lay down on his bed and closed his eyes while Mingjuan was professing her love for Black just before she had an orgasm. She let out a cry that Black loved to hear when he made love to her.

Down the hall in another room, Rolf Rhinehard held Patel in his arms, kissing her tenderly. He was worried for her safety and hoped to convince her to remain behind at the space station. He waited until after they made love before he brought up the subject.

While Rolf was running his hands through her hair and looking into her eyes, he decided to be direct with her. "Supreet, you should not come with us to the moon. You should get off at the space station."

Patel raised her left eyebrow, "Why? You are staying. I will stay, too."

"I don't want you to be hurt or killed."

Patel smiled, "Rolf Rhinehard, are you trying to tell me that you actually care about what happens to me? You?"

Rolf nodded, "Just because I am not a man that commits to a woman does not mean that I am incapable of caring. Of course I care for you and I do not want to see you harmed. Please go back to Clovis City."

"I will if you do. I care about you as well. Rolf, if you leave I will. If you stay, I stay."

Realizing that she was not going to listen to his request, he told her that they should sleep on it. He cuddled up next to her and held her in his arms. Rolf had never felt any form of romantic love for a woman before. He had felt lust for women; he had felt love for his mother and his sisters. But never romantic love for any of his partners. What frightened him the most was that he had feelings for Patel. He was afraid of those feelings, but he was more afraid of losing her. Keeping his thoughts to himself, Rolf positioned himself on top of Patel and looked into her eyes as he began having intercourse with her.

Patel moaned as she felt his erection entering her. The rhythm of his thrusts inside of her began slow and were methodical. As his animal lust grew in intensity, so did his number of thrusts inside of the woman. Rolf panted heavily as he made love to her, savoring every second as he drove her to climax. Patel buried her face into his muscular chest and groaned out loud. Rolf eventually was moved to orgasm as well. He kissed her lips several times as he tried to catch his breath.

Fenster kept his thoughts to himself as Lupita settled into the co-pilot seat next to him. He knew she was staring at him.

"Dirk, why won't you allow any of us to know what you are really thinking? All we want to do is help you."

Fenster gripped his pilots steering column tightly as he searched for the right words, "It is not that I don't appreciate all of you volunteering to help me. The problem is that I plan on taking some alternative routes to the Blood Moon, routes that are considered top secret clearance level. By having all of you on this ship, you are slowing me down."

"Because you cannot use these mysterious routes you are referring to?"

"Correct."

"If they are top secret clearance level routes, then how do you know about their existence?"

Fenster sighed and faced her, "Because I am a Fenster. My family has more money than you can imagine. With wealth, one becomes more connected. The hidden mysteries of life are not mysteries to me or my family. We learn things that the leadership of humanity would hope to keep to themselves. I trust you, Lupita. I don't know what it is about you, but I trust you. There are areas in space where you can access folds in space."

"What do you mean by that?" Lupita frowned at him.

"What I mean is, a pilot can fly their ship into an entrance of the fold, some people refer to them as worm holes. Others call them other titles. I call them folds. You enter the fold and you can travel several AU in seconds."

"How come we never were told about these folds at the Academy? As pilot candidates, we should all know about them."

"You see, Lupita, the Glorious Leader and his family stole the locations of the folds from the Akarzdamedians. He has kept it to his family and revealed them to a select few Admiral's and commanders. He wants to keep them secret."

"Why keep them secret?"

Fenster shrugged, "Well, if all of the ships in the eight solar systems started using them, it would cause a problem with the economies of several planets. The main reason is that the Royal Family wants to know exactly where every ship is at every second. So, if I use one of those folds now, with all of the others on this ship, they will be exposed to information that could get them arrested. That is why I did not want you all coming with me."

Lupita nodded, "Well, I would have come regardless of

what you say. You are a good man, Dirk Fenster."

"Thanks. You are quite a lady yourself."

She laughed, "Really?"

"Yes, you are. Whoever ends up with you will be a very lucky man."

She blushed, "Thank you. Could you ever date a woman like me? I mean, a lower economic class girl from a Latin family?"

Fenster nodded, "My mother is from a Latin family. So yes, I could date you. Or someone like you."

"I am only talking about me," Lupita wagged her index finger in his direction.

"Yes, I could date you, Lupita."

She smiled and took his hand in hers, "So when we get back to Clovis City, where would you take me out on our first date?"

"Anywhere your heart desires," Fenster smiled and took her hand in his. "

"Good," she smiled. "I really like you."

"I really like you, too."

CHAPTER TEN

Ginger Collins O'Grady had fallen asleep at her table in O'Malley's. She had been awake for almost thirty-four hours, keeping vigil to learn some news regarding her husband and the Clovis Academy Team. The staff at the restaurant/bar allowed her to sleep, as did one of her constant companions, Cara Perez Guerrero. At three in the afternoon, the large sixty and eighty foot long screens came to life with static. The sound was loud and caused everyone present to stop in their tracks. The static noise continued for several minutes. One of the O'Malley girls was asleep on the bar and she slowly raised her head up to the sound of the noise and squinted her eyes. She sat up quickly when she saw the static on the screens.

Perez Guerrero was drinking a decaffeinated coffee when the sound of static had started. She immediately shook Ginger Collins O'Grady awake.

"What?" Ginger opened her eyes. "What is that noise?"

"Static," Perez Guerrero told her excitedly. "That means the source is no longer jammed. We should be getting live broadcasts very soon!"

And she had been correct. As if she were a fortune teller, everyone saw live action of Yuri Gorski dismantling a small Jammer device. All of the occupants erupted in applause.

"Only one?" Perez Guerrero asked. "Where are the others? Which one is it?"

Piotr Gorski had been sitting in another booth with Mia Nguyen, Stella Andolini and Flora Evart. He had jumped to his feet when the screens came to life. He ran toward one of the large screens and was standing about three feet from it. He concentrated on the lone figure in the enviro-suit as he slowly deduced his identification.

"That's my brother, Yuri!" Piotr announced with pride.

"What is he doing?" Perez Guerrero asked.

"He figured out the problem," Ginger observed. "He is destroying the jamming devices so we can see him."

The news spread over the Clovis Academy faculty and student body like an avalanche. Several different views of the Moon of Semiramis were coming to life. As each Jammer was eliminated another angle of the moon was visible via the broadcasts over the Satellite system.

Lila Zapata and Sophia DuBravac were in a lecture regarding terra-forming technology when the announcement came over the University wide system. Dean Harvard announced that they were receiving broadcasts from the Moon of Semiramis and that at least on Clovis cadet, Yuri Gorski, was confirmed to be alive and well.

Several citizens on distant planets viewed the same scene as the Jammers were slowly dismantled. News reporters throughout the eight solar systems began to broadcast live, speculating as to which of the Clovis Academy cadets was the one that was coming through the satellite system.

On the United Nations Space Command *Cortez*, Colonel Jamal Lincoln received word from military intelligence officer First Lieutenant Jim Shigeta that live feed was coming through the satellite system again. Colonel Lincoln immediately ordered all of the broadcasts to be sent to the screens in the Executive Meeting Room. Colonel Lincoln urged his staff to push their Battle Cruiser to the limit and get to the moon as soon as possible. He had to get to his daughter to safety. His crew of just under fifteen hundred women and men did not argue against the orders and the huge space craft changed course and began a long journey toward the Blood Moon.

Jurgen Doernitz had worked for several hours removing the pulsar weapons from each of the fighter ships and replacing them with real laser batteries. Each of the others had to assist in holding the laser battery steady as Doernitz mounted the weapons inside the belly of each ship. It was a long and tedious process.

"How many hours have we gone without sleep?" Marco asked.

"Thirty-six," Porfirio Cardenas answered.

"Let's get the armor piercing rockets installed," Lincoln urged.

The four cadets began walking back and forth from the weapons storage units and back to their ships, carrying as many of the deadly missiles as they dared. Unlike the laser batteries, the missiles were surprisingly light. Doernitz began attaching them one at a time to the bottom wings of each ship, two to a side.

David Rosenburg woke up and brushed his teeth in the communal bathroom sink. All of the other cadets in the Achilles headquarters were sound asleep. After he brushed his teeth and changed his clothes, he walked down the stairs. He saw Avery Jackson passed out on the floor, Cleon Alexander was asleep on a sofa, Rutger Stenerud was asleep on one of the tables. The entire room had the smell of alcohol and sweaty bodies. Keith Austin was passed out on a table; his flight suit was covered with dried vomit. David saw that the hybrid human and bear cadet Neal Giamatti was sprawled out on the floor, snoring loudly. David picked up his jacket from his chair and pulled out his small computer from the breast pocket of his jacket.

He saw the red light on his device blinking.

His eyes widened in surprise. Someone had been removing their Jammer devices. David Rosenburg felt as if his heart had fallen to his stomach. If the Jammers were disabled, then the rest of the Earth Empire would be able to see everything.

He cursed out loud. While they were all drinking, eating to excess, partying and being complacent, the enemy cadets were working. The fact that at least one of the opposing teams was disabling the Jammer devices meant only one thing, they had figured out at least some of the plot. And most importantly, the Communication Towers would now be able to broadcast to the rest of the eight solar systems the events as they played out. The beautiful framing of the Clovis Academy cadets would be ruined.

"Hey! Everyone!" David yelled. "Wake up! Wake up!"

The others began sitting, holding their heads and groaning. Most of them had hang overs from drinking too much. Giamatti waived his brown furry arm at David Rosenburg as if to dismiss him.

"What the hell is wrong with you? It's early you asshole. Let us sleep!" Keith Austin demanded as he sat up and was holding his head in his hands.

"Someone is removing our Jammers!" David yelled. "Damn! Computer, on screen. Are there any audio or visuals being broadcast from the moon to the rest of the star systems?"

"Yes, for the last several hours," the computer responded.

"Damn!" David yelled again, his stress level was rising. "Everyone get up! Now! They are on to us!"

Caine Rosenburg was up, rubbing his head due to a massive hang over from all of the wine and liquor he had consumed. "Computer, display on our screens what has been happening?"

All of the Achilles team saw visions of Yuri Gorski removing the Jammers and cutting their internal wires, rendering them all useless.

"It's Gorski," Avery Jackson mumbled.

"We need to get ready for a fight," Caine told the others. "Get your weapons ready. Lomax, get those twenty-four fighters airborne. We need to strike the Newton cadets and then finish off Gorski."

"But we used up most of our rockets when we killed the judges and the Tyr Academy Team," Lomax protested.

"Then get your lazy asses over to the weapons storage units and re-load!" Caine ordered him. "We gotta finish this fast! If he gets all the Jammers removed, our frame up is history! Don't you understand? We have to finish this now!"

"All twenty-four ships?" Clive Doornink asked as he put on his boots. "Isn't that a little over kill?"

"Do not question me!" Caine answered sternly. "Get the Akarzdamedian slave pilots and get in the air. I want the Newton cadets annihilated within the hour."

Doornink groaned but began to put on his enviro-suit. He was also suffering from a headache from the night long celebration. He followed Stenerud, Lomax and Austin out the front entrance, grabbing a laser pistol on the table near the door as he ran. The four humans would lead the twenty Akarzdamedian slaves to the Newton Academy building and do as Caine had directed. After all, the Rosenburg's were paying a good sum for them to kill all of the other cadets.

Les Gillis had waited over an hour for the underground light rail train to arrive at his location. The engine car in the front had fifteen box cars attached to it. Gillis boarded the lead box car where he knew the computerized controls were located. He wasted no time and quickly spliced into the main computer and began typing in commands. It took a few seconds, but Gillis was able to gain access to the controls.

Gillis then downloaded the commands to his own holo-com. He smiled to himself as the computer programs finished their download. He could now command the rail train by using his computer device and from several thousand kilometers distance. Gillis then pulled out a solar powered screw driver and knelt down before the metal plating covering the atomic powered engine. He unscrewed the ten screws, removed the plating and began inspecting the wiring.

"Computer, set the atomic engine to detonate on my command." Gillis instructed.

"Is that wise?" The computer voice responded.

"Normally no," Gillis hated it when the computer would talk back. "But we are in a bad situation and I need to be able to detonate the engine from a remote location. Our survival depends on it."

"I will comply," the computer answered.

Gillis nodded and then asked for the computer to patch

him into Harrison. "Drew, I am ready. Lower down those canisters of concentrated fuel."

Harrison had been able to locate ten metal canisters of rocket fuel in the Tyr Academy Headquarters. Each of the containers held fifty gallons that were compressed into five gallons. He had tied them to ropes and began to slowly slide each of them down to the tunnel so that Gillis could manufacture his bomb. Harrison could feel the fatigue from the lack of sleep. They had been up for a day and a half without rest. He closed his eyes and shook his head to keep himself awake.

Gillis worked for another hour, wiring the fuel containers to the engine. Then he heard Gorski's voice come over his enviro-suit communication device. "Les, this is Yuri. I have almost all the Jammer's disabled. You are on. Make it good."

"Thanks Yuri," Gillis answered. "I will do my best. Drew! Rope!"

Harrison dropped the rope down to him and he climbed up. Gillis waived for Harrison to follow him.

"What's the rush?" Harrison wanted to know.

"Yuri said we are now broadcasting live. I need you and Julia to hide where I told you. Stay out of sight." Gillis gave his instructions as he moved toward the headquarters.

Gillis ran into the Tyr Academy Headquarters and ordered all of the computers to come to life. One of the baby Saharakaree leaped onto his right shoulder.

"Computer, this is for universal broadcast. I will be giving a speech to the eight solar systems," Gillis instructed.

"Yes Mister Gillis."

"I want my speech sent to every corner of the Empire of humanity," Gillis said and stood before one of the cameras. "Every solar system, every space station and every single space craft. Ready?"

"You are on," the computer informed him.

As they had planned in advance, Steiner and Harrison stood out of range of the camera. Gorski had determined that it would be to their advantage if the enemy believed them to be dead.

The rest of the United Nations saw the image of Les Gillis appear on their screens.

Penelope Rosenburg had been keeping up with the tragic events on the Blood Moon while she flew to her destination. She was in the pilot's seat of her Super Raumschiff when she saw the image of Lew Gillis appear on one of her four large monitors. She smiled, recalling how kind he had been to her. She wished she could have been there in his hour of need to help. One of the replicants of Drayton Love-Easter was sitting next to her. He also smiled, seeing his best friend.

"You really liked Les, didn't you?" The Love-Easter Replicant asked.

Penelope looked at the duplicate of Love-Easter and smiled, "Yes, I was drawn to him. If it had been a different life time, if things had been different, I think he and I might have shared something special. But I know he would never have been able to forgive me for my part in all that has happened."

Love-Easter laughed for a moment, "I think he would have surprised you."

Penelope thought for a moment and nodded, "I wish we could have helped him. He will die soon along with any of his friends that are left alive. I know how much you cared for him, Dray. I am sorry."

"Don't count Les out yet," the clone gave her a wry smile. "He is a fighter and he will never surrender. If anyone can survive what is going on over there, Les can."

Admiral Seward and the rest of the staff at Clovis Academy watched in anticipation as to what Gillis would say. Dean Harvard wondered why O'Grady was not the one to speak for the Clovis cadets.

O'Malley's had a packed house. All of the Gorski Gang was surrounded by hundreds of cadets and civilians. It was standing room only. The vision of Les Gillis caused many of the cadets to yell and applaud. Sophia DuBravac wept with joy seeing him alive.

"Ladies and gentlemen," Gillis began. "My name is Les Gillis. I am a cadet senior at Clovis Academy. I was honored to be selected to compete at the annual tournament on the moon orbiting planet Semiramis. My team mates were equally honored to represent our school. As you all know, each and every military academy has a similar competition at different times of the year. This was supposed to be our time to shine in the spotlight. But when we arrived on this moon, something went terribly wrong."

The Newton Academy cadets watched with interest. Alan Anderson was sitting forward in his chair listening to every word. Nicolas Curtis was next to him, leaning over another chair.

"When we arrived here on the moon," Gillis continued, "we were attacked by a pack of Saharakaree. Several of my team lost their lives in the attack. We were ambushed. We later learned that the Tyr Academy cadets were attacked by the same cowards that had us ambushed. The judges on this moon were also killed without warning by the same perpetrators."

At O'Malley's, the cadets began murmuring about the casualty comment. The news media began to speculate that only Gillis and Gorski were still alive from the Clovis Academy team as they were the only two that had been seen.

Caine and David Rosenburg watched the speech without comment. Kai Chin shook his head with dread. He had warned the others to finish what they had started. But Caine and the others ignored Chin. Their over confidence was now coming back to haunt them.

"The few survivors of my team and I have uncovered that we were being framed for the killings here," Gillis stated plainly. "Our conclusion is that the cadets from the Achilles Academy are the perpetrators. They placed Jammers on the broadcast towers so that you would see only what they wished you to see. They painted their ships to look like ours and they wore uniforms with our colors to fool everyone. They have murdered without warning.

"I personally removed a microchip from the brain of one of the dead Saharakaree that attacked my team. The Saharakaree were slaves, being forced to kill against their will. As we all know, slavery is illegal and a direct affront to all we hold dear in our society. I have concluded that there are very few families in this Empire capable of containing slaves such as these. The microchip we removed from one of our Saharakaree attackers was manufactured by the Rosenburg Corporation. I formally accuse the Rosenburg family of violation of United Nations laws.

"My dear friend, Yuri Gorski, has located and removed the majority of devices that were blocking the transmissions from this moon to the rest of humanity. He has risked his very life to ensure that each of you would know the truth of the events on this moon. Yuri and I have discussed the fact that we are outnumbered. We have no weapons to fight the Rosenburg killers on this moon. I know that within twenty-four hours I will be dead. Yuri also has come to the conclusion that his life will soon end. But we will not go without a fight, that is, if the cowards we face will give us a fight.

"You see, ladies and gentlemen, the men we face have no courage. They are not men of honor. They have killed others by sneak attacks. You saw what kind of men they are before they severed the transmissions. These men beat and rape defenseless women. They are animals.

"So I now challenge the cowards of Achilles Academy. Come meet me and my friend Yuri Gorski. Fight us hand to hand. If you do so, I promise that you will lose.

"I know you will not meet my challenge because you are cowards. Yuri and I will die today because you will attack with premiere weaponry that we cannot defend against. How brave of you.

"I ask that all of you of the eight solar systems remember this day. We will not surrender to these animals. I am prepared to die fighting for life and liberty. I can say that because I came from a wonderful family. I have had gracious and decent friends and I have been fortunate enough to love and be loved by an amazing woman. Sophia, if you are out there listening, I love you more than words can express. I am sorry that I will not be coming home to you. I hope you will be able to move on and find happiness in your life. My only regret is that I will not grow old with you at my side." Gillis began pressing buttons on his hand held computer, setting the rail train engine detonation timer. He had dispatched the train toward the Achilles Academy headquarters before his speech had started.

"I also humbly request that all of you listening honor what we do here in the next few hours," Gillis continued. "We will fight back and give our lives for the freedom we all deserve.

I will shed every drop of my blood and every last breath in my lungs against these men that have no morals and no values. Throughout the history of humanity, men and women have been forced to rise up against the immoral and meet them on the field of battle. This conflict is one of those moments. It has been written that those of us that are burdened with morality will always lose to evil. I disagree with that saying. I may die here today, but my death will ensure that the evil ones on this Moon will be punished. Morality is not a weakness, it is a strength. I am proud that my parents raised me to know the difference and to choose the correct path in life. You see, when you fight for a righteous cause, for the common good, it makes you a stronger man and a stronger woman. You will be able to battle for something greater than yourselves. That is what Yuri and I will do here. We fight now to show the rest of you that standing up to evil is the right thing to do.

"You will all be witnesses. We will die with dignity and honor. But we will not bow down to these individuals who have killed and raped innocents. I gladly go to my end standing up to these men. If you honor life and freedom as we do, honor my team mates and I. Honor us as men and women who fought and died with principle. Honor us as fellow men and women that lived amongst you. Honor us because we had the audacity to fight against impossible odds. But do not mourn us. Celebrate us instead.

"The attack against the cowards begins..." Gillis paused

and looked at a time piece on the wall. "It begins in about twelve seconds. I bid each of you farewell."

Gillis walked away from the screen and picked up his hand held computer and spoke into the device. "Computer, are you ready? Begin."

As Gillis was giving his speech, Caine Rosenburg and Avery Jackson were cursing him, screaming many obscenities at the screen. Their plan had been ruined and they had been outed to the farthest reaches of humankind.

"We kill them now!" Caine yelled at the others, his face was red with anger. "Lomax, get those ships off the ground and kill the Newton cadets and then bring me the heads of Gillis and Gorski!"

The reactions to Gillis' speech were mixed across the United Nations. Admiral Yamamoto and his wife were subdued. They felt in their hearts that their son, Jurgen, was either dead or would soon be soon. Colonel Lincoln urged his pilots and engineers to push his Battle Cruiser to the limits. Sophia DuBravac and Lila Zapata were holding each other throughout the speech, weeping. The other Gorski Gang members were stunned.

Lomax, his pilots and the Akarzdamedian slaves lifted off. The twenty-four small one man fighter space ships began heading toward the Newton Academy cadet headquarters.

The rest of humanity could see the show of force from the Achilles cadets. Twenty four armed fighter space ships were clear on every screen in all those that watched in the numerous conquered solar systems. Any one that had doubted Gillis' words no longer could do so. The evidence was too powerful and overwhelming.

Twenty-four small fighter ships were rising into the sky of the Blood Moon. The Akarzdamedian slaves in twenty of the ships were excellent pilots. Although the slaves did not wish to participate in the blood bath, they had no choice. The micros chips in their brains, placed there by Rosenburg family surgeons, controlled their will power.

The remaining cadets at the Achilles headquarters began arming themselves. They were shouldering laser rifles and retrieving other weapons.

"Do you feel that?" Neal Giammatti asked.

"Feel what?" Caine demanded.

"The ground, its' moving," Giamatti told them.

David Rosenburg looked at the floor of the building. He could feel the ground shaking.

"The underground rail system," David said. "Someone activated one of the rail trains. It feels like it is coming this way."

"The rail runs underneath our headquarters," Kai Chin told the others. "Probably Gillis trying to escape."

The shaking increased in intensity. When the rail train was under the Achilles headquarters it came to an abrupt stop.

Caine gave his brother David an inquisitive look. "What the hell?"

"Is Gillis insane? Why would he stop under our building?" Avery Jackson asked.

Then they heard the next words over the satellite system from Les Gillis. "Fire in the hole."

"Run!" David Rosenburg realized that somehow Gillis was bringing the fight to them.

Before Gillis had sent the rail car to come to a dead stop under the Achilles headquarters, he had wired the nuclear engine to detonate on his command. Gillis pressed the button on his holo-com device to set off the explosion.

Caine Rosenburg ran for the exit as the underground train erupted. The containers of fuel ignited in the explosion shaking the ground for about a radius of two kilometers. The moon rock split and was blasted into the sky. The metal and concrete foundation of the Achilles safe house cracked under the force of the explosion and was lifted several feet off the ground. The force of the destructive wave caused the metal and synthetic materials of the headquarters to be spread outwards in all directions. Many of the Achilles team made it out by a narrow margin. Giamatti was not so fortunate. The explosion threw his torn and twisted corpse into the air. Cleon Alexander was thrown by the blast and twisted his ankle. Several of the Saharakaree slaves were ripped to shreds in the blast.

Burton Stapler had been the first one out of the building when David Rosenburg ordered everyone to flee. Like the others, he had not had time to grab his enviro-suit. He kept his head above the chlorine gas as he ran. Stapler was able to get about thirty feet from the building when he felt the explosion. The force of the concussion sent Stapler sprawling to the ground. He rolled for several feet as he inhaled he felt the burning of the chlorine gas in his lungs. He tried his best to hold his breath and covered his head with his hands as debris began pelting the lunar surface.

Dell Ragnarsson was relaxing in his Raumschiff during the explosion. He was thrown against the metal hull of his space craft as the explosive force threw his Raumschiff tumbling end over end. The rear engines of the vessel were damaged. His space craft landed upside down and slid for several more feet before coming to a stop. Dell gashed his forehead as he hit the walls and was rendered unconscious. His loyal crew members were all killed as the ship was thrown into the sky and hit the lunar surface.

The Achilles Raumschiff fared better as it was not as close to the annihilated building as Ragnarsson's craft had been. Alfred Rosenburg, II, had been asleep on the ship when the explosion took place. He felt the blast, but was not injured. Cursing, he ran to the observation window to see the remains of the Achilles headquarters flying in each direction. He saw a red-orange fire ball rising into the sky line, with black smoke and shades of yellow. The debris of the walls, floors, foundation, fixtures and furniture were flying in all directions. The Achilles Academy Headquarters were completely destroyed.

Alfred cursed and ran to the back of his ship. Several of the cadets were lying on the ground. His first concern was of his two sons, Caine and David, as he rushed out onto the lunar surface toward the cadets to render aid.

The rest of the eight solar systems witnessed the explosion. There was stunned silence at O'Malley's. The Clovis Academy cadets watching the three dimensional broadcast could not pull away from the scene. Many of them knew Les Gillis and Yuri Gorski. Sophia DuBravac always knew that Gillis was capable of out smarting anyone. She also was aware that when attacked, Yuri Gorski would not back down.

The events the other citizens of the United Nations Empire just witnessed proved what DuBravac and the other Gorski Gang members already understood. If one attacked the Gorski Gang, be ready to answer for it.

Colonel Nikolai Gorski watched the events from his office at the United Nations Building. He was monitoring many events that were occurring throughout the eight solar systems. One of the events that had led him to make a very difficult decision was one that involved the *Lysander*. The Commander of the Battle Cruiser kept her word and had fired several R-5 rockets at a transport ship that was owned by a Kotek named Alonzo Bauslaugh. According to the news reports, Bauslaugh had left his home on the Robert Andrews moon to attempt a rescue mission on the Blood Moon. Once his small ship and his crew of seven came within range, the *Lysander* fired upon it without warning. The ship exploded in deep space and all lives were lost. Based on that event, Nikolai Gorski recalled Mark Lund and ordered him to abandon their mission to the Blood Moon. Gorski did not want the blood of Aura Lynda Glenn and the others on his hands. His order meant that his son and the other cadets were on their own.

CHAPTER ELEVEN

The routine in the underground prison cell that she had been held in had grown monotonous. She was told when to eat, what to eat, when to sleep and when to wake up. Her freedom to do as she wished was gone, so when Ella Ragnarsson had been told she had a visitor, she was both intrigued and relieved that the person that had come to see her would at least break up the predictable and boring schedule that had become her life. She had been transported to numerous prisons in an effort to conceal her location to make any further rescue attempts impossible. Each time she was forced to move to a new facility, she was drugged and rendered unconscious. Ella knew it was to keep her in the dark as to her exact whereabouts. She did not even know if she was still on New Edinburgh or not. She had not seen her brother Ivar in months. Likewise, she had not heard from her lawyer and brother, Ellis. It had been quite some time since any of the lawyers working for Sean Collins came to her to demand information. Each time the lawyers would interview her, Ella refused to talk to them and she refused their offers of witness protection if she agreed to testify against the others. She was loyal to her family and would not betray them.

The one person that Ella feared was the one that had almost killed her, the gypsy cadet named Jen Staszko.

Ella said nothing to the guards as she was taken from her cell to an interview room. She was escorted by two large Marine Corps soldiers. They had cuffed her hands and put chains on her legs. Clearly the correctional employees had learned their lesson from Ella's many escape attempts which had resulted in several guards needing medical treatment. The guards took no chances with her. The interview room had a metal six foot long and four foot wide table with four metal chairs. Ella was placed in one of the chairs and her restraints were chained to a chain that was imbedded in the cement floor.

Ella looked over the interview room. And observed that there was a one way mirror to her left. The walls were grey; there were no pictures, just that drab grey wall. The ceiling was twenty feet from the floor. She noted that two cameras were on the ceiling probably filming everything. She raised both of her middle fingers at the cameras.

The door to the interview room slid open at that moment.

"Very mature," Jen Staszko said as she walked into the room. The door slid shut behind her. "A super assassin reduced to flipping off cameras in prison."

Ella was terrified of Staszko, the last time they had faced off, Ella came seconds away from death. She forced herself to control her breathing and masked her facial expression to avoid revealing her fear of Jen Staszko.

Ella watched the female cadet sit down across from her. The table was the only thing separating them. Ella recalled the feeling of Staszko's knife cutting into her. She recalled lying face first on the Clovis Academy cemetery grounds, bleeding to death. She only survived her wounds due to the talented medical staff that operated on her at the Clovis City Hospital. Ella had been living in dread that she would one day cross paths with Staszko again.

Jen Staszko had arranged the meeting with lawyer Sean Collins. Staszko had used the assistance of Collins' daughter, Ginger, to explain the reason for the meeting. Collins and Military Intelligence Sergeant First Class Mark Lund agreed to give Staszko the chance to interrogate Ella Ragnarsson in the underground jail that she had been held at. Collins had prepared Staszko for about two hours on questions he needed answered by the Ragnarsson woman. Staszko agreed with Collins and Lund to push the prisoner to her limits and get her to talk.

"I know you are a fantastic actress," Staszko smiled at her. "You are doing a great job hiding the fact that you are afraid of me. You cannot hide the fear that is in your eyes. I have seen it before, when I looked you in the eyes when I thrust my knives into you."

"Fuck you!" Ella Ragnarsson yelled and spit at Staszko.

Staszko wiped the spit from her cheek, "Another mature act. My how you have fallen. You were once one of the best killers on the planet, hell the entire solar system. Now you are nothing but a frightened lab rat."

"Why are you even here?" Ella demanded. "Did they send you here to threaten or taunt me?"

"No," Staszko reached into her jacket and pulled out a foot long knife. She laid the knife on the table and allowed two minutes to tick by before speaking again, glaring into Ella's eyes the entire time. "I asked to come to see you."

"To finish me off?" Ella laughed nervously.

"Maybe. Whether you live or die right now depends entirely on you." Staszko's voice was even and calm. "We are going to play a game."

Ella swallowed as her eyes focused on the knife, "What kind of game?"

"The kind that you answer my questions truthfully or I carve your body up." Staszko picked the knife up by the hilt and she noticed Ella's eyes were following the knife. Staszko concluded that Ella was very much intimidated.

"Okay, what kind of questions are you talking about?" Ella was now fidgeting in her chair.

"I want you to tell me all you know about technological advances in the Rosenburg Corporation regarding communication jamming devices," Staszko said, waving her knife.

"I know very little of the Rosenburg Corporation..." Ella began to lie. She was cut off when Staszko jumped onto the table and put the knife to her throat. Staszko grabbed Ella's hair and forcefully pulled her head back. Ella cried out in fear.

"Speak bitch before I cut your throat!" Staszko screamed.

Ella began to talk, rapidly. She told Staszko everything she knew about communication jamming devices. She confirmed that the Rosenburg's had perfected the technology by using old radio wave technology and stolen alien equipment from the Danaraja space craft under Rosenburg's Ranch to create the Jammer's. Ella continued to talk, even though Staszko had not asked further questions. She admitted that it was the Rosenburg's that had been behind the attempted rape of Elektra. She confessed that she was one of the members of the conspiracy that covered up the attack after the fact. Ella admitted that Daryl Rosenburg died in the attack. As she gave out all of the critical information her bladder gave way and she urinated on her chair.

"Is that why you and your family have been trying to kill Yuri and me all this time?" Staszko demanded.

"Yes," Ella's voice was stammering as the knife was still at her throat. "Alfred Rosenburg, II, hired my father and brother to kill you, Gorski, Gillis, Evart, Harrison and Elektra."

"And you went along with it all," Staszko concluded.

"I was well paid," Ella shot back defiantly. "You see,

when you and your friends killed Daryl Rosenburg and injured the other brother, Caine, you started a war. A blood feud, bigger than the historical Hatfield and McCoy's. You are dealing with very dangerous people and you have no clue what levels of effort the Rosenburg family will go through to get revenge. Alfred Rosenburg and his sons do not like being beaten. They are narcissistic and full of pride and there is nothing they will not do to kill you, Yuri Gorski, Les Gillis and all the others."

"Such as the Transport ship that was blown up leaving Space Station Cy-7?" Staszko recalled Collins needed to know about that issue.

"Yes, my sister Emma placed the explosive device on the Transport," Ella confirmed what Dulce Ragnarsson had already told them. "We all thought you would be on board. You out smarted us on that one."

"During the sand storm there was an attack on the dormitories. Who was behind that?" Staszko demanded.

"Alfred Rosenburg and my father," she blurted out.

Staszko released Ella's hair and pulled the knife away from her throat. Out of shame for betraying her family, Ella began weeping.

Staszko jumped off of the table. "Thank you for being honest with me. Now, tell me what you know of the ambush on the Blood Moon."

"Nothing. I swear, I know nothing." Ella hid her face in her hands. "They must have planned the Blood Moon attack after you arrested me."

Staszko watched the woman's reaction and nodded to the window. "Okay, I believe you."

"What happens to me now?" Ella asked between sobs. She had done the unthinkable; she had betrayed her father and her family. Never in her life had she felt so alone.

"That is for the courts to decide," Staszko said as she walked toward the door. "But if I ever see you again, I will kill you."

As Ella Ragnarsson told Jen Staszko all she knew, Sean Collins, Mark Lund and several of his investigators watched from the outside, looking through the one way mirror.

"When she graduates," Lund whispered to Collins, "She should be hired by Military Intelligence. She's a natural."

Collins nodded thoughtfully. The confession was just about all he needed to bring the cases to trial. "Yes she is."

Lomax had his ship soaring into the lunar skyline when Gillis detonated the explosives on the underground train. He was leading his pack of twenty-four fighter ships toward the Newton Academy Headquarters for the lone purpose of wiping the cadets from the face of existence. He and Stenerud, Doornink and Austin knew nothing of the explosion caused by Gillis. Their engines were roaring as they flew at maximum speed in the direction of the helpless cadets.

"No prisoners!" Lomax directed his flight team. "Kill them all once we are done we need to get to the Clovis HQ and take out Gillis and Gorski!"

The four young cadets from Achilles Academy knew that the attack on the Newton Academy cadets would be simple. The opponents had no weaponry other than stun lasers and pulsar blasts. Alan Anderson and his team of cadets would be wiped out in seconds.

"It almost seems unfair," Stenerud remarked out loud.

Austin grunted, "So what? The Rosenburg's are paying us good money. It's only ten lousy cadets and none of them are friends of mine. A few years from now, no one will even miss them."

Doornink agreed, "Screw them. I can't wait to get paid."

Porfirio Cardenas was checking his instruments on his small ship when his on board computer warned that the twenty-four ships had launched. He looked over his tactical display of the twenty-four moving triangles that represented the enemy ships.

"What direction are they heading in?" Cardenas asked his computer.

"They are on an intercept course for the Newton Academy cadets," the computer informed him.

Cardenas looked over at Marco, Lincoln and Doernitz. "They are going to kill the other team. We cannot let that happen."

"Porfirio, I agree. We need to protect Anderson and the Newton team," Marco said as he pressed a button in his cockpit to open his canopy.

"We have to fight them," Lincoln agreed.

"We are outnumbered twenty-four against four," Cardenas warned. "We most likely will all die."

"I know everyone thinks I am a coward because I always refused to fight," Doernitz said softly. "But when I came to Clovis Academy I never had a fight worth fighting, until now. We have to defend the others."

Cardenas cleared his throat with pride, "Jurgen, you have seen real combat when you were a young teen. You told me last year how you and Admiral Yamamoto were in a battle, in small fighters just like ours and against triple the odds. What do you suggest we do? How do we fight twenty-four against four?"

Doernitz looked over at Marco and Lincoln and chose his words wisely. "We use the element of surprise. The enemy has no clue that we are armed. We first target the ships that have the highest number of armor piercing rockets. We blow them out of the sky with our rockets before they have time to realize we are also armed. Once we fire on them, the element of surprise will be gone. It will be a high speed ship to ship laser fight after that."

"We have sixteen rockets between us," Marco observed. "With any luck, we can cut their number down to eight."

"If we hit with all sixteen rockets," Lincoln added.

Marco looked at Doernitz. "You really saw combat, before you came to the Academy?"

"Yes, I did," Doernitz confirmed. "My adopted father, Admiral Yamamoto, and I were ambushed by an alien attack. We were outnumbered three to one. We won, they lost."

"So we can all four come out of this alive," Cardenas added. "The odds are against us, but, the four of us saved Tina Martinson in the Forbidden Region against similar odds. We are a great team if we stick together. We can survive this."

"I love your optimism," Marco said climbing on board his ship.

"Have faith, Marco," Cardenas called out to him. "I want each of you to do something while we are in flight. Broadcast to your friends and loved ones and tell them why you decided to fight, why we had to make a stand at this very moment. I think it will be important to explain our actions today. Besides, the people that we loved in this life deserve to know what our thoughts were at this moment, just in case."

Lincoln and Doernitz nodded and boarded their individual ships. They had heard Gillis' speech and they watched on their individual monitors the attack he had unleashed on the Achilles team. The battle could not be avoided now.

Cardenas was silent for a moment as he prayed for forgiveness for his sins. He asked his computer to broadcast his order for the rest of the United Nations to hear.

"This is Cadet Porfirio Cardenas of Clovis Academy. We are about to engage the enemy. They are on course to murder the cadets of Newton Academy. We cannot stand by and allow then to kill these innocent cadets. We will make our final stand now. To my wife Freya, I love you more than life. To my children, I hope the Lord blesses each of you and that you will grow to be good law abiding citizens. Lift off!"

Cardenas guided his space craft upward. He was followed by his wing man, Doernitz.

Marco felt he needed to say something, to his friends and family before he died. He asked his on board computer to broadcast his last words. "Dominic, mother, father. This is good bye. I love all of you. Dominic, you and Harumi make lots of babies and name one after me, okay? Stella, Venus and Giola, I want you two to live long a fruitful lives. Tell all of our other brothers and sisters how much I loved each of them. Stella, if you are listening, be strong and work hard and try and keep the others out of trouble. To my dear friends at the Academy, I send each of you all my best."

Mary Lincoln did the same, with a lump in her throat. "Father, mother, if you are out there, I want you to know how much I love you both. I guess my dream of being an officer will never happen for me. I hope you understand, I have to do this. Those other cadets have no one to defend them. It comes down to us. Daddy, if you are out there, I know that you would have done as I am doing now. You were always the bravest man and you raised me to be the same. I am so proud that I was your daughter and I hope that you have always been just as proud of me."

"Jurgen, any last words?" Cardenas offered.

Doernitz was numb as he struggled to find any words at all. "I just want to tell my sister, don't cry for us. Porfirio and I get to die as men. We get to die fighting for something important which is defending our fellow man. I hope the way I fight today and the way I die brings honor to the House of Yamamoto." He paused and swallowed. "Lila, this is farewell. Thank you, Lila, for just being yourself. I die knowing that I was loved in this life. I wish I could hold you one last time, to hear your laugh again. My biggest regret is that we will never meet the children that I know we would have created together. Besos mi amor."

After the four pilots broadcasted their farewells, they flew their space craft at full speed to intercept Lomax and his large squadron.

At the Newton Academy, Alan Anderson had ordered his cadets to retreat to the Raumschiff. He was aware that they would not be able to escape and that they were all as good as dead. "Alan?" Ellen Benson spoke on her head set as she was flying her single fighter ship above.

"Yes Ellen?" Anderson responded.

"I request permission to join the Clovis cadets and engage the enemy." Benson told him.

Anderson looked up into the sky at the four small ships and then spoke into his holo-com. "You are all armed with only pulse blasts. The enemy is armed with rockets and lasers."

"We will give them hell anyway," Benson promised. "It

is twenty-four against four. We can help them."

"Please sir," Hal Palmer added. "We cannot let them fight alone. They are moving into position to protect us. They will need our help."

Alan Anderson felt his heart swell with pride. Up til the current events, Anderson had been mobilizing his team to attempt to escape the Blood Moon and flee to the nearest Empire space station for protection. Hearing that his team members would rather stay and fight against impossible odds in response to the speech given by Gillis caused Anderson to decide on a different course.

"Permission to engage the enemy is granted. Good luck my friends," Anderson said for the entire eight solar systems to hear. "If we are to die, then we should do so with our faces to the enemy."

Anderson watched in silence as Ellen Benson, Hal Palmer, Torch Woods and Jeff "June" Carter flew their small fighter ships up into the sky. Anderson looked at his second in command, Nicolas Curtis and motioned to the Raumschiff. It was time to form an alliance with Yuri Gorski and his surviving team members. Their only chance at making it off the Blood Moon depended on them working together against the common enemy.

CHAPTER TWELVE

Hearing the last good-byes of the four cadet pilots caused a spike in the ratings for the news networks. The cameras were on the Clovis Academy cadets at O'Malley's. The United Nations citizens were treated to Sophia DuBravac consoling and hugging Lila Zapata.

Many of the other cadets and family members were sobbing from the speeches given. The news media were now speculating that six members of the Clovis Team were still alive. They began broadcasting obituaries for Eamon O'Grady, Julia Steiner, Pierre Zerbe and Drew Harrison.

As the premature reports were being released, Les Gillis, Drew Harrison and Julia Steiner continued digging around their new headquarters and preparing metal barricades and a redoubt. They each had their one foot long solar powered Allen Corporation Magnetizer devices in their hands. The "Magnetizers" as they were referred to were able to magnetically pick up and move any metal up to a ton in weight without straining the person directing the action. Using the hand held devices Steiner and Gillis began placing metal barricades around the perimeter. Gillis directed them to secure a sheet of metal and then count ten feet and secure another metal piece into the lunar surface. In the ten feet spacing between the metal barricades, Gillis placed trip wire to connect to the homemade explosives that he, Steiner and Harrison had spent their spare time preparing.

Steiner and Gillis had found several chemicals in the Headquarters to construct explosives. Harrison assisted in placing the home made traps around the entire radius.

"Les," Harrison said. "Why didn't you warn us you were going to blow up their building right now? I thought we were going to wait before we did anything."

"You disapprove?" Gillis asked as he slammed a large sheet of Raumschiff metal into the moon surface. He turned off his Magnetizer. "Yuri approved it."

"Hell no!" Harrison laughed. "That was beautiful man."

"We really are going to kill them all," Steiner observed. "That was a great chess move, Les. You took out their two Rooks in one move."

"But they still have their superior fire power," Gillis lamented. "And now they will be really pissed off."

"Which will work to our advantage," Harrison added as he picked up a solar powered trench digging machine and began digging more to complete a hole he started earlier. "If they are angry, they will not think. They will rush in and attack out of rage."

"And that is how we can beat them," Steiner finished the thought.

In the distance, the three cadets saw their Raumschiff that was piloted by Yuri Gorski was returning. Gorski was in a long distance communication with Jen Staszko while he flew the ship. She informed him of the true players behind the attack. Gorski took the information calmly as he guided the Raumschiff to a safe landing. All this death just because Elektra stabbed Daryl Rosenburg and because Caine Rosenburg was injured and their father wanted retribution. Gorski expressed his love to Staszko and thanked her for the information. He un-buckled his safety harness and rushed to the exit of the Raumschiff. He had heard the statements made by his friends that were preparing to take on the approaching enemy ships. The war now was going to be fought in earnest.

Gorski walked to the exit of the Raumschiff and was met by Steiner, Gillis and Harrison. Gorski marveled at their handy-work. He saw a complete wall of metal around the headquarters building made of eight foot wide sections and a few feet of space between that was about twenty feet from the structure. The cadets were placing metal about one hundred feet out now in a similar circular pattern with metal pieces and ten foot spaces in between.

"Impressive," Gorski told them.

Steiner approached him and pulled out a hyper dermic

needle from her medical pouch. "Take off your helmet. I need to inject you."

"What is it?" Gorski asked.

"It is a vitamin energy injection. I already injected myself, Les and Drew." Steiner explained as she showed him the hyper dermic needle. "We are all going on almost two days without sleep. Your body needs the additional energy. The injection will fool your body and rid you of any feelings of fatigue."

Gorski allowed her to proceed.

On Sikorsky's Planet, the Glorious Leader, Vladimir Sikorsky watched the drama play out on his holographic view screens. His damned great grandson had failed and the public relations damage could be immense. Sikorsky knew he had to deliver a speech in support of the Clovis Academy Cadets and turn on Alfred Rosenburg, II.

Sikorsky had no choice. If his involvement in this affair became public it could lead to enough outcries to start a rebellion against his two hundred year rule. Sikorsky would not allow that to happen. He summoned his best speech writers to prepare a short presentation for the media. The Glorious Leader had to act swiftly to be on the side of the citizens.

Clive Doornink heard his ship computer warning of an approaching contact. He had been ordered by Lomax to be the point ship and was leading the pack of twenty-four ships. They were flying about five hundred feet above the surface. He noticed his red warning light flashing. "Computer, what is wrong?"

"Four ships approaching directly ahead," the computer informed him.

"Lomax, Austin, Stenerud, you guys get that message?" Doornink was laughing. "Four heroes that want to die are blocking our path to the Newton Headquarters."

"No problem," Keith Austin told them. "When they get in range, let's toy with them. They have no weapons other than worthless pulsar blasts. I think we deserve to have some fun."

Porfirio Cardenas felt his mouth dry up and his palms were beginning to sweat. They were less than one minute away from engaging the enemy. He licked his lips and looked down at the five by seven color photograph of his wife Freya and his children on his control board. He closed his eyes for a second and took in a deep breath. The time had come to see how good a pilot he really was and whether or not he would live to see his family again.

"Everyone locked onto the ships with the most rockets?" Cardenas asked his team mates.

"Ready." Marco said with a steady voice. He ordered his computer to lock onto the four outer ships on the left flank and glanced at his tactical screen to make certain that his missiles were locked on the proper targets.

"All set," Lincoln reported. Her computer had programmed her four rockets to hit some of the ships in the back of the group.

"Let's do it," Doernitz affirmed. He had his rockets ready to hit the right flank of the approaching ships.

Cardenas took in another deep breath, "Computer, open a direct channel to the opposing ships." He waited until the computer confirmed it had done so. "This is Cadet Porfirio Cardenas from Clovis Academy. I order you to land your ships and surrender. No one else needs to die today. We can all walk away from this and avoid further bloodshed. What is your response?"

Peter Lomax could not believe his ears. The fools were demanding that they actually consider surrender. "Fuck you! You all die today!" He laughed as he responded.

Cardenas cut off the communication with the other team. He felt he had to try and give them the chance to end the conflict peacefully. Predictably, it did not work.

"Okay, we do it the hard way," Cardenas said to himself. His computer signaled that the twenty-four ships were now in range of their rockets. He switched open his communications to his team. "Fire your rockets."

Marco, Lincoln and Doernitz did not hesitate. All four ships fired their armor piercing rockets. Sixteen armor piercing rockets were sent at high speed in the direction of their targets.

Peter Lomax thought he was dreaming when he heard his computer sirens sound off, warning him of incoming rockets. He looked up from his dash to the cockpit windows and observed the flashes of light from the opposing four ships ahead of him. Sixteen rockets had been fired simultaneously at Lomax and his team.

The cadets at O'Malley's watched in awe. Dozens were holding hands, praying for their friends.

"How the hell did they get weapons?" Reynita Calderon asked John Gauthier at the Bragg Gang round table. Gauthier shrugged and stared at the three dimensional screen before him, not wanting to miss a second of the events on that moon.

At the Hospital in Clovis City, Cadet Lynn Goldsmith found Freya Cardenas doing her rounds with some of the patients. She informed her as to what was happening on the Blood Moon. Freya stopped her duties and ran downstairs to the cafeteria where many members of the medical staff were watching the three dimensional broadcast. Freya stood next to Doctor Harding and they immediately held hands. Harding felt horrible for her colleague. Her husband and her brother were both in harm's way.

Peter Lomax and his team were slow to react when they realized live armor piercing rockets had been fired upon them. They had not been prepared for such an offensive action. None of them had considered the possibility that the other cadets on the moon would be able to arm themselves and fight back. Lomax was frightened enough that he urinated into his enviro-suit.

"They have weapons!" Keith Austin screamed. "How?"

"It doesn't matter how, dammit! Evasive maneuvers!" Lomax yelled as he pulled his ship upwards into the sky to avoid being hit by one of the deadly rockets.

Rutger Stenerud tried to avoid being hit but was not fast enough on his reflexes. He screamed as a rocket fired by Mary Lincoln impacted the front hull of his ship and caused a massive explosion, leaving the remains of his body torn and burned. The metal of his small craft scattered in the fireball created by the eruption.

The other fifteen rockets were also on target. Two of the rockets hit and destroyed the same vessel. The doomed Akarzdamedian slave pilots of those fourteen small space craft never had a chance to avoid the attack. Each of their ships erupted in blasts that tore their ships to pieces. Their bodies were practically vaporized by the heat of the exploding rockets. The skyline of the moon seemed to resemble a fireworks display with the numerous bursts. Burnt metal fell to the lunar surface to the dismay of Lomax and his fellow pilots.

"Our surprise attack worked!" Marco yelled to the others. The odds were down to nine against four.

"Press our advantage!" Porfirio Cardenas ordered as he steered his ship and increased his speed. "Stay with your partner. Light them up!"

Cardenas and Doernitz flew their ships next to each other and began to pursue a block of opponents that had ascended to avoid being hit by the rockets. Marco and Lincoln grouped together and concentrated on Lomax and two Akarzdamedian pilots that were seemingly in disarray. They were not flying in tight formation which was the combat recommended pattern.

The four Clovis Academy cadets began firing their laser batteries at the remaining nine ships.

Austin and Lomax were yelling at the others to regroup and fire back.

Doornink was swinging his ship around to face the four Clovis cadets. It was a fight to the death, Doornink told himself. "This is not what we signed up for."

Alfred Rosenburg, II, had been able to pull his son Caine from the rubble of the demolished Achilles Academy building. Caine was coughing due to his inhalation of chlorine gas. On the lunar surface, there were still pockets of fire and smoldering ash around. The elder Rosenburg was relieved to discover Caine was unharmed. Caine stood and brushed the dirt and pieces of sheet rock from his clothing.

Alfred Rosenburg noticed that his other son, David, was helping Cleon Alexander to his feet. Alexander was limping, favoring his left leg.

"How the hell did this happen to us?" Alexander was demanding with rage in his voice, not directing his question to any person in particular.

Burton Stapler and Avery Jackson had suffered some minor cuts and bruises. But were mostly angry about the attack on their lives. Jackson was cussing while Stapler was coughing due to his exposure to the chlorine gas.

Kai Chin was walking with difficulty with two Saharakaree next to him. The alien slaves had been astute enough to not look at the bright flash of the bomb blast. Some of the other Saharakaree had not been as fortunate. Chin had a piece of wood stuck in his right arm. He acted as though it did not bother him at all.

"Everyone get to the Raumschiffs!" Alfred Rosenburg instructed the survivors. "Hurry! Our pilots need help! They were ambushed!"

"How?" David Rosenburg demanded.

"The Clovis cadets must have taken our weapons lockers." His father responded. "Our pilots are getting their asses kicked!"

Keith Austin flew his ship downward and then sharp right and back upwards. He fired his lasers at the closest Clovis Academy ship. After firing the laser burst, Austin fired his second to last armor piercing rocket at the same Clovis ship. Jurgen Doernitz saw the maneuver made by Austin and turned his ship right and watched as the armor piercing rocket narrowly missed him. Doernitz pressed the laser weapon on his tactical screen when another enemy ship came within range, firing a set of laser beams at the craft.

Two of the laser blasts impacted the side of Doernitz ship, on the rear, and left scorch marks on the metal hull. The impact shook Doernitz' small vessel causing him to let out several curse words. Doernitz then guided his ship down toward the surface to avoid another missile that Austin had fired at him. Doernitz gripped his half-moon steering wheel and spun his ship left to right. The missile followed and was closing on him. Doernitz swerved his ship left and the missile continued to stay on him. It was a heat seeking projectile which would stay on Doernitz until it impacted the ship or some other object.

Doernitz decided to try a new tactic. He flew his ship in the direction of one of the geysers that secreted chlorine gas onto the moon's surface. Doernitz increased his speed as the missile was closing in on him. He spied the geyser below him that was erupting with olive colored gas. Doernitz flew his ship to five feet off the surface and directly into the spewing gas. The missile followed and entered the gas cloud behind Doernitz' space craft. The missile tracking device lost the heat signal that emanated from the ship. The missile slammed onto the moon and exploded harmlessly.

Doernitz then turned his ship back to rejoin the battle. He made a mental note to remember the pilot of the ship that had hit him with the lasers. He was a better than average pilot and in a dog fight such as the one they were in, it was always the best strategy to shoot down the best pilots first.

Clive Doornink brought his ship around in a wide right curve and followed Austin's example, firing wildly at the two in coming ships. Porfirio Cardenas saw the ship flanking him, but could not move in time as he was firing on another ship piloted by an Akarzdamedian slave. Cardenas was a great shot. His laser blasts caught the Akarzdamedian ship in the rear and left side. The solid black, jackal-like alien growled a death cry as his ship erupted into flames and was sent spiraling toward the lunar surface, out of control. The alien was able to eject before his ship crashed and was demolished on the ground below.

Doornink fired again on Cardenas ship with several volleys of deadly laser fire. Cardenas felt the impact as his ship was hit a dozen times causing his hull to have enough holes in it to resemble a block of Swiss cheese. Cardenas heard his computer warning him that the engines were on fire and crash landing was imminent.

"Jurgen! I am hit!" Cardenas reached for his ejection lever. The fire was spreading to his cockpit. He only had a few seconds. He pulled on his ejection lever and watched as his cockpit entrance popped open and felt himself tossed into the sky. Only a second after he was ejected, Cardenas' ship exploded. Cardenas screamed in pain as searing hot metal shards ripped into his torso and his legs. His enviro-suit was torn in several places. A piece of shrapnel hit the visor to Cardenas' helmet and caused a crack in the glass. The impact of the shrapnel whipped his head backwards and sent him spinning out of control. Cardenas knew from the numerous pieces of metal in his body that he had been injured badly. He did his best to use his gliding device to land safely on the surface. He prayed that

Doernitz and the others would fare better than he had. He looked down at the wounds on his body and winced in pain.

Lomax had been able to recover from his initial shock of the rocket attack on his small fleet. Lomax rounded up three of the Akarzdamedian slave pilots to follow him. He led the three aliens in a pursuit of Andolini and Lincoln. Lincoln saw them coming on their right flank.

"Marco! We are being flanked!" Lincoln warned as she fired at the three approaching ships. Her laser blasts impacted the front of one of the Akarzdamedian ships. The laser shots cut through metal and the cockpit glass and the pilot was sliced to pieces. The ship spiraled out of control and crashed onto the surface erupting into a fireball.

Marco had swerved his ship in an arcing motion to join Lincoln on the other side of her vessel. He watched helplessly as Lomax and the other Akarzdamedian pilots were firing mercilessly at Lincoln's ship. Marco heard Lincoln cry out in pain as fifteen laser blasts impacted her small ship.

Lincoln felt her left leg burn as a lasers cut through the hull of her craft and tore two gashes into her upper leg. Her engine was hit several times and smoke and flames billowed out in front of her, obscuring her view. She kept telling herself to not pass out. But it was in vain. The intensity of the pain in her leg caused her to black out. She did not hear Marco screaming for her to wake up and eject. He watched helplessly as her space craft spiraled down toward the surface of the Blood Moon.

Marco screamed in rage. He loved Mary Lincoln, and in a split second she was gone. He pressed down on his laser control button and fired at the two ships that had hit Lincoln's ship. The Akarzdamedian space ship received ten laser hits and one was a direct shot on the engine. The alien and his space craft were gone in a brilliant flash of fire and flying metal.

Lomax swerved to avoid the barrage of laser fire of Marco Andolini. Lomax began flying full speed away from Marco, believing the opposing cadet would not follow him.

Lomax was dead wrong.

Lomax heard his computer warning him that Marco Andolini's ship was on his rear, traveling at eight hundred kilometers an hour and increasing his speed.

Lomax heard Marco scream at him, "Take this you sorry bastard!"

Marco pressed down on his laser controls and began firing a volley of death on the ship of Peter Lomax. Lomax felt his vessel shaking as the laser fire impacted the rear of his hull. Lomax instinctively reached down for his ejection lever, but he was too slow. The lasers fired by Marco hit the reserve atomic fuel tanks and Lomax died as his body was incinerated. Lomax was already dead when his ship fell toward the surface. The ship exploded in the sky, about fifty feet before it would have impacted the moon. Marco watched with gratification as the metal pieces of Peter Lomax' ship fell to the ground.

Marco turned his ship back toward the battle to assist

Doernitz and hopefully rescue Lincoln and Cardenas, if they were still alive. Marco noticed that another Akarzdamedian had been pursuing him. He decided to play "chicken" with the opposing ship and flew head on for her. He opened fire with his lasers and the Akarzdamedian began firing back at him. Marco moved his ship to the right and avoided the laser blasts. The Akarzdamedian did not move out of the firing lane. The yellow colored alien let out a growl as his ship was hit by twenty different laser beams which caused the engine to explode.

Marco continued on his flight plan to help Doernitz. He did not see the large Raumschiff of Alfred Rosenburg, II, approaching from his left. The ship computer warned him of an incoming vessel.

"Another fighter ship?" Marco demanded of the computer.

"No, a Raumschiff," the computer replied. "It is locking armor piercing rockets on you."

"Shit!" Marco yelled out loud, turning his head looking in every direction to see where the Raumschiff was. He began to wish had at least one of his armor piercing rockets left. Firing lasers on a Raumschiff could be effective but the explosive capability of a rocket would bring the larger craft down with more efficiency.

Caine and David Rosenburg were standing on the pilot command section of their Raumschiff. They had Cadet Marco Andolini in their target sights. David fired three armor piercing rockets at Andolini's ship. They watched as Andolini did his best to avoid being hit. But his efforts were for naught and the three tracer rockets proved to be too much for him.

Realizing his ship was about to be blown out of the sky, Marco pulled up hard on his ejection lever. His canopy popped open, but the seat did not eject as it was supposed to.

"My ejection mechanism has malfunctioned!" Marco cried out. He continued pulling on the lever with all of his strength. His computer continued to warn him that he only had seconds before impact.

At O'Malley's Bar in Clovis City, Dominic Andolini and his younger siblings all watched as Marco Andolini's space craft erupted in a massive red-orange ball of fire. All three rockets hit dead center on the ship.

"Marco!" Dominic cried out as he fell to his knees on the floor of O'Malley's. "No!"

The Andolini family was holding hands when the ship flown by Marco Andolini exploded. Lucius Andolini dropped his head and stared at the ground. Venus and Lucrezia Andolini hugged each other as they wept. Giola Andolini stood silently and stared at the large screen before her. She did not attempt to hide or wipe her tears that were running down her cheeks.

Elektra Papanikolaou, Harumi Shigeta and April Mejia wept openly as they cried for Marco, Mary Lincoln and for Porfirio Cardenas.

At the hospital, Freya Doernitz Cardenas was on her

knees, crying over the loss of her beloved husband and hoping her little brother could out fox the four remaining enemy combatants.

Yuri Gorski, Les Gillis, Drew Harrison and Julia Steiner continued to build their barricades, knowing full well that the battle would soon come their way. They had programmed their headquarters computer broadcast the three dimensional events before them as the placed their sheets of metal around the headquarters. The loss of their three friends hurt them all to the bone.

"They sacrificed themselves to buy us time," Steiner lamented. She could not wipe the tears from her eyes as she was in her enviro-suit, her face covered by the patented, unbreakable transparent metal and glass. She kept working, using her Magnetizer to place metal sheets in the locations Gillis directed. She never noticed that the three men with her were also shedding tears over the loss of their friends.

CHAPTER TWELVE

Jurgen Doernitz knew he was the only one left. It was four against him and he could not allow any of the enemy to survive or escape. If he did, they would easily wipe out his friends. He had no choice but to kill them all or die trying. Doernitz determined that he could not go in the direction of the approaching Raumschiff as that would be suicide. He decided to lead the four ships up and away from where his remaining friends were hiding. With the Raumschiff that shot down Marco on its' way, Doernitz would be dead very soon. He increased his ship speed to two thousand kilometers an hour and flew straight up into space. He angled his ship to fly directly into the sunlight.

"He's trying to escape!" Doornink yelled.

"Follow him and let's finish this!" Austin responded.

Doornink, Austin and the two remaining Akarzdamedian slave pilots increased their speed and pursued Doernitz upward.

The news media began speculating that Doernitz had decided to run away.

James Cobb and Bret Bragg were laughing as they sat on bar stools at O'Malley's.

"I told all of you that Doernitz is nothing but a coward,"

Cobb yelled out to the others. "All of you loser Gorski Gangers! All your leaders are going to die!"

Sophia DuBravac had enough of the Bragg gang and their insults. They were both verbally and physically abusive to others. Their words were cruel and unwarranted. DuBravac stood up from her chair and began walking toward the cluster of cadets that were loyal to Bret Bragg with Lila Zapata walking next to her. Without a word DuBravac stopped in front of Cobb and stood just inches from his face.

"Say that again," DuBravac hissed.

"I say I love watching all your friends die," Cobb sneered at her.

Cobb hit the floor on his back, holding his broken nose. DuBravac downed him with one punch from her right fist. Bret Bragg and the other Bragg gang members began to stand up. Bragg noticed the Gorski Gang members were also standing up. But this time the Gorski Gang was not alone. The Collins faction was with them and about a hundred neutral cadets were joining in, standing to show their support.

Bret Bragg realized he and his gang were about to receive the biggest whipping of their lives. They were outnumbered about twenty to one. He watched as long time Bragg Gang member Reynita Calderon walked away from their side of the bar and she stopped next to DuBravac and Zapata. At first, DuBravac thought Calderon was going to start something. But her demeanor indicated she did not want to fight. Calderon's hands were not balled up into fists.

"I am so sick of you both," Reynita Calderon said to Bragg and Cobb. She pointed at one of the screens. "Those are our friends over there dying, our fellow classmates! What is wrong with you? Take your gang and shove it. I am out!"

Bragg swallowed as he looked at Reynita Calderon in disbelief. She had been one of the original members along with his older brother William. He never would have believed that the day would pass that Reynita would abandon them. "Sophia, I apologize for Cobb. He is out of line. I really am sorry."

DuBravac examined Bragg's face and determined that he was not being sincere. So she punched him in the mouth, sending him to the floor next to Cobb. She regarded the rest of the Bragg gang. Most of the Lipinski sisters were looking down at the floor, ashamed of themselves. "Any of you want to try me?"

The other Bragg members shook their heads "no." DuBravac and Zapata slowly returned to their seats, walking backwards so none of the Bragg Gang could jump them from behind. Bret Bragg spit out one of his bottom teeth.

As the altercation ended none of the patrons of O'Malley's realized that in the next few seconds they were about to see that Doernitz was not a coward at all.

In fact, they and all that were watching were about to see young Doernitz prove himself to be the greatest fighter pilot in the entire conquered eight solar systems and old Earth.

Doornink and Austin pushed their space craft to their limits, flying at full speed in pursuit, their two slave pilots next to them. They were getting close to leaving the atmosphere of the Blood Moon and enter the space vacuum.

"Where is that little bastard?" Austin yelled as he was blinded by the sun light.

"I don't see him!" Doornink replied, his voice sounded as if he was panic stricken. "He must have fled the moon to get away."

Doernitz was able to hear their conversation as his on board computer had spliced into the communication devices of his opponents.

Doornink and Austin heard Doernitz' voice tell them: "Wrong. I just had you follow me where I could kill you once and for all."

Keith Austin did not see the laser blasts coming due to the sunlight in his face. Doernitz had been able to outdistance his opponents circle back and then dive down at them. Doernitz was patient to attack when the opportunity was sure to yield a high percentage point of hits versus misses. As a young teenager, Admiral Yamamoto trained him to make each and every laser shot count. Doernitz opened fire when he was in range. He wanted to kill Austin first, due to his observation that he was the better pilot left on the side of the enemy. His laser blasts hit the side of Austin's ship thirty times. Every single shot fired by Doernitz made a direct hit. Austin screamed as laser blasts entered through the metallic hull of his space craft and cut into his body. His chest and abdomen were ripped open before his skull was impacted by a direct hit. His head was vaporized just seconds before his ship exploded. Keith Austin was finished.

Doornink roared with rage after witnessing his best friend Austin die. "I'm going to kill you for that you bastard!"

"Come get some!" Doernitz responded as he fired upon the next closest ship. One of the Akarzdamedian slave pilots cried out as he suffered the same death as Austin had. The space craft exploded violently.

Doornink watched helplessly as Doernitz flew by his position at a speed of three thousand kilometers an hour.

"Get him!" Doornink ordered his remaining Akarzdamedian pilot. The two ships pursued Doernitz down toward the moon. The speeds were increasing due to the gravitational pull of the moon below.

The cadets at O'Malley's found themselves cheering Doernitz on as he led the final two opposing pilots on a spiraling chase straight at the lunar surface.

"How will he pull out in time?" Lila Zapata worried out loud.

The others watched as Doernitz increased his speed to five thousand kilometers an hour. Doornink and the Akarzdamedian followed suit and matched his speed. Doornink began firing lasers at Doernitz, missing him.

"Warning!" Doernitz heard his on board computer

announce. "Impact with lunar surface in five minutes. Recommend you pull out now."

"Not yet," Doernitz gritted his teeth. "Not yet." He watched as the surface grew closer and closer. He knew his computer was correct. He had to pull out soon or he would not be able to avoid the impact.

"Four minutes," his computer warned.

"Not yet," Doernitz held his steering column tight. He would have to negotiate the turn and lift at the last second.

"Three minutes."

"Not yet!" Doernitz waited for the call of two minutes.

"Two minutes."

With that time warning, Doernitz twisted his steering column to the left and upwards. His ship was shaking as it tried to break the gravitational pull and the trajectory. He struggled with his half-moon steering column to avoid impact on the surface. His whole body was shaking from the strain. Slowly, Doernitz was able to pull his ship upwards. The belly of Doernitz ship missed the lunar surface by about twenty feet. Doernitz ship shot upward as he strained with his controls. He heard himself screaming as he narrowly avoided crashing on the moon.

"Computer!" Doernitz yelled. "What about the other two ships?"

"One has crashed on the surface," the computer reported. "The other is pursuing us."

Clive Doornink strained his limits to avoid smashing his

ship onto the surface of the Blood Moon. He watched helplessly as the last Akarzdamedian slave ship slammed into the ground, exploding on impact. Doornink realized now that he was in over his head. The other pilot was far superior in his talents and had taken out three ships quickly.

Doornink decided it was in his own personal interests to flee. He turned his ship to cease his pursuit of Doernitz and began flying toward the safety of the Raumschiff of Alfred Rosenburg, II. Doornink was beside himself with grief. Four pilots took out twenty-three ships. Impossible, he thought. He began to relax before he received a communication from the Doernitz kid.

"Where do you think you are going?" Doernitz asked him.

"Leave me alone!" Doornink yelled back. His heart was pounding in his chest. "I don't want anything to do with this anymore!"

"You know I cannot do that," Doernitz told him. "You and your friends started a war when you killed those judges and the other cadets. But you made it personal for me. Several people I love and care about are now dead. I will stop pursuing you only if you get the rest of your people to surrender right now. Otherwise you will die. As you saw, I never miss and right now I have my cross hairs trained on you."

"I will try to get them to surrender!" Doornink screamed in desperation. "Please don't fire on me!" Doornink then contacted the Raumschiff. "Mister Rosenburg! Please come in!"

"Yes?" Caine Rosenburg responded. He and his brother had been watching the aerial combat talents of Doernitz on their multiple monitors in the pilot command section of their Raumschiff. The brothers were impressed and David Rosenburg had commented that they would not leave the moon alive if they had to face the Doernitz kid in face to face combat.

"We need to surrender!" Doornink begged them. "If we don't I am going to die!"

Before Caine could respond, his Raumschiff was hit by a volley of pulsar blasts. His Raumschiff rocked left and right.

"What the hell!" David Rosenburg demanded as he fell to the left and slid on the metal floor. Caine was jolted as well and fell on his buttocks.

Ellen Benson, Hal Palmer, Torch Woods and Jeff "June" Carter had fired their pulsar weapons on the Raumschiff. The Rosenburg's failed to notice their approach on their tactical screens because they had been so intent on viewing the battle between Doernitz and the other pilots.

"They are the ones that fired those rockets on the lone pilot!" Benson yelled to her fellow pilots. "Hit them again and again until they go down!"

Benson and her three men simultaneously fired their ship pulsar blasts again, causing the Raumschiff to spin out of control.

Caine pulled himself up into the pilot's seat and saw

from the corner of his eyes that David Rosenburg was able to sit in the co-pilot chair. David used his fingers to expand the weapons targeting screen before him and began typing in commands to the Raumschiff weapons control.

"Firing heat seeking rockets!" David announced. He pressed the fire button on his control panel as the Raumschiff continued to spin in circles.

"Rockets launched!" Torch Woods warned. "Coming in our direction!"

"Take evasive action!" Ellen Benson yelled.

Five armor piercing rockets were shot from the Raumschiff at the four brave cadets from Newton Academy. Jeff "June" Carter had turned twenty-one years old. His twenty-second birthday was to be in June. He would never see that day. He died as his ship was hit by two of the deadly rockets. The force of the explosion caused his wing man, Hal Palmer, to lose momentary control of his own ship.

Torch Woods saw that two of the rockets were on a collision course with Ellen Benson. He screamed as he throttled his small ship at full speed in the direction of the missiles. Instead of blowing Benson's space craft out of the sky, the two rockets annihilated Torch Woods' ship.

Benson tried to cry out to Woods, to stop him from sacrificing himself. Her cries were never heard by Woods as he died in the explosion.

Hal Palmer realized one of the rockets was coming in his

direction. He turned his ship in the direction of the missile and fired his pulsar blast in the direction of the projectile. The missile detonated harmlessly in the air. Palmer had learned that defensive tactic from his Academy training. Palmer had been holding his breath but allowed himself to breathe easier when he saw the rocket detonate.

Benson and Palmer begin firing pulsar blasts at the Raumschiff again and again and again. They watched with hope as the Raumschiff seemed to rock with each pulse blast.

Caine and David Rosenburg cursed out loud as the pulsar attack worked. The Raumschiff electrical power ceased and the solar power cells became inoperable.

"What is going on here?" Alfred demanded of his two sons.

"Power failure!" Caine had panic in his voice. "We are going to crash!"

David placed his hands on the computer control panel before him and braced for the crash.

Benson and Palmer watched as the Raumschiff slammed onto the surface of the moon. Chlorine gas, dust and rock were thrown as the larger space craft slid for about two hundred yards before twisting to a halt. The three Rosenburg's on the ship were knocked unconscious by the crash landing.

"Alan!" Benson reported. "We were able to down the Raumschiff. I am leaving Hal here to monitor for survivors. I am going to go help the last pilot!"

"Understood," Anderson responded. "I will send our Raumschiff to collect prisoners if there are any. Palmer, take no chances. If any one comes out of that Raumschiff holding anything that resembles a weapon, even a squirt gun, drop them."

"Yes sir." Palmer affirmed that he had received the orders.

Benson pushed her ship in the direction of Jurgen Doernitz.

As she approached, Benson noticed that Doernitz was tailing Doornink.

"Pilots!" Benson attempted to contact them using a general term since she was uncertain as to their real names. "The Raumschiff is down. It is time to surrender. Repeat the Raumschiff is down."

Doornink snarled when he saw the Newton ship approaching from the east. Doornink formulated the conclusion that he was about to be fired upon. The Rosenburg Raumschiff was shot down and now the Newton Academy cadets were joining forces with the Clovis cadets. Doornink took in the news that he was now all alone and panicked.

Benson was communicating with Doernitz that she had been scanning and picked up two life signs several kilometers south and they should end this quickly to render aid to whoever the two survivors were. Doornink heard the message exchange and then fired a laser burst at Benson's ship.

Doornink's aim was true and Benson's ship suffered irreparable damage. Her rear engine was hit by Doornink's laser fire. Her on board computer warned her to eject. She pulled on her ejection lever and was shot out of her space craft, flying freely into the sky as her ship exploded. Benson screamed as she flew through the sky. She had a fear of heights that kicked in whenever she was not inside a ship. She cursed herself for having been so careless in approaching the enemy ship.

Doernitz, seeing Doornink's unprovoked attack on the Newton cadet's ship, opened fire with his laser batteries. Doornink screamed like a child as his space craft was blown to metal shards from the accurate firing of Doernitz. His dying thoughts were that Caine had promised him that nothing would go wrong if he joined them on the Blood Moon.

"Pilot? Are you injured?" Doernitz attempted to raise Benson on her holo-com.

Benson responded, holding her holo-com in one hand and was brushing dirt and small pebbles off of her with the other. She had safely landed on the surface. "I am fine. Go to your two friends at the coordinates I sent to you. They might need medical attention. Go."

"Thank you for coming to our aid," Doernitz told her.

"We should be thanking you and your friends," Benson said. "In all my life, I never saw such courage. I really hope your friends are not hurt."

Doernitz throttled his space craft forward toward the

coordinates Benson had given him. Two life forms were confirmed by his computer scanner. Was it Porfirio, Mary or Marco? Doernitz wished that none of them had been harmed. One was missing. But who?

After docking with Space Station Cy-5, Dirk Fenster said farewell to cadets Gleaia Chin and Ristina Bedrosian. The two female cadets accepted money from Fenster to pay for a transport flight back to New Edinburgh. The remainder of the cadets on his ship elected to stay the course and continue on to the Blood Moon in an attempt to rescue the Clovis Academy cadets.

CHAPTER THIRTEEN

Doernitz landed his space craft about ten yards from the first life form that Benson had informed him of. Doernitz pressed the button on his control panel to open his canopy and unbuckled his safety harnesses. He drew his hand laser, just in case, and then jumped from his ship to the surface of the moon. He could feel the loose lunar rocks move under his feet as he ran as fast as he could to the prone figure lying on the ground. When he made it to the pilot he saw who it was.

Porfirio Cardenas.

Doernitz observed that Cardenas' enviro-suit had several small slivers of metal stuck in it. There were patches of blood where the metal had penetrated Cardenas' body. Doernitz knelt down next to his brother in law and took his hand.

"Porfirio. It's me, Jurgen."

Cardenas slowly turned his head and looked up at Doernitz. Cardenas had blood on his chin, his breathing was labored. Doernitz noticed that his helmet had several cracks that resembled a spider's web.

"Jurgen," Cardenas swallowed with difficulty. "Thank

the Lord you made it."

"You will to. I am going to take you to Julia and she can help you." Doernitz said hopefully.

Cardenas smiled and squeezed his hand. "No. I am dying. I saw Mary's ship just crash over that hill. She might be alive. Take her."

Cardenas pointed with his free hand in the direction he saw Mary Lincoln's ship crash. Doernitz began to pick Cardenas up in his arms. Cardenas cried out in agony. His back had been broken from the impact with the lunar surface. Several of his internal organs were torn open by the metal pieces.

"Porfirio, hold on. My sister and your children need you." Doernitz realized that tears were flowing down his cheeks. He loved his brother in law. He was a good man, a great friend, a wonderful father and had been a fantastic husband to Freya.

Cardenas coughed up some fresh blood. "Jurgen. Go to Mary. When you make it back, tell Freya how much... how much I loved her. Take care of...of my children."

Doernitz realized that Cardenas was about to die. He held his hand tight. "Do not worry about anything. I will take care of them all. I promise."

Cardenas nodded, "Lila, she loves you. She is a good person. Never let her go."

"I won't, Porfirio. I promise."

"Good," Cardenas was coughing more blood. "Go to Mary. Hurry."

Doernitz was about to respond when Cardenas head slumped to his left side. He exhaled his last breath and died in Doernitz' arms. Doernitz screamed out loud due to his anger and frustration.

Doernitz laid his dead brother in law on the surface and stood up. He looked in the direction that Cardenas had been begging him to go toward. Doernitz ran as fast as he could. If Lincoln was alive, he needed to help her.

Hal Palmer had boarded the downed Raumschiff and found three occupants. Using cuffs and restraints, Palmer bound all three. He went to the command station of the Raumschiff and contacted Alan Anderson.

"Sir, Palmer here. I have secured the Raumschiff. We have three prisoners and they are bound. I don't know if Ellen informed you sir, but Carter and Woods didn't make it."

"Good job Hal," Anderson responded. Everyone from the Newton Academy team already knew that Carter and Woods had died. "Ellen was shot down but she was able to eject. I am sending our Raumschiff over so we can take possession of the three prisoners. Take your fighter ship, pick up Ellen and bring her in. You did great out there."

"Thank you, sir." Palmer tapped his fingers on the command control desk. "Palmer out."

Anderson turned to his remaining team members, "Nic, get everyone on our Raumschiff. We are going to pick up the three prisoners and then rendezvous with Gorski's team."

Nicolas Curtis turned and looked at LeClair, Thompson, Riley and Myers. "You heard the man! Let's move out!"

In the distance, Doernitz saw one of the Clovis Academy space craft resting on the lunar surface. The ship was badly damaged with several laser burns on the hull; the metal in some locations was torn and twisted due to the ship rolling over and over again upon impact. There was still some smoke rising from the engine area. It was about fifty feet distance away. Doernitz ran to the side of the crashed vessel and then climbed up her side to the top of the hull. He gazed into the canopy and saw Mary Lincoln in her pilot's seat. Her eyes were closed and her arms were resting at her sides. Her head was leaning back against her pilot's seat headrest. Doernitz was relieved when he noticed that she was breathing.

Doernitz tried to pry open Lincoln's canopy, but it would not budge. He used his laser pistol to melt the metal braces holding the canopy down. Once he had finished melting the metal, Doernitz pushed the transparent metal canopy off of the space craft. It slammed onto the lunar rock with a loud clanging noise. Doernitz gazed at Lincoln and saw that her left leg was cut open in two locations. Doernitz could see Lincoln's bone through the wounds. He speculated she might lose her leg.

Doernitz unbuckled Lincoln's safety belts and lifted her up into his arms. He stood upright while carrying her and stepped onto the side wing before he jumped onto the surface. Doernitz carried her toward his space craft. In the distance,

Doernitz observed a Newton Academy space craft landing next to his. The canopy of the ship opened and Ellen Benson and Hal Palmer jumped out of the ship. The two cadet pilots from Newton Academy ran toward Doernitz.

"She is hurt really bad," Doernitz informed the two Newton students as they closed the distance between them. "I have to get her to our safe house for treatment."

"We'll go with you," Benson told Doernitz as she scanned Lincoln with a hand held medical life signs device. Benson had been studying search and rescue classes which included some medical training. "Her left leg is broken in two places and she is in shock. She has bruises in several locations on her ribs and shoulders."

"I can take her," Doernitz told them as he looked into Lincoln's face. Losing Andolini and Cardenas cut like a knife through his heart. He hoped that he would be able to save the kind hearted Mary Lincoln. "I need you all to go to a location on the dark side of the moon. Do it quick. There are some large metal lockers filled with weaponry. Laser rifles, hand lasers, stun darts, thermite grenades. All kinds of useful weapons for a war that we need if we are going to survive. Use your tow cable and bring it with you. I have a sinking feeling we are going to get hit by the survivors of the Achilles group."

"That was where you and your friends found the rockets and laser batteries?" Palmer concluded.

"Yes," Doernitz said as he lifted Lincoln onto his ship

and placed her gently in the back seat. "Hurry. They must know that we raided their stash of weapons. You need to get there before they do. We need to be ready."

Palmer and Benson nodded and jumped onto their space craft. Time was of the essence.

Colonel Jamal Lincoln watched in silence as the screen before him showed the young Doernitz carrying his injured daughter in his arms. Although relieved that his daughter was not dead, Lincoln grieved for her friends that had died. In his many computer chats with Mary, he recalled her mentioning how close she was to her friends. Especially Gorski and Andolini.

Lincoln had received orders from the Space Command on Sikorsky's Planet to turn his ship, the U.N.S.C *Cortez*, around and not go to Semiramis and her moon. Lincoln disobeyed the direct order. His daughter was in danger. She was injured and needed him to get to her. Colonel Lincoln cared little for any potential court martial or conviction for disregarding orders. Mary was his child and he was determined to protect her no matter what the consequences.

Colonel Lincoln met with his top officers in the Executive Conference Room. Lincoln was wearing his one-piece standard military issued Marine Corps uniform. It was green, black and brown, the colors swirled in patterns. There was a black zipper line from the bottom of his neck to his midriff. He had on his issued black boots.

Captain Mara Sowa, in command of Military

Intelligence, was already seated at the long rectangular table when Lincoln walked in. Sowa was wearing the standard uniform as well, but hers was black to signify Military Intelligence. Chief Pilot for the *Cortez*, Lieutenant Commander Clarissa Marywood was also present. Her uniform was the color of the Pilot Corps, dark blue. Next to her was second in command of Military Intelligence, First Lieutenant Jim Shigeta, who also was wearing a solid black uniform. Lieutenant Paula Vela, another pilot was also seated at the table. Next to Vela was Lieutenant Hans Streicher another pilot.

Professor Simon Brennan, a renowned Astro-physicist, was standing in the background. He was wearing civilian clothing as he was not a part of the military structure. Brennan was bald, sported a mustache and had a slender build. He was in his late seventies. The crew understood and respected the fact that Lincoln valued Brennan's advice in all matters.

Lincoln noticed Shigeta and walked to him and hugged the young officer in front of the others. "I am so sorry for your loss," Lincoln told him. Lincoln was a well-respected commander. One of the reasons for the admiration he received from his crew members was because he took time to get to know about all of his officers and non-commissioned officers. He knew the names of their spouses and he took time to get to know about all of their children and families. Lincoln had even approved leave for Lieutenant Jim Shigeta to travel to New Edinburgh to participate in his little sister's wedding to Dominic Andolini.

"Thank you sir," Jim Shigeta responded and hugged Lincoln back.

"You were related to one of the kids on that moon?" Marywood asked.

"My little sister is getting married," Shigeta told them all. "Her soon to be husband is the twin brother of Marco Andolini."

The officers all began to express their condolences to Shigeta.

After all of the officers sat down, Colonel Lincoln got down to business. "We have been ordered to make best speed to the moon at Semiramis. We are to take the Rosenburg conspirators into custody and save the remaining Clovis and Newton Academy cadets. Captain Sowa, I am putting you in charge of the arrests and the transportation accommodations for the criminals. Those of you in space command and engineering, I want you to move this ship faster than she has ever done before. No excuses. Dismissed."

The officers began jumping to their feet as they had their orders from their commander. Each of them had been watching the drama as it played out on the Blood Moon and for each of the senior staff serving under Colonel Lincoln there was a common thought regarding the event and that was that there were cadets on that moon worth saving.

Alan Anderson and his team landed their Raumschiff next to the Rosenburg Raumschiff. After Thompson and LeClair determined that the enemy space craft could be flown safely, Anderson ordered Curtis and Riley to pilot the enemy Raumschiff to the Tyr Academy headquarters. Anderson took LeClair, Thompson and Myers on the Newton Academy ship.

"Where are the others?" Anderson asked himself. "There should have been several more Achilles members. Where are they?"

Dell Ragnarsson had suffered a head injury in the blast that Les Gillis caused. His Raumschiff had also been damaged, the main engine was destroyed, his back up engine was operable, but needed to be wired into the hybrid nuclear-solar powered engine.

His dunkle materie, also known as dark matter, converter was irreparably damaged. His long time crew that had been on board were all dead. Kai Chin, Avery Jackson, Burton Stapler and Cleon Alexander had stayed behind to help him with the necessary repairs.

The four men listened to the radio transmissions of the space battle. They were disturbed about the fact that their friend, Keith Austin, had died in the battle. The other three pilots that lost their lives had not been close friends of theirs. They knew Lomax, but he was not really one that the other men had confided in much. But the death of Austin left them all silently questioning their allegiance to Caine Rosenburg. He had promised them a quick adventure and good pay. Now Giamatti, Lomax, Austin, Stenerud and Doornink were dead. It caused each man to realize that perhaps they had gotten into an event much larger than they could control.   Several of the surviving Saharakaree were also on board the Raumschiff, watching the cadets work on the repairs. Their long and deadly tails were wagging left and right.

Dell had his head bandaged with white medical gauze. A spot of blood was present on his bandage from the location he had hit his head. His number one concern was that his dark matter converter was destroyed. That meant any lengthy space travel would be out of the question. His ship could still function with the normal nuclear-solar hybrid engine.

Ragnarsson directed the cadets on how to make the necessary changes. He had grown to despise the cadets, other than Kai Chin. The rest were sadistic idiots. Dell had contemplated killing them all, except for Chin, and fleeing. Gorski and his friends had turned the tide on the situation. While the Rosenburg's and their friends partied and rested on their laurels, Gorski and his team demonstrated how valuable hard work and preparation were in fighting a battle. Chin understood that lesson. The others did not have enough intelligence to learn from their error.

Dell left them to continue to work on the engines and he ran down to one of his large storage rooms in the belly of his vessel. He ordered the computer to open the door to Storage Room B and walked in after the doors slid open. The doors slid shut behind him.

"Lights," he ordered his ship's computer.

The lights slowly switched on and illuminated the entire storage area. Dell walked in circles in the center of the storage room and inspected the seven foot tall cryo-sleep chambers before him. There were fifty of them. He looked over each one individually to make sure that they had not been damaged. In each of the cryo-sleep chambers were duplicates of his son, Junior. The cloning process had been completed many days earlier, but Dell did not want to unleash the small army of replicas of his son unless necessary.

Based on the Clovis Academy Cadets cunning and their demonstrated willingness to outwork an opponent, it was now time to wake the fifty clones so that they could join in on the battle. Dell had downloaded his own memories into each of the fifty duplicates. They were perfect physical copies of his son with one exception; their skin was the wrong color. Dell speculated that the duplication process had not been perfected. He looked into each individual cryo-sleep container. All of the duplicates were a light green color.

On the upper level of the Raumschiff, the other cadets finished wiring in the replacement engine. Kai Chin and Avery Jackson gave each other a high five.

"I think it is ready," Burton Stapler announced proudly into the communication system. "Fire up the engine and see if it works."

Dell nodded, quickly left the storage room and began

climbing the series of ladders to get to the pilots section. He was met by Chin and the two men continued the short walk upwards. They sat down in the pilot and co-pilot seats as Dell ordered the computer to begin checking the engine. Everything was coming up with a positive response. The engines started without a problem.

"Now what do we do?" Chin asked.

"Now we end this charade," Dell growled. "We rescue the Rosenburg's and then we kill Gorski, Anderson and the remaining cadets."

"And after that?" Chin was thinking ahead. Their identities had been exposed, thanks to Gorski destroying the Jammer devices. Chin was smart enough to realize that he would be a fugitive for the rest of his life.

"After that," Dell pondered the question for a moment, "it is a large universe out there. We have plenty of locations that we can hide at until the heat dies down. Stick with me; I have been on the outs with the law my whole life. I am still standing."

Chin nodded and watched as Dell began flying his Raumschiff up into the sky. The final battle was coming. Chin began checking his weapons to make sure he was ready for the challenge.

Rear Admiral Alejandro Cardenas had been the commander of his own Fleet of Battle Cruisers for two years. He had raised his children to become officers in the space command, as he had. The highly decorated Admiral hoped that each of his children would follow in the footsteps of their father. One by one, his children left their temporary homes which were space craft that the Admiral had been assigned to, and they became students at the various military schools across the eight solar systems. Now, his youngest son, Porfirio, was dead.

After his son died on the moon of Semiramis, the Rear Admiral locked himself into his quarters on his flagship, the United Nations Space Command Battle Cruiser *Cleopatra*. The *Cleopatra* had a crew of over one thousand three hundred men and women. The majority of the crew consisted of fighter pilots. The *Cleopatra* was a war ship, one of the best ever designed and manufactured by the Fenster Corporation. She had one of the best weapons sections of the entire fleet and was capable of unleashing enough missiles and laser fire to destroy a small planet.

Cardenas did not want his crew to observe him in a state of grief, so he sat in his self-imposed solitary confinement, tears flowing down his cheeks. He blamed himself for the death of Porfirio. Had he encouraged his son to seek a different path, another career, then he would still be alive. As he grieved he heard his computer announce that he had a visitor at his door. Rear Admiral Cardenas wiped the tears from his face and composed himself. When he felt ready, he asked the computer to open the doors to his quarters.

Standing in his door way was perhaps the most beautiful woman Cardenas had ever laid eyes on. She was wearing a grey and black striped sweater that accentuated her large breasts and flat stomach. Her tight black leather pants and knee high black boots left little to the imagination. The woman had a laser rifle slung over her right shoulder and a large black belt with a hand laser, a few knives and sun dart attached. She looked as if she were ready for war.

"Do I know you?" Rear Admiral Cardenas asked.

"No, but you will know me well when I explain why I am here. May I come in?" Penelope Rosenburg responded.

"Please," Cardenas motioned with his arm. He watched as the woman walked gracefully into his quarters. His doors slid shut behind her.

"My name is Penelope Rosenburg," she reached out to shake his hand. He cautiously took her hand in his.

"How did you get on board my ship?" Cardenas asked. "You are not a part of my crew."

"I can board any Space Command ship at any time or location I so choose," Penelope said confidently. "My family developed most of the security systems on all of the Battle Cruisers. I can bypass all of those protocols."

"What do you want from me Miss Rosenburg?" Cardenas asked as he watched her inspect his quarters. She seemed particularly interested in several of his paintings on his wall.

Penelope turned and smiled at him, "Paintings by Florez and Severinsson. You have very good taste in art. Admiral, I will be blunt with you. Your son died as a hero. He was a good man. I am here to recruit you to make certain that your son will be remembered."

"Why do you care about my son?" Cardenas half asked and half demanded.

"Sit down, Admiral. Please." She requested calmly. "I have a very long story to tell you and when I finish my tale, you will not only know who was responsible for the death of your son, but you will join with me in our war to stop them from ever harming another person like Porfirio."

"War?" Cardenas sat down.

"Yes, Admiral. A war is coming." Penelope told him calmly. "Your son already chose a side in the war, or I should say, the events of the last several months put him on a side. He and his friends got tangled up in a web of universal intrigue and political cover-ups. I hope that when I finish telling you about the events leading up to today that you will join my side."

"And what is your side?" Cardenas asked cautiously.

"I am going to over throw the current government and install free elections for every person in the Earth United Nations system."

"That is treason!"

Penelope smiled, "Yes. Yes it is. Before you have me arrested and executed, will you be gentleman enough to hear me out?"

Rear Admiral Cardenas swallowed, finding that he

trusted the stranger by the firmness of her voice and the manner that she made eye contact with him. He knew his oath of service required him to arrest the woman and turn her over for immediate torture and execution. But she had his attention. He had previously received and watched a computer diskette that had been sent to him by an officer that had formerly served under his command named Garrison. Cardenas had already been exposed to information by the Garrison disk that had Cardenas questioning the validity of Sikorsky rule. Due to the death of his son, Cardenas felt that he needed to hear what the woman had to say.

"Go on. I am listening."

Penelope pulled out a chair that was in front of his roll-top desk and sat down. "Admiral, all you were taught about the history of humanity was a lie. The alien race called the Akarzdamedians attacked us, which was true. But when we attacked them they begged to surrender. Vladimir Sikorsky refused to accept their total surrender because he wanted to punish them as an example to all of the other alien races in the universe. Humanity, under the Sikorsky rule, has become a cancer to all other races."

"That is not so!" Cardenas shook his head, recalling that his entire preparatory classes had drilled into his head that humanity barely defeated the Akarzdamedians.

"Fix yourself a drink and have a seat, Admiral." Penelope advised him. "We have much to discuss together."

"You have proof of what you say?"

She smiled and pulled her long hair back. "Yes, Admiral. I have evidence to back up everything that I say."

Cardenas walked over to his small bar that was beside his bed. He poured himself a double shot of straight up whiskey, offered her some which she declined. He sat down at the foot of his bed and faced the woman. "Tell me everything."

The Glorious Leader, Vladimir Sikorsky, issued a prepared statement to the citizens of the united eight solar systems. He asked his prosecutors on Sikorsky's Planet to formally charge the Rosenburg's for murder and conspiracy based on the events on the Blood Moon. Sikorsky ordered that Colonel Jamal Lincoln make best time to the moon and arrest the Rosenburg conspirators, bring them to justice and rescue the surviving cadets from Newton and Clovis Academy. His statement was met with rising approval ratings from the masses.

Freya Doernitz Cardenas was granted leave for the next two weeks due to the death of her husband. She had been able to bring her two children home with the help of several friends. Most attentive to the needs of the Cardenas family were the Gorski gang members. Jack Harcourt and the recovering Michel Evart helped with the children. Elektra Papanikolaou and April Mejia began helping with the chores of cleaning the house, cooking and running errands for the widow. Yesenia Guevara and Drayton Love-Easter would bring their son over so they could have the children play together. Blossom Li and her family would send food from their restaurants. Freya was struck by how much the other cadets had loved and respected Porfirio. The amount of kindness shown in her time of grief was more than generous.

As the cadets helped out, Freya stayed in her bed room and would spend most of her time crying. The love of her life was gone and she had little to no will to face the rest of the world. She would need time to come to terms with all that had happened. She prayed that Jurgen would soon be out of harm's way.

The Andolini family handled their grief privately. Harumi Shigeta, as Dominic Andolini's fiancé, was allowed to attend the private burial ceremony. Colonel Gorski and his son Piotr were allowed to attend and Shigeta learned from the conversations before and after the services that the Gorski's and Andolini's had been very close. All other outsiders were asked to stay away by Dominic and Marco's parents. They even excluded the remaining members of Gorski's Gang. They promised that there would be a larger, more public ceremony for Marco Andolini at a later date.

CHAPTER FOURTEEN

Jurgen Doernitz had landed his small fighter ship just outside of the impressive metal walls that Les Gillis, Drew Harrison and Julia Steiner had constructed. As he opened his canopy he was met by Yuri Gorski. The two men carefully lifted Mary Lincoln, slowly lowered her from the ship and rushed her to the Headquarters Building. Inside they found that Steiner and Harrison were ready to perform surgery on their injured team mate. Gorski and Doernitz laid the unconscious Lincoln on the operating table next to where Sara Barnes was still drugged so she could sleep. Eamon O'Grady was still recovering from his wounds, sleeping on another bed.

"Both of you out of here," Steiner ordered as she put on her medical mask, covering her mouth and nose. Harrison already had his mask on and both were wearing sterilized clothing and had caps on the keep their hair from falling onto the patient.

Gorski and Doernitz walked out of the medical area.

"Kid, that was some of the best flying I have ever seen," Gorski put his hand on his shoulder. "I am so sorry about

Porfirio."

"Me too," Doernitz said softly. "I wish I had been good enough to save him and Marco. I feel like I failed them both."

"This is war. They knew the risks and blaming yourself will solve nothing. You need to let it go," Gorski said sharply. "Marco was one of my best friends and I will miss him. He and I met when we were both six years old and he was like a brother to me. We can mourn them all later. But right now we still have a fight on our hands, so sit down and relax. I think the Newton cadets will be arriving soon and we all need to have our minds clear so we can formulate a plan that gets the rest of us off this moon alive."

Doernitz nodded and sat down on a couch. Two of the baby Saharakaree crawled onto Doernitz lap and began making cooing sounds. Doernitz wondered if the two infant creatures understood his pain.

Gorski walked back out onto the moon and saw that Les Gillis was still putting up wires around his metal barricades. The two men watched as the Newton Academy small fighter ship approached from the west, with one of the ammunition lockers attached to its' tow cable.

"How stupid our opponents must be," Gillis said. "They leave those weapons out there and expected that we would not find them."

"They were arrogant," Gorski agreed with Gillis. "They thought we would get our noses bloodied by the Saharakaree attack and we would not fight back. They were wrong."

The locker hit the ground with a thud when Hal Palmer released it from his magnetic cable. Palmer landed his space craft and opened his canopy. Gillis and Gorski watched as Ellen Benson and Palmer climbed down the side of their space craft. The two Newton cadets approached them. After introductions and handshakes were completed, the four walked toward the weapons locker and found that there were plenty of laser rifles and other offensive weapons to be used in their defense.

"Let's get these passed out to everyone," Gorski recommended. "Everyone gets a rifle and hand laser. Everyone gets knives, stun darts, flame darts and any other weapon they wish."

"I am going to wire the thermite grenades to my barricades," Gillis warned the others. "When the rest of the Rosenburg group comes, they won't be able to see my trip wires due to the chlorine gas."

"Good," Gorski smiled.

"What can we do to help?" Benson followed Gillis.

"Help me wire these explosives to the metal walls we set up," Gillis gestured in the direction of the grenades. "When they attack us, I want to have several trip wires so that we can even the odds. I will show you how to do it."

Palmer took a handful of thermite grenades in his hands and followed Gillis toward the circle of metal around the headquarters.

The two Raumschiff's that were now under control of Alan Anderson and his cadets were flying in the direction of the Tyr Academy Headquarters. The cadets were anxious to see Palmer and Benson again and mourning the loss of their two friends at the same time.

Laurence Thompson reported to the others that he had picked up the news reports that the *Cortez* had been ordered to come to their rescue. LeClair and the others began cheering and clapping at the announcement.

Their celebration was short lived.

As the two space craft flew over the moon they were surprised by an explosion.

They had flown into an ambush.

Dell Ragnarsson had anticipated the flight pattern Anderson and his cadets would use to rendezvous with Gorski. With his topography maps of the lunar surface, Dell prepared to ambush them before they could join Gorski and create a more formidable defense. Dell had been waiting at the location he chose, his Raumschiff was hovering just one hundred feet above the surface.

When Anderson and his two Raumschiffs approached, Dell and Kai Chin began firing armor piercing rockets in their direction. On the lunar surface, Dell had placed Avery Jackson, Burton Stapler, and Cleon Alexander in strategic locations and armed all three of the men with laser rifles and shoulder propelled rocket launchers. The three men synchronized their attack with Dell and were firing on the two ships under Alan Anderson's command.

Dell had given Jackson, Stapler and Alexander strict instructions not to cause the Raumschiff's to explode. He had ordered them to target the engines so that the two space craft would be forced to the ground. The reason for the caution was that three Rosenburg's were on board one of the two ships. First order of business was to get the Rosenburg's to safety so that he and the remaining cadets could be paid for their troubles on this mission. Dell's secondary reason was that the Rosenburg's were members of the Royal Family and were their only hope at avoiding prosecution for the crimes that they had committed.

The Rosenburg Raumschiff was hit by three rockets, two from the men on the ground and one from the Raumschiff. The hull just below the engine room was the target of the attack. The explosions destroyed the engines and sent the large Raumschiff spinning out of control. Curtis and Riley began sending out a May Day signal as they both braced for impact. Their ship collided with the moon surface, the metal hull of the space craft buckling on impact. Both Curtis and Riley suffered injuries as the ship flipped twice, end over end, before coming to a rest. Riley's right arm was broken. Nicolas Curtis suffered two broken ribs.

The May Day was received by Gorski and his team.

"Anderson is under attack!" Gorski alerted the pilots that were helping Gillis on the surface.

Palmer and Doernitz looked at each other with alarm in their eyes. Their friends were in danger and they were needed.

"Let's go!" Palmer urged.

Gorski nodded to the two younger cadets, "Do what you can for them."

Doernitz and Palmer ran toward their small space craft and were airborne in seconds.

Anderson's Raumschiff was hit by several rockets from the ambush. He urged his crew to buckle their safety harnesses. The explosions inside of the Raumschiff were devastating. Laurence Thompson and Angelique LeClair were both injured by shrapnel. Mary Myers was in the engine room monitoring the solar power batteries when one of the rockets made a direct hit on the hull. The engine room exploded with fire and metal shooting in every direction. Myers was blown into several pieces. Most of the remains of her body were burned in the fire.

With the engine now inoperable, Anderson struggled with the Raumschiff steering controls. He tightened his safety harness in preparation for the crash landing. His ship slammed into the surface, dirt and rock flying in several directions. Anderson felt a metal beam collide with his head. Everything went black as Anderson fell forward, unconscious.

Avery Jackson did not wait for Ragnarsson to issue any further orders and rushed in the direction of the Rosenburg Raumschiff. He was followed by Burton Stapler. The two men fired their rifle lasers at the rear door to blow a hole through it.

Once they were successful, Jackson jumped inside the Raumschiff. Jackson ran up the stairs that began at the lower level of the space craft to the second level. When he arrived there he saw all three of the Rosenburg men, cuffed to the rails at the rear entrance to the computer room.

"Get us the hell out of here!" Caine Rosenburg demanded when he recognized Jackson.

"We found them!" Jackson reported through his enviro-suit communication system.

He and Stapler drew knives from their utility belts and began cutting the Rosenburg men free.

"We found the Rosenburg's. They are alive," Jackson reported.

"Good job," Dell told them. "Get them over to my ship and let's get a move on. The other cadets have dispatched two small fighter ships. We need to move out."

Stapler searched the rest of the Raumschiff with Alexander, who joined them later due to his sprained ankle. They located Riley and Curtis in the pilot command section. Both were unconscious.

"Hostages?" Alexander thought out loud.

"Why not?" Stapler answered. "Let's get them out of here. We can use them to negotiate our freedom if need be."

Stapler lifted Riley over his shoulder and Alexander did the same with Curtis. They moved as fast as they could with the extra weight of the two captured cadets. It was urgent that they cleared out of their current location with the two small fighter ships en route. They did not want to be easy targets to the approaching small fighter ships, especially the fighter pilot that never missed.

"Too bad that kid with the Clovis cadets wasn't one of our pilots," Stapler said as he ran.

Alexander thought of Lomax and Austin. They had been good pilots but were clearly out of their league with the Clovis pilots. "Yeah, too bad we have to kill him."

Jackson, using smelling salts, revived the other two Rosenburg's.

"Wake up!" Jackson urged them.

David Rosenburg opened his eyes first and then took in a deep breath. He grinned when he recognized Jackson and then stood to his feet. He looked at his father and lifted him in his arms. "What took you so long?"

"Don't ask," Jackson responded as Caine was screaming out curse words. "We need to get moving, an attack is on its' way."

David Rosenburg did not ask questions, the urgency in Jackson's voice was enough to motivate him to run. He followed Jackson out and all of the men were running through a four foot wall of chlorine gas toward Ragnarsson's Raumschiff.

Caine was wide eyed and awake and grateful to be alive. He had thought for certain that Gorski or Anderson would have killed him. Caine hated Gorski and his friends for how Daryl had died and for all of the trouble they had caused for him. They were weak in Caine's estimation because they had failed to kill him when they had the chance. Caine would not have hesitated to slash the throat of a helpless fallen adversary.

Dell waited until the entire group plus the Rosenburg's and the two hostages were on board before flying his Raumschiff up into the sky. Like the others, he had no desire to tangle with Doernitz. The elder assassin wished he could have met Doernitz under other circumstances. He would have made an effective ally. Dell pushed his ship to full speed as Chin watched the four tactical monitor screens to chart the location of the enemy ships.

CHAPTER FIFTEEN

Julia Steiner and Drew Harrison did all they could to save Mary Lincoln's left leg. Their efforts were in vain. The damage from the laser cuts, the broken and crushed bones along with the shrapnel pieces left Steiner and Harrison only one alternative. They had to amputate the leg. Steiner worked quietly as Harrison assisted her. If they ever got Lincoln off of the rock called the Blood Moon, she could get a new metallic leg just like Papanikolaou had received a brand new arm.

In the upstairs of the headquarters, Yuri Gorski was on a three dimensional communication with his father and Admiral Seward. They were informing Gorski of the news that the Glorious Leader had dispatched the U.N.S.C. *Cortez* to rescue them.

"That is good news," Gorski said, somewhat relieved.

"Son, when was the last time you slept?" Colonel Gorski saw the fatigue in his sons face.

"Three days dad," Gorski responded to his father. "Julia has been injecting us all with energy supplements, to keep us going.”

“You need your sleep,” the elder Gorski rebuked.

“Dad, you don’t understand. We are outnumbered and suffered some terrible ambushes. We have been working day and night to prepare a defense and fight back against a better armed and motivated enemy. Once we can sleep, we will. Right now, we do not have that luxury.”

“Without sleep, you might be unable to pay attention to details,” Seward warned. “Can you give yourselves some rotations? Let one or two cadets sleep for an hour or two so they can at least rest some. It is not good to go as long as you have without rest.”

“I will see what I can do,” Yuri Gorski nodded. “I heard from Julia and she said that it looks like Mary will make it.”

“But?” Colonel Nikolai Gorski knew his son. The tone of his voice led him to believe there was more to the news.

“But she is going to lose her leg,” Gorski said sadly.

“Son, you and your crew did a great job of surviving this attack. Don’t feel guilty about any of this. So far you have seven of your original ten crew members alive. After the attacks you and your team endured, that is amazing. Mary is fortunate to be alive.”

“I know dad. I love you. I have to go.”

“Be careful son.”

The three dimensional images of the two men disappeared. Yuri Gorski was weary from the lack of sleep. He walked down the stairs to see Ellen Benson and Les Gillis walking in.

"All the thermite traps are set," Gillis said proudly.

"Good," Gorski told him. "Now go upstairs and get some sleep."

"But what if they attack?" Gillis protested.

"Then we will wake you. We will all sleep in intervals. You know we cannot keep this up. I need you thinking, Les. Now go upstairs and I will wake you up in a few hours."

Gillis nodded as he agreed with Gorski's order. He was exhausted but was too proud to admit it. He climbed the stair case, found a bed and lay down. He was asleep in seconds.

"Any news from Doernitz and Palmer?" Gorski asked Benson.

"None," Benson said as a small Saharakaree leaped onto her shoulder. She laughed as the little baby alien licked her cheek. "I think he likes me."

Hal Palmer and Jurgen Doernitz saw the wreckage of the two large Raumschiff's in the distance. Doernitz told Palmer to land and check the Newton ship as there were three life forms coming from there. Doernitz, who was flying the ship with laser batteries attached, would stay airborne in case the enemy returned. Palmer landed his space craft as instructed and rushed to the Raumschiff. Doernitz watched Palmer from the sky to cover him just in case.

Palmer was almost at the back entrance of the

Raumschiff when he saw Alan Anderson walking out the back entrance waving at him. Anderson's forehead was covered with blood from the wounds he suffered in the crash.

"Hal!" Anderson called out. "It is good to see you. I have two of our team injured. Help me out!"

Palmer ran to Anderson and saw LeClair and Thompson lying on bed mattresses. Both of their heads were bandaged. Thompson had a gash on his right cheek that would probably leave a scar. Anderson had treated the two cadets for their injuries as best he could using the training he had received in his search and rescue courses.

"The others?" Palmer asked.

"Myers is dead. They took Curtis and Riley," Anderson responded. "I need you and the other ship to take Thompson and LeClair for medical attention."

"What about you? It looks like you might need some attention as well." Palmer said as he was lifting Thompson up into his arms.

"I will start walking," Anderson smiled. "We do that sometimes in Australia. Once you get Larry and Angelique to safety, come back for me. I will be just fine, just had a few scratches on my head from the crash. Go on, get them to the new hideaway and come back for me."

Palmer nodded and waved for Doernitz to land.

Doernitz guided his ship to the surface and did not turn off the engine as he ordered his canopy to open. He leaped out of his cockpit and ran toward Anderson and Palmer, to assist them.

"We have two more injured cadets for Julia Steiner's make shift hospital," Palmer informed him.

Anderson introduced himself to Doernitz and then handed him the sleeping LeClair that he had been cradling in his arms.

Seeing the concern in Anderson's eyes, Doernitz held the woman carefully and noticed that she was light in weight. "Do not worry, sir. Julia will take good care of them and we will come right back for you."

"I have no doubt that they will be in capable hands," Anderson nodded. "You are one hell of a pilot, mate. I would love to have you as my wingman one day."

"Thank you, sir. We will return for you."

Anderson watched as Palmer and Doernitz loaded LeClair and Thompson onto their ships. He waived at them as they began to launch their ships into the sky. Anderson looked back at the two wrecked Raumschiff's, "What a damn mess."

Dell Ragnarsson landed his Raumschiff at the Clovis Academy Headquarters. He ordered Kai Chin and Burton Stapler to fire a few armor piercing rockets at the structure. All on board watched the cadet building erupt. Metal, sheet rock and wood were rising into the skyline in a funeral pyre. Their next stop was the Newton cadet building. Dell's plan was to destroy all of the dwellings so that the survivors could not find refuge on the chlorine gas filled lunar surface.

When Palmer and Doernitz arrived at the Tyr headquarters, Gorski and Benson assisted in bringing in LeClair and Thompson. Since they had communicated with Gorski during their flight back, Steiner and Harrison had made two more recovery beds for the new injured cadets. Steiner began using the medical equipment to scan her two new patients for any life threatening injuries.

After the two patients were in the capable hands of Steiner, Palmer and Doernitz began to walk back toward their ships to pick up Anderson.

"Wait," Gorski stopped them. "Palmer, take Benson with you."

"But Anderson is still out there and we have to go get him." Doernitz began to protest.

"No buts. You get upstairs, lie down and sleep," Gorski ordered.

"But the enemy might return and Anderson is out there all alone," Doernitz continued his protest.

"The enemy will still be there when you wake up," Gorski said calmly. "Hal and Ellen are capable of doing this. You have been awake for almost three days, Jurgen. You cannot continue to operate at one hundred percent without rest. Now go to sleep."

Doernitz nodded and joined Gillis upstairs. Just as Gillis had done, Doernitz was sound asleep minutes after he laid his head on a pillow.

Palmer and Benson ran to the two fighter ships. Palmer told her that Anderson was alone on the surface. They climbed up the sides of the ships and started the engines. Benson gave Palmer a thumbs up to let him know she was ready. Palmer wanted to pick up Anderson and then hurry back, just in case. No one knew when the final attack would come, but they were all certain it would be soon.

Yuri Gorski moved into the headquarter building and observed that Steiner and Harrison were getting ready to brew some coffee.

"How are the two new patients?" Gorski asked.

"They are sedated. Minor scrapes on both, no brain injuries according to the scans," Steiner reported. Gorski could hear the fatigue in her voice. "They just need to rest."

"So do you two," Gorski pointed upstairs. "Get up there and get some sleep. Both of you. I am not kidding."

"Yuri, if they attack us, you will be all alone," Harrison protested.

"No, I will have the baby Saharakaree to help me fight." Gorski laughed to himself. Harrison and Steiner glared at him, failing to find the humor in that statement.

"Look, Benson and Palmer will be back soon with Anderson. The four of us will keep watch and in a few hours I will wake you two, Les and Jurgen and then it will be your turn to monitor the long range scanners. We all need to rest. That is an order. We have gone over three days, non-stop. The building has its' defenses ready, your patients are stable. Go to sleep."

"All right," Steiner agreed reluctantly. She knew that Gorski was correct. She could feel her legs aching and her head was pounding. Sleep would do her a world of good. She followed Harrison upstairs to see Gillis and Doernitz already asleep. Each man had two Saharakaree children cuddled up next to them. Steiner and Harrison lay down in separate beds and were dreaming in no time.

Yuri Gorski was now all alone. He put on his enviro-suit helmet and began patrolling the outside of the building. He walked the perimeter, not out of necessity but rather to keep him awake and alert. Gorski then began placing hand lasers and laser rifles in strategic locations, behind the barricades they had built with the metal of the destroyed space craft. He similarly put weapons and under the tables inside the safe house. Once the battle began, Gorski envisioned he and his team would need to run for, and retrieve, a weapon quickly. When the Rosenburg team did arrive, it would be as if the gates of hell were opened before them.

Gorski finally stood at the front entrance of the building. The powerful fans were keeping the chlorine gas about fifteen feet from the perimeter of the building. Gorski removed his enviro-suit helmet and sat it on the wooden floor. Gorski took a moment to look over his suit. It was covered in blood from the Saharakaree and O'Grady.

He looked up into the sky, "Mother. I miss you so much.

Did you feel the same way, when the missiles were fired at you and your platoon? Knowing that you were being fired upon and could not escape death? I would give anything to ask you about this. Dad had many battles in the Dinosaur Wars on New Edinburgh. But the reptiles had no ability to fight back with the weaponry that the humans had. These men, they are cruel and evil. They have already caused me to kill one man by throwing him to his death. I am not afraid of dying but I am afraid of becoming something that is not what you and father raised me to be. I am afraid that I will become a killer, just like them."

Gorski stopped his conversation with the skyline when his holo-com device began to vibrate. He pulled it from his pocked and flipped it open. The contact code of the person attempting to contact him was not one he recognized. He ordered his device to take the incoming communication.

"Yuri, thank the Stars we got through to you!" Dirk Fenster's familiar image appeared before him.

"Dirk? It is so good to see your face and hear your voice. How are all of the gang members doing?" Gorski always worried about everyone else first.

"Well, Rolf and Arch are with me and we are two days away from the moon. We are on an illegal rescue mission, you could say."

Gorski sat down on the porch of the headquarters and sighed. "Dirk, you should all be in school and attending class. How were you able to convince some pilot to violate the quarantine?"

Fenster laughed, "We are flying in my own ship, Yuri. We have a crew of cadets and we all ditched class to come to your defense. I have been trying to get through to you for three days. How badly were you and the team hit?"

Gorski wanted to order Fenster to return back to New Edinburgh, but they were closer to the moon than the *Cortez* and a rescue was a rescue, no matter how it happened.

"Pierre, Marco and Porfirio are dead. Eamon is in critical condition and Mary lost her left leg. Things are bleak here, Dirk. The survivors of the Newton Academy have joined up with us and we have prepared a defense. I hope we can hold out."

"Please do hold out my friend," Fenster said quickly. "We have Dino and Lupita with us to help with any fighter pilot issues. Katerina joined up and she is amazing with what she can do on the computer monitors. I think she could kill all of the bad guys by herself. Just stay alive, Yuri. We are coming for you."

Gorski swallowed and wanted to break down and cry due to the showing by the other cadets that they were willing to be expelled to come to their aid. He fought the coming emotional outburst and smiled. "Dirk, I cannot thank you enough. We are all ready to fight back and will do so. I hope that we are all still alive by the time you get here."

"Hang in there, Yuri. Help is on the way."

"Thank you, Dirk. I will see you in two days."

Gorski watched the image of his friend fade away as the

link was severed.

He continued walking, to keep himself awake. He hoped Anderson and the others would return soon. He desperately needed the rest and the company.

Dell Ragnarsson's Raumschiff unleashed metallic death upon the Newton Academy headquarters. Several rockets rained on the structure causing it to be leveled to the foundation. Once the deed was done, Dell climbed down the ladder from the pilot section to the command area. All three of the Rosenburg men were present, eating fruits. Avery Jackson was there as well. Kai Chin, Burton Stapler and Cleon Alexander were in the engine room. The five surviving Saharakaree slaves were guarding the two prisoners.

"So now we attack Gorski and finish this?" Caine more demanded than asked.

"No," Dell told him.

"No?" Caine stood up and waived his index finger in Dell's face. "You do not get to tell us no. You do as we tell you to do!"

Dell backhanded Caine on the right cheek. The younger Rosenburg fell to the floor holding his face.

"I said no," Dell glared at the other men.

Jackson looked as if he was going to jump Ragnarsson, his fists were balled up and his shoulders were leaning in the direction of the assassin.

"If you know what is good for you, you will stay where

you are," Dell pointed at Jackson. "I have killed men like you without raising a sweat. Do not fuck with me."

Dell stared down Jackson and watched as Jackson raised his hands up as if he were surrendering. "Hey, we are on the same side. Right?"

Dell nodded in the affirmative, "Yes, we are on the same side. But attacking those cadets right now while we are all exhausted would be suicidal. We need to rest. Everyone take a nap. We will attack in a few hours' time. Gorski is not going anywhere. We just eliminated the remaining food sources on the moon. Now they have nowhere to run. They will get hungry in a few days. If they beat us somehow, the dehydration and hunger may get revenge for you. So, everyone go to sleep. Now."

Jackson picked Caine up to his feet with one hand. Jackson whispered to Caine, "He is right. Let's go."

Everyone departed except for David Rosenburg. When it was just the two men in the room, Dell shrugged at him. "What is on your mind?"

"You were with my father for a long time," David began. "Were you one of the crew that went to the alien tunnels in the Rosenburg Ranch territories?"

"Yes. Yes I was." Dell answered, not sure where the young man was going with his questions. "Why do you ask?"

"Remember that metal alloy that was discovered there? The metal that could not bend or break or melt unless the temperatures were more than a body could withstand?"

"Yes I do remember that."

"Because my entire skeleton structure is made from that metal. My whole body was re-made by my brothers Cush and Matthew. I am practically indestructible." David stood up. He was much taller than the assassin. "You ever hit me, like you did my brother, I will kill you."

Dell laughed, "David, I would not hit you. You are not an idiot like your brother Caine. Caine is the reason we are here. He was the one that picked a fight he could not win. You and I are here as garbage men. We are cleaning up the mess left over by that narcissist you call a brother. You should be threatening Caine with death, not me. Now go get some rest. You need to be ready for the fight of your life tomorrow. I can say without question that Gorski and his group are the best adversaries I have ever faced."

David grunted his agreement. When the battle began, the Rosenburg group had superior numbers, superior fire power and the element of surprise. But yet everything had gone wrong for them. It should have been so easy to kill all of the defenseless cadets. David was still dumfounded that things had transpired as they had.

Although David was trying to determine how and why everything had gone so wrong for them, his father was concerned with a bigger issue. Now that the Glorious Leader had declared them all to be outlaws and excommunicated them from the Royal Family, Alfred Rosenburg spent hours attempting to contact his family members, begging for help. He found that all of his children at the Rosenburg Ranch had either been arrested or fled. He contacted his brother John who gave him a ten minute barrage of verbal abuse and then refused any requests to render aid.

Alfred attempted to locate his daughter Penelope and she would not respond to him. Alfred made several attempts to contact the Glorious Leader so that he could plead with him to change his mind. Alfred felt pains in his chest as each of his attempts to contact Vladimir Sikorsky were thwarted by one of his underlings on Sikorsky's Planet. The message was clear; the Glorious Leader wanted nothing to do with Alfred Rosenburg or his sons on the Blood Moon. He ordered the *Lysander* to return and he lifted the quarantine on the moon. The Glorious leader had been a master at following public opinion so that he could use the mobs of people to love him while he did their bidding on minor issues which gave off the impression that he actually cared.

CHAPTER SIXTEEN

Five hours after he had gone to sleep, Drew Harrison felt someone nudging his shoulder. He woke up, sitting straight up on his bed. Harrison had a hand laser under his pillow, just in case. He grabbed the weapon and was ready to shoot. He saw Yuri Gorski looking at him.

"Calm down big guy," Gorski laughed. Gorski had been able to sleep for three hours when Anderson had arrived with Benson and Palmer. The three Newton Academy cadets had taken over the watch.

Harrison looked around and noticed the others were all gone. "Where are Julia and Les?"

"Downstairs," Gorski motioned with his head. "Come on. Our defenses are ready. The time has come for us to finish this."

Harrison jumped to his feet, "They are on their way?"

"Not yet," Gorski told him as he was walking down the stairs. "But they will be after I taunt them."

Harrison frowned at his friend, "What do you mean by

that? How are you going to taunt them?"

"I mean that you need to suit up and get your weapons ready," Gorski told him. "This war ends today."

Harrison saw that all of the remaining cadets that could walk were present. They were all in enviro-suits, except for Steiner, who was still in a set of blue medical sweats. Laser rifles and laser pistols were on the table top. Harrison began putting on his enviro-suit. The baby Saharakaree were all watching the humans with interest.

"Sleep well, Drew?" Gillis handed Harrison a cup of warm coffee as he greeted him.

"Yes, thanks for the coffee." Harrison took the warm mug and found a fold out chair and sat down.

"Drew, we were contacted by Dirk Fenster," Steiner told him to get him up to date on the current events. "His parents gave him a Super Raumschiff for his birthday."

"It must really suck to be wealthy," Palmer commented.

Gorski took over from that point, "Dirk rounded up a handful of cadets and they are on their way here. He has delusions of grandeur that he can use his new toy and whip up on the Rosenburg's here. The only military tactician he brought with him was a sophomore cadet named Katerina Strahovski. I hear she is quite good with weapons systems, but she has no real combat experience at all and I worry that the Rosenburg's would wipe her and Dirk out."

"Hal and I are sophomores and we handled ourselves

quite well," Doernitz blurted out.

"I did not mean it that way, Jurgen." Gorski patted Doernitz on the shoulder. "So, we could wait for them to arrive and see how we could fight the enemy together, or we take them down, right now."

"And there is another issue," Steiner cut in. "When I was scanning the moon for life forms, my computers caught some of the surface of planet Semiramis. I found the scans to be interesting so I scanned the entire planet. Now, the Glorious Leader always reported that Semiramis was a dead planet and that the efforts to terraform her were in vain. But I found thousands of life forms down on that planet with numerous ships and buildings. The planet is covered by gas, which the government always said was lethal, and it obscures the scans and the naked eye cannot pierce it. I think that the Glorious Leader is hiding something from us all and that was the reason he quarantined the moon. He does not want the rest of humanity to know what is being done on planet Semiramis."

"If that is so, and Dirk's ship passes close by the planet, then he might stumble onto something that is top secret?" Harrison asked after he sucked down his coffee.

"I do not know what is down there, Drew. It could be scientists working on the reforming of the planetary climate or something else. The point is that I do not want to put Dirk and his crew at any kind of risk."

Gorski stood in the center of the room, "I feel the same

as Julia. We cannot wait for Dirk to arrive. We have to end this now. I think we are as ready as we will be. Les has assured me he has all of his traps ready. We have decided how to proceed. Jurgen and Hal will pilot the last two fighter ships. Ellen, you will take the Raumschiff. I am going to bait the Rosenburg's to come and fight us. According to Julia's scans, there are eight human enemy combatants left and five Saharakaree. She also found fifty faint life signs that are in their vicinity. The fifty could be another form of alien life that we do not know of. They are all clustered on the southern part of the moon. We believe them all to be on the last Raumschiff they have operable."

Gorski had the computer display a three dimensional view of their headquarters. "Now, we have two walls of separation. One wall has booby traps all over it and in between the ten foot gaps. We hope that the enemy will be weakened by those traps. Our last wall, the redoubt as Les calls it, has several weapons behind the walls ready for you to pick up and use. Do not hesitate. Shoot these bastards to kill.

"I am going to play on their vanity, their narcissism," Gorski told the others. "I am going to get their leaders so angry that they will ignore safety and charge in."

"Like waiving a red flag at a bull fight," Benson nodded.

"Exactly," Gorski said. "Now when they come in, our Raumschiff is loaded with some rockets now. Ellen can fire upon them. Hal and Jurgen can fire lasers and pulsar blasts. The goal is to knock that flying war machine out of the sky. Once you succeed in that, the enemy will be on foot. That is what we must have to win. No matter what, that enemy space craft must be knocked down. Ellen, Hal, Jurgen, you all understand? Bring that ship crashing down to the surface."

"You can count on us," Doernitz said with confidence.

"Good," Gorski continued. "We have about ten extra enviro-suits. Les, Drew, I want you two to put them on the roof, to be decoys. Make the enemy believe we have armed cadets up there. That will draw some of their fire. Once you do that, get down and take your places behind the barricades.

"Julia, if any of the enemy gets through us, you will be here to defend the patients," Gorski told her. "Shoot to kill."

Steiner grabbed a hand held laser pistol from the table. "Don't worry about me. If they get through those doors, they're dead."

"My father and Admiral Seward think we should try and take some prisoners. They feel that would look good for us if we are not cold blooded killers. It will also allow the justice system to bring them before a criminal court for indictment and conviction." Gorski continued. "So, if any of the enemy surrenders to you, give them either a stun blast or inject them with a Stun Dart. Everyone with me?"

All of the team was nodding in agreement.

"We have several empty enviro-suits on the rooftop and out on the outer flanks," Gillis added. "Drew, you and I will be hiding behind the metal barricades at the redoubt. Yuri and Alan will be at the far wall, to lure the enemy in. Drew, we must not reveal ourselves until after the enemy passes the outer barricades."

Harrison nodded, "No problem. How will we know they have gotten past the first barricade?"

"The thermite devices will detonate when they step into the trip wires. The explosions will be loud as hell and the temperature will rise all around us." Gillis told them. "We will all know."

"All right," Gorski said as he continued pacing. "Now, let me contact their ship and push all of their buttons."

Dell Ragnarsson was asleep on his pilot seat. Sitting in the co-pilot seat next to him was Kai Chin. They were both awakened by the sound of static.

"What was that?" Chin mumbled.

"Someone is trying to contact us," Dell sat up and moved toward the ladder.

He descended the ladder quickly and found that Caine Rosenburg and Avery Jackson were already awake, waiting for him in the large command station of the space craft. They were sitting at the large center table, leaning back in their chairs and had their feet up on the table. Unknown to Dell, Caine and Jackson were there to mutiny and take control of his ship. After Dell had slapped Caine, the younger man convinced Jackson that the time had come to get rid of the old man and take control of the Raumschiff. Jackson agreed as he had concluded Caine was his best chance at getting revenge against Gorski.

"Someone is trying to contact us," Dell told them. The two men followed him into the communication room and they watched as Dell pressed some of the buttons on the control panel. He secured the location of the incoming communication.

The ship computer indicated that it was from the Tyr Academy building, where Gorski and his team were hiding.

"What do they want?" Jackson growled.

"Let's find out," Dell suggested and flipped on his Receive/Send control and leaned back in his seat. "This is the Achilles team, over."

"Don't you mean the cowardly Achilles team?" It was the voice of Yuri Gorski. "This is the Clovis Academy Team. We wish to discuss terms of our surrender."

"What?" Caine was incredulous at the statement. He was rubbing his hands together and pacing back and forth. He did not want a surrender, he wanted to kill them all off. "After all the fighting back they did?"

"Shut up!" Dell glared at him. "Gorski, we are ready to have you surrender. When can we come collect you and your fellow survivors?"

"First I need assurances," Gorski said.

"Of course," Dell sounded bored. "What do you want?"

"First, the two hostages, are they still alive?"

Caine finally had enough and pushed Dell out of his seat. "Why? You think we are a pack of animals like your friend

Gillis said? Huh? You think we just kill for no reason!"

"Actually, yes I do think that of you, Caine Rosenburg," Gorski responded calmly. "You are not even worth my time to speak with, Caine. You are not even a man. Any man that rapes and beats women should be taken out into space and thrown out of an airlock. But I will settle for thrusting a knife into your evil heart."

Caine was seething with rage; his lips were pulled back revealing his teeth. "How the hell do you know my name?"

"Because some of your own family sold you out," Gorski began laughing which infuriated Caine even more. Gorski did not reveal that Sean Collins had obtained all the information he needed about the Rosenburg family from Dulce Ragnarsson and Ella Ragnarsson. "Even your own family wants you dead you little sniveling piece of shit. The entire population of the eight solar systems wants to see you die badly."

"You Russian prick! I will kill you and all of your friends! I will go back to Clovis City and rape your girlfriend Staszko and then eat her raw intestines!" Caine was losing his temper, his face was red.

Dell was getting to his feet, but Avery Jackson stood between him and Caine.

"No," Gorski responded. "I think I will not die today. You see, my friends and I are coming for you. I will personally skin you alive. I am going to castrate you and show the world your less than an inch long penis. Then I will go to the

Rosenburg Ranch and I will have all of your sisters raped by poggie's."

Caine began banging his fists on the communication command board. "Fuck you! I will kill you!"

"Come try and take us," Gorski was laughing at him. "You are nothing. You had us out numbered and you had weapons when we had none. You should have been able to beat me easily, but you failed. You are the biggest loser in the solar system. The news media is laughing at you. No woman will ever want you now. You are nothing, Caine Rosenburg. I have proven that I am the better man. I have already won this contest. You lost."

"I am coming for you!" Caine was screaming. Spit was coming from his mouth as he yelled at the desk. "You fucking Russian! I am coming! You hear me!"

"You are a joke, Caine. Everyone knows that you are a nobody. If you were not born a Rosenburg you would be some grunt cleaning toilets and finding a way to screw that up, too." Gorski said and cut off the communication.

Dell pushed Avery Jackson out of his way to get to Caine and remove him from the communication system, "Caine! Calm yourself. Calm down."

"I want everyone awake! We attack them now!" Caine's face was red with rage. "No more of this bull shit waiting! We go and blow them all to hell! Now!"

Dell grabbed Caine by his shirt, "Calm down, don't you

see, this is what they want. They want you to rush in!"

Caine pulled out his hand laser from his thick belt and jammed the barrel into Dell's abdomen. "Get out of my face, old man! Big Bad, cuff him."

Jackson took out some cuffs from his breast pocket and secured Dell's hands behind his back.

"You idiots will get us all killed!" Dell hissed just before Jackson hit him over the back of the head with the stock of his laser rifle. Dell hit the floor and was not moving.

"Wake the others," Caine instructed Jackson. "Today you get to kill Gorski."

"About damn time," Jackson was elated to hear that news.   He ran down the spiral stair case yelling for everyone to wake up.

Caine ascended the ladder to the pilot section and he sat down in the pilot seat next to Kai Chin. He started pressing buttons to start the engines.

"Where is Ragnarsson?" Chin asked.

"He's retired," Caine laughed as he took hold of the half-moon steering mechanism and began flying the Raumschiff in the direction of the Tyr Academy Headquarters.

In the lower level of Ragnarsson's Raumschiff, Nicolas Curtis was sitting next to Cadet Riley. Both of the cadets had their hands tied behind their backs. Across the room from them sat five adult Saharakaree that watched over the prisoners every move, their deadly tails waiving in different directions.

"You think they understand English?" Riley whispered to Curtis.

"I doubt it," Curtis whispered back to him. "When the time comes, we need to make a run for it. You understand?"

Riley nodded.

"If something happens to me, do not let these bastard's use you for any kind of leverage against Alan and the others." Curtis instructed.

"I would rather be dead," Riley said softly.

"For what it is worth, it has been an honor to know you," Curtis told him.

"For me, too." Riley seconded.

Julia Steiner checked on her patients. Sara Barnes was still asleep as was Mary Lincoln. LeClair and Thompson were injured to some extent and needed more rest. Steiner pulled out some large knives and set them in counter tops and taped a few under the beds of the patients, just in case. She holstered her laser pistol in the belt around her waist. She realized something was missing, or rather someone. Eamon O'Grady was gone.

"Eamon?"

His bed was empty. Steiner looked under the counters feverishly. "Eamon. Where are you?"

"Here," O'Grady answered, his voice was weak. He was leaning against the wall, breathing heavily. "What is happening? Where are the others?"

"Eamon, you need to lie down." Steiner said as she ran

to him and guided him back to a bed.

"How long have I been out?"

"Four days," Steiner told him. "You had been poisoned by a Saharakaree. You are lucky to be alive."

O'Grady lay down and was looking all around him, "Where are we? Where are the others?"

"They are around," Steiner said softly. "Now relax. I am going to give you something to help you rest. You should not be on your feet for at least another three days. Do you understand me Eamon?"

O'Grady nodded slowly to her as he allowed her to cover his torso with a blanket. He could remember the Saharakaree. He remembered that he was impaled in his shoulder. He also remembered Pierre Zerbe had been hurt by one of the creatures as well. "Pierre, did he make it?"

"No, Eamon. I am sorry. He died." Steiner said as she injected him.

She was amazed at the strength of the man. Most men would be unconscious for a minimum of seven days after being poisoned by a Saharakaree and then being injected with the anti-venom. She watched as O'Grady slowly drifted asleep. Steiner covered him with additional blankets and checked his pulse and blood pressure.

Hal Palmer and Jurgen Doernitz had their small fighter ships in the sky. Ellen Benson had been able to pilot the Clovis Academy Raumschiff about fifty kilometers up in the sky. The hope was that her ship would avoid detection by the enemy.

Down below, Gorski, Anderson, Gillis and Harrison were ready to defend their turf. Each man had a laser rifle ready and was hidden behind metal walls constructed from the ruins of all of the Tyr Academy space ships. They waited for the attack.

"Bingo!" Palmer yelled. "I have them on radar. They are coming in from the north."

"Then let's make sure they never get that ship close to our friends," Doernitz said, gritting his teeth. "Full speed ahead!"

Gorski watched as the two youngest cadets throttled their small fighter ships in the direction of imminent harm. The final battle against the Rosenburg's was about to begin.

CHAPTER SEVENTEEN

The crowd at O'Malley's watched as the deadly drama was unfolding before them. Some could not bear to watch. Many of the crowd applauded when they observed the small fighter ships flown by Doernitz and Palmer speed directly at the enemy Raumschiff. Sophia DuBravac and Jen Staszko were sitting at a round table with Lila Zapata between them. Zapata was covering her eyes by keeping her head on the table. The other two women were encouraging her to relax. Staszko assured her that Gorski knew exactly what he was doing. He would not send Doernitz at that ship unless he had every confidence in him. The duplicate of Drayton Love-Easter and Yesenia Guevara Love-Easter were present with their son. The couple had married the previous day at a private ceremony and they promised the others that they would have a more formal ceremony when Gillis and Gorski returned.

The tension in O'Malley's was intense. Even the Bragg gang members had joined in, cheering for Gorski and his team.

Hal Palmer and Jurgen Doernitz received the warnings from their space craft computers that the Ragnarsson Raumschiff was flying in their direction. Estimated time of arrival was five minutes. Ellen Benson, who was flying the Clovis Academy Raumschiff, received similar reports regarding the other space craft. She warned Gorski and the others that the opposing team was on the way. She flew the Raumschiff upwards, about two kilometers higher, and began traveling toward the enemy ship.

Palmer and Doernitz kept their ships at about fifty feet off the ground and also began flying full speed in the direction of Ragnarsson's Raumschiff.

Kai Chin observed the three dimensional display that revealed that three space craft were approaching rapidly. Caine Rosenburg had also looked upon the computer data screen which revealed the same information.

"Prepare to launch all of our remaining armor piercing rockets," Caine instructed. "Fire upon those three ships when ready."

"If we do that," Chin warned him, "then we will have no missiles to fire upon the ground forces that Gorski may have assembled."

"Fine with me," Caine responded without emotion. "I want to see Gorski and the rest of his team die in hand to hand combat against us. No more missiles. We cut them; torture them I want to eat their brains. We make them die slowly."

Chin looked at Caine with concern. Chin wished he had never agreed to join this trip. In fact, Chin began to wish he had never met Caine Rosenburg at all. Without comment, Chin complied with the order and began pressing buttons on the pilot control dash board. He had the eight remaining rockets armed and aimed them at the two smaller space craft and the opposite Raumschiff. When the computer broadcasted that the eight missiles were ready, Chin launched them at their targets.

Palmer and Doernitz saw that five rockets had been launched at them. Their computer warning systems aboard their small fighter ships also began sending verbal warnings of the incoming missiles. Three other rockets were shooting in the direction of Ellen Benson and the Raumschiff she was flying.

Palmer began firing his pulsar waves at the incoming projectiles while Doernitz began firing his laser batteries. Their efforts caused two of the five rockets to harmlessly explode in mid-air. The other three were on target.

At the last possible second, Palmer and Doernitz both swerved right and left respectively. They three rockets flew past them, but began to curve back due to the computerized heat seeking mechanism on each of the missiles.

"Fly right at the enemy!" Doernitz told Palmer. "At the last second, eject."

"Why?" Palmer was bewildered.

"Because the rockets will follow our ships, which will be on a collision course with the enemy Raumschiff."

Palmer nodded, "So if our ships crashing into theirs does not bring them down, then their own rockets will finish the job?"

"Exactly," Doernitz affirmed.

Ellen Benson did her best to avoid the three rockets that had been fired upon her. She flew the Raumschiff straight up into the dark sky, increasing her speed as the three rockets gained on her ship with each passing second.

"This is Benson!" She said through her communication device for the benefit of Gorski and Anderson. "We managed to make them waste their last rockets. I can't avoid the three coming my way. Best wishes to all of you."

Benson put on the helmet of her enviro-suit and climbed down the ladder from the pilot control section. She ran to the ladder to the lower level and slid down it. She pressed the red button on the wall of the storage area and waited as the rear exit opened. As the bay doors began to open, Benson grabbed a jet pack and pulled the straps over her shoulders. Her only chance to survive was to jump out and activate the jet pack after all three missiles hit the Raumschiff. If she was lucky, she could guide herself to a safe location on the lunar surface without detection by the enemy. She could feel the force of the winds as the bay doors were now opened. The computer warned her she had only thirty seconds before impact.

Benson ran toward the exit and jumped out of the ship like a diver in an Olympic competition might. She let out a scream as she was flying in the air. She looked back at the Raumschiff, which was still ascending toward space. She saw the brilliant flashes of fire and metal when the three missiles hit the space craft. The explosion was so bright in the night sky that

Benson had to close her eyes. Benson activated the jet pack and slowed her descent. At least we got rid of the most powerful weapons the enemy possessed to attack us with, Benson thought to herself.

Doernitz and Palmer flew their ships in direct collision course with the Raumschiff piloted by Caine Rosenburg.

Chin and Caine watched the screens and observed the two craft flying right at them.

"They are crazy," Caine said.

"No, they are smart." Chin disagreed. "Their goal is to ground us and kill as many as they can in doing so. We should all jump. If either of those ships hit us, we might not survive the impact."

"Jump? Are you kidding me?" Caine demanded. "Fire the laser batteries at them! Bring them down!"

Chin did as directed and began firing lasers at the two smaller ships. The vast majority of the laser fire missed.

As the battle raged on, Dell Ragnarsson stood up and walked out of the command area. Avery Jackson was looking up at the pilot section and was no longer paying attention. He never noticed that Dell had been able to sneak away to the lower level.

"Crap!" Palmer yelled as his ship sustained several laser blast hits in the front hull. Smoke began flowing over his observation window, making his ability to see impossible. His on board computer was warning that the ship was losing power.

"Jurgen! I have to eject." Palmer reported.

"I'll see you on the ground!" Doernitz responded as he kept his ship moving. Out of the corner of his eyes, he watched as Hal Palmer's observation canopy popped open. A split second following that, Palmer was jettisoned into the air from his ship.

Doernitz increased his speed and began to move his ship left to right and up and down to avoid the laser barrage that was being fired at him. One of the two rockets that had been following him and Palmer slammed into Palmer's damaged space craft. The ship exploded on impact. The final two rockets continued their deadly chase of Doernitz' craft. Doernitz began firing his laser batteries back at the Raumschiff.

Alfred Rosenburg, II, and the others were gathering at the rear of the Raumschiff near the bay doors. Alexander, Stapler and the others were pulling on jet packs to help guide them safely to the planet surface. They felt the brunt of the laser fire hitting the hull of their Raumschiff.

"That pilot is damn accurate," David observed. He pressed the wall controls to open the back bay doors. Two of the five Saharakaree had the two prisoners, Curtis and Riley in their grasp, ready to jump and bring the captives to the surface with the rest. More lasers from Doernitz hit the Raumschiff.

Unknown to the rest of them, Dell Ragnarsson had previously activated the fifty cryo-sleep chambers so that the occupants would wake up. Dell had downloaded his own memories into the fifty cloned bodies of his son, Junior. Other than the light green skin color, they would all look like Junior but have the knowledge of father and part of that knowledge was that Yuri Gorski had killed the original Junior.

After continuing his recommendations to flee, Chin finally convinced Caine that it would be wise to abandon their post. They moved as quickly as possible to the lower level and to the bay doors. They arrived in time to see Cleon Alexander and Avery Jackson be the first two to abandon ship. Burton Stapler followed behind them, jumping as if he were in an Olympic Diving competition. The computer was warning of the imminent impact with Doernitz' space craft. It was counting down the estimated time. Caine cursed when the computer announced impact would occur in less than thirty seconds. The five Saharakaree jumped out next, with the two hostages, Curtis and Riley. David Rosenburg and his father were next. The last two to leap were Chin and Caine.

Jurgen Doernitz knew it was now or never. He pulled up on his ejection lever which sent him spiraling high into the sky. He looked downward and saw his small fighter ship hit the front of the Raumschiff. The resulting explosion increased the temperature around the surrounding area. The two missiles hit the Raumschiff a few seconds later. More explosions could be observed on the lunar surface. Gorski and Anderson were already in position behind some of the metal slabs that had been secured into trenches by Gillis, Steiner and Harrison. They saw the explosions light up the night sky. They knew that Doernitz and Palmer had done their duty. They had brought down the enemy

Raumschiff and switched the advantage in the battle.

Now the odds were even.

Moments before the Raumschiff collided with Doernitz' smaller space craft, Dell Ragnarsson struggled to remove the restraints placed on him by Avery Jackson. Dell, using a small laser pen, cut through the binding chains around his wrists. The fifty clones of his son, Junior, were obediently standing by, each holding a jet pack.

The first explosion caused Dell to lose his footing and he fell to the cold, metal floor. He could hear the ship computer warning of the two missiles heading his way. Dell cursed. He ordered the fifty duplicates of his son to jump. They all did as commanded, rushing down to the lower level and leaping from the crashing space ship. Dell dived down the shaft to the lower level of the ship. He didn't waste precious seconds by climbing down the ladder. He landed on his side on the metal floor and felt shooting pain as a result of the impact. He could feel the wind due to the open bay doors and saw that all of the fifty clones were gone.

Dell searched the storage bay feverishly and found that all of the jet packs were gone. He spied upon three of his Hover-Cycles that were secured on the wall farthest from him. They were the size of motorcycles, but these had no wheels. They were created to travel twenty feet above ground at rates of speed above two hundred kilometers an hour.

Ragnarsson mounted his favorite Hover-Cycle, a black

machine with red trim manufactured by the Brackenridge Corporation in 2331. It was in excellent condition. Dell knew that he would free fall for several feet, but he had no choice. If he remained on board the Raumschiff he would be dead when the two missiles impacted and exploded. He started his Hover-Cycle and throttled it toward the open bay doors. As he flew out into the open skyline, the missiles impacted the Raumschiff. The explosions sent Dell Ragnarsson spinning out of control. He struggled to maintain his grip on his Hover-Cycle. He could see the ground below growing closer to him as he fell. He hoped the machine would stop the free fall when it was twenty feet from the surface. If it did not, Ragnarsson would surely die from the impact. Not a romantic manner for the world's greatest assassin to die, he mused to himself.

Les Gillis and Drew Harrison remained crouched down behind their chosen metal slabs. Harrison had chosen one that was six feet tall, four feet thick and nine feet wide of solid iron and tungsten. He held his laser rifle in his right hand, a large knife with a blade of over twelve inches in his left. Harrison could see Gillis several metal slabs away on his left. Gillis had two hand lasers in his hands. All around them sticking out of the lunar surface were several long slivers of metal that Gillis had sharpened into knives around his feet. Gillis was crouched behind a similarly sized and shaped piece of metal as Harrison. Harrison hoped that the battle would begin soon, the waiting was killing him.

Cleon Alexander rolled onto the lunar surface, favoring his sprained ankle. He was cursing due to the pain and struggled to stand upright. He saw that Burton Stapler was already standing, readying his laser rifle, Avery Jackson had a short sword in one hand and a laser rifle in the other. The Saharakaree landed near them with the two hostages, Curtis and Riley, firmly in the grip of two of the aliens. Soon the three Rosenburg men were on the ground and Kai Chin landed last.

Caine pulled his laser rifle off of his shoulder and ran his left forearm around the strap, to keep the rifle tight to his body. His right hand was at the trigger. He nodded to the others that he was ready. David took the lead and began running toward the Tyr Academy headquarter building where Anderson, Gorski and the others were waiting.

Alexander was in the rear of the group and he heard the loud rumble of the jet packs behind him. He turned around and saw the fifty exact duplicates of Junior Ragnarsson flying toward him.

"Uh, Caine! Mister Rosenburg!" Alexander yelled out.

Alfred Rosenburg and his sons Caine and David turned and saw the fifty duplicates of Junior Ragnarsson landing on the lunar surface.

"What the hell?" David removed his protective helmet to make sure he was seeing things properly.

"They must have been hidden in Ragnarsson's ship in a secret compartment," Alfred speculated. He walked toward the group of clones as they all dropped their jet packs to the surface. The senior Rosenburg noticed that the duplicates had green skin and he immediately understood what had gone wrong. Dell had not obtained the updated technological advances from Nicolette and Matthew Rosenburg. The earlier clones had many problems with skin pigmentation. Further testing and study perfected the process and the errors of the color of the skin were rectified.

"Dell! Great to see all of you! Are you ready?" Alfred Rosenburg asked them.

Rosenburg watched the fifty all move and face him in unison. They were all pulling laser rifles from their backs and holding them ready for combat in their hands.

"Where are we?" One of the clones demanded.

"On the Blood Moon!" Alfred Rosenburg told them. "We are in the middle of a war against Yuri Gorski and his friends!"

"Gorski?" Another clone smiled at the mention of the name. Their memories were of Dell and not Junior. All of the clones knew that Yuri Gorski had killed the son. "Where?"

Alfred pointed in the direction of the Academy Headquarter. "In the building over there. We intend to kill him and everyone else there. Care to join us?"

All fifty of the green skinned clones nodded in unison. "Lead the way!"

Jurgen Doernitz slammed onto the lunar surface due to his glider seat not functioning properly. He felt his lower right leg snap upon impact. Doernitz screamed out loud in pain and rolled on the ground for a moment, trying to put the agony he felt from his broken leg out of his mind. He released his safety harness and asked his enviro-suit computer to scan his leg. The computerized voice informed Doernitz of what he already he knew, his leg was broken. Doernitz pulled out his hand laser and tried to ignore the pain. If any of the enemy survived, they would be nearby, perhaps as close as a hundred or so yards.

Doernitz heard a warning from his enviro-suit computer that a lone figure was approaching from the west. Doernitz aimed his hand laser and set it for stun only. It could be Palmer or Benson or it could be one of them, the adversaries from the Rosenburg team. Doernitz could see the outline of a figure approaching him. He prepared to fire.

David Rosenburg instructed his team to spread out as they charged the building. They were about twenty feet away from the metal pieces imbedded in the lunar rock. "Some one's been busy," David said to himself a she spied upon the many large pieces of metal circling around the perimeter of the Tyr Headquarters. He estimated it was about two hundred feet from the actual structure. He could see the second metal perimeter, about fifty feet from the building.

The clones of Junior Ragnarsson began to spread out and make a circle around the Tyr Headquarters. They each had their laser rifles ready for revenge against Gorski. Killing him would be the best way to begin their new lives.

"Stop here," David said softly. He began to make a head count. "Who is missing? We are short one person."

"Ragnarsson," Caine responded softly so that the fifty clones would not hear. "He did not make it off the ship."

Avery Jackson gave Alexander a sharp look. He wondered why the younger Rosenburg would not just tell the truth about Ragnarsson's fate. He looked up at the sky and observed that the sun was rising in the east. It would be bright in a matter of twenty minutes.

"I think we should threaten them into surrendering." Alfred said. He was also wary of the sunlight revealing their position. "Tell them we will execute the two hostages if they fail to throw down their weapons and give up."

David motioned for the two Saharakaree to bring Curtis and Riley forward. The two enslaved aliens complied, dragging the two Newton Academy cadets forward. David instructed his enviro-suit computer to open communications with the occupants of the Tyr Academy building.

"You have all suffered much!" David began. "It is time to cease hostilities between us. We have two of your people, Curtis and Riley. Surrender now and we let them live. If you fail to throw down your weapons, we will kill them both. What say you?"

Anderson and Gorski were behind metal protection at the two hundred foot wall. Anderson, who was now the ranking cadet, shook his head from side to side. They knew that if they surrendered, the Rosenburg's would kill them anyway.

Anderson cleared his throat, "A Rosenburg does not keep his word! We will not surrender to you!"

The two cadets had made a pact that they would not allow their captors to use them as bait. Both Riley and Curtis head butted their respective Saharakaree guards. The aliens released each man, mostly because they were surprised by the humans attempting any move at that point. Curtis and Riley both began running as fast as they could toward the Tyr Academy building.

Anderson and Gorski leaned over their protective metal slabs and aimed their laser rifles and began firing, attempting to give Riley and Curtis cover fire. The Rosenburg men dived to the ground to avoid the laser blasts.

Anderson hit one of the Ragnarsson clones and obliterated his upper body. Gorski also hit a Ragnarsson in the left upper torso, blowing the clone in half.

"Attack!" Alfred directed his five Saharakaree slaves. The five aliens began leaping into the air and within three long jumps, they were behind the two hundred foot barricades and behind Gorski and Anderson. The remaining forty-eight Ragnarsson clones also began charging at the Tyr Headquarters.

Jackson and Alexander began firing at the two fleeing hostages. Jackson, using his laser rifle, split Riley in half, just below the rib cage, with two shots. Riley's body crumpled to the ground, the doomed cadet did not scream as he was hit.

Alexander fired his laser pistols at Curtis and hit the running cadet three times, severing Curtis' left arm and blowing small holes in his back. Curtis did scream as his arm was hit. His chest exploded from the exit wounds. The body of Nicolas Curtis twisted in the air and slid to a stop on the rocky surface.

Jackson and the others begin to advance under the cover fire of the Rosenburg's.

The Ragnarsson clones were running at the positions held by Anderson and Gorski. The two cadets kept firing their laser rifles at the charging adversaries, cutting down several of them. The Ragnarsson clones were firing back, their blasts hitting the large metal sheets that Gillis and the others had spent so much time placing around the building.

The five Saharakaree were faster than their human counterparts. They were able to leap several feet and were able to make it to the metal barricades quickly and the jumped over them with ease.

Anderson and Gorski were forced to turn and face the five Saharakaree. Anderson fired at the nearest alien and his aim was true. The alien creature died as the laser blast cut it in half. Gorski was also fortunate enough to kill the Saharakaree closest to him. While the two men successfully parried the two aliens, two of the remaining Saharakaree began jumping at Gorski and Anderson.

Anderson fired two laser bursts at the Saharakaree charging at him. The creature landed on Anderson's chest and kicked him to the surface. Anderson slid on the ground for several feet. The alien pressed its' advantage and jumped on top of him, aiming its' pointed tail at the Australian. Anderson could feel the hind claws of the creature ripping through his enviro-suit and cutting the flesh of his chest. Anderson had lost his laser rifle in the fall, but had his hand laser drawn. He fired his weapon at the alien simultaneously with the creature's tail shooting down toward him. Both hit their targets. Anderson's laser blast blew a hole through the chest of the Saharakaree. The point of the alien's tail stabbed through Anderson's chest, just below his clavicle. The force of the laser blast sent the Saharakaree flying backwards, dead.

Anderson felt the cut in his chest and immediately knew he was poisoned and would need the anti-venom soon, or he would be dead. He was also losing oxygen from his torn enviro-suit. His suit computer warned him that he was losing blood and that his air capacity was down to eighty percent.

Gorski jumped to his left to avoid the attack of another Saharakaree. The alien landed without incident at the spot where Gorski had been. There was laser fire coming from the Rosenburg's as Gorski crouched down behind the metal slab. The alien snarled and charged at Gorski. Gorski fired his laser rifle and his aim was true. The Saharakaree cried out as its left leg was blown off. The alien fell to the ground crying in agony. Gorski felt sorry for the creature as he ran for what Gillis had called the redoubt, the second barricade, as the Rosenburg's pressed their advantage and charged at them, closing the distance. Gorski saw that Anderson was crawling, holding his chest. He was injured and Gorski ran to the man to give assistance.

The last alien had sensed danger behind the other metal slabs and jumped toward the other row of metal. After four jumps, the Saharakaree landed on Drew Harrison's back. Harrison rolled as the creature pushed him to the rocky surface. Harrison landed a punch with his right hand in the face of the alien. The Saharakaree fell backwards and Harrison jumped onto his opponent, his knife ready.

Harrison pinned the alien down and stabbed his knife into its neck. The blood from the Saharakaree spattered all over Harrison's enviro-suit as he stabbed the creature a second time. The legs and arms of the alien were kicking and pounding the surface as it's' blood spilled. The Saharakaree bled out in less than two minutes.

The clones of Ragnarsson were rushing through the openings in between the slabs of metal. They did not see the trip wires that were waiting for them. Many of the Ragnarsson clones unwittingly activated the explosives that had been planted by Gillis and the others. The explosions began rocking the lunar surface. Massive fireballs spread in every direction, roasting alive any human caught within the circumference of the blast. Many of the Ragnarsson clones perished in that initial part of the battle and their numbers were decreased substantially.

Jackson, Chin, Stapler and Alexander made it to the first row of metal slabs and did not hesitate to run through the openings. Gorski had lifted Anderson over his shoulder and was running, keeping low to the ground, to get the injured cadet to Julia Steiner for a dose of anti-venom. The three Rosenburg men were right behind them, firing their laser weapons wildly and occasionally stumbling and falling when one of the trap bombs would be detonated by one of the Ragnarsson clones. Gorski turned and fired on the men as he dived for cover behind one of the other metal slabs. Several laser blasts hit the protective metal chunk that Gorski had found safety behind. He sat Anderson onto the surface and pulled out his hand lasers. Gorski began to return fire at the men as they charged, hoping to dispatch them quickly and continue his attempt to get medical attention for Anderson.

Alfred Rosenburg, II, sensed that victory was theirs. He led the men forward, screaming at them to kill everyone that they found inside the building. He did not see the trip wire that Les Gillis had placed on the surface because the green hue of the chlorine gas obfuscated his view. The elder Rosenburg fell to the surface as five thermite grenades rolled toward him. Avery Jackson observed the deadly round explosives rolling out, their pins pulled by the force of Rosenburg hitting the trip wire.

"Shit!" Jackson yelled as he shoved Caine Rosenburg down to the ground. "Everyone down!"

The other men dove for cover. Alfred Rosenburg, II,

screamed helplessly as he saw his death coming in the form of the thermite devices, bouncing and rolling in his direction. He had lived for over one hundred sixty years, fathered over forty children and he had killed or caused to be killed hundreds. He laughed out loud at what he considered the impossible, that his death was imminent. The thermite grenades ignited and spewed out huge fireballs. Alfred Rosenburg's screams could be heard by all as his body was burned to a crisp. It was a horrible and agonizing death for the elder Rosenburg. When the blasts subsided, all that remained were charred pieces of his skeleton.

The force and the heat from the blasts shook the earth below them all. Caine rolled to his right for several feet and then crawled to the safety of the last barricade. He pulled himself over one of the metal walls and found himself facing the entrance to the Tyr Academy Headquarters. They had killed his father and now he would make them pay, not that he needed the further motivation. Caine charged the doors to the building and to his surprise, he met no opposition.

The explosion was the sign Les Gillis had been waiting for. He was on his feet, firing at the smoke caused by the explosion. He did not see Caine Rosenburg jump over the protective wall. Gillis also did not see that Anderson was crawling on the surface, the Saharakaree venom weakening the man. Gillis focused on killing as many of the enemy as he could and his shots were on target. In less than fifteen seconds he killed seven Ragnarsson clones that were charging his position.

Gorski and Harrison were also firing at their opponents. Harrison took out six of the Ragnarsson clones with his accurate aim.   The body pieces from those he hit were scattered throughout the air and lunar surface. Gorski also fired on four others and the Ragnarsson clones died on impact.

Cleon Alexander and Burton Stapler were firing laser rifles at the decoys on the roof of the building. The empty enviro-suits would collapse when hit by the laser blasts.

Kai Chin noticed that Les Gillis was attempting to aim at David Rosenburg. Chin, using the fact that Gillis was not facing him, ran at his position and dived in the air. He easily cleared the metal wall that Gillis was using as cover. Chin landed his right foot into Gillis, sending him sprawling to the ground. As Gillis was rolling on the surface, Chin pulled out one of his several knives from his utility belt and stabbed down at the prone Gillis. Gillis moved to the side and the blade struck the side of his right shoulder, cutting into his enviro-suit. Gillis felt his flesh tear, but was not certain whether the wound he received was serious or not. Gillis twisted his body and flipped Chin off of him. Chin rolled and came to his feet, crouching. He had two knives drawn.

"You," Gillis said, looking through Chin's visor of his enviro-suit helmet. "You were on the space station when Dray and Elektra were attacked!"

Chin laughed, "Yes I was, and now you die. We kill your friends later!"

Chin dived at Gillis. The Irishman rolled out of the way

and kicked Chin in the back of his left leg. Chin fell to the ground a turned back to face Gillis. He watched Gillis rise to his feet, holding two pieces of metal that had been sharpened on one end into sharp points. Gillis faced Chin, gritting his teeth. Chin was a good fighter, one of the best Gillis had ever faced.

"What are you waiting for?" Chin taunted him. "You are bleeding. Soon your strength will fade and give me the advantage. You better take me out soon."

Gillis said nothing in return as they circled each other, just like two predators before a deadly fight. They were sizing each other up, looking for an advantage or an opening. Both men gripped their deadly weapons in their hands. Gillis kept his eyes locked on Chin's as they continued their assessment of each other.

Burton Stapler followed Chin's example and charged the wall in the direction of Yuri Gorski. Gorski saw Stapler running at him. Remembering what his father had told him about taking prisoners for trial, Gorski switched his hand laser to stun mode and fired upon Stapler as the man was jumping in the air. Gorski's stun blast hit Stapler in the chest, sending him flying backwards, head over heels. Stapler landed on the lunar rocks and rolled a few times before stopping. He did not get back up.

Gorski had no time to celebrate taking Stapler out of the battle as Avery Jackson was on him. Jackson had been charging in Gorski's direction at the same time Stapler had. Jackson tackled Gorski from his blind side and threw the shorter man to the ground with significant force. Gorski felt the wind knocked out of him by the impact from the fall. He rolled to his left as Jackson tried to stomp his foot on Gorski's face plate. Gorski rolled out of the way of the incoming foot. Jackson had his knife ready and ran at Gorski again. Gorski struggled to his feet as Jackson closed the short distance between them. Gorski quickly formulated in his mind a defense as Jackson was almost on him. Jackson snarled with rage when Gorski stepped to his left and tripped Jackson by kicking the bigger man's legs out from under him.

Jackson rolled for several feet and pushed himself back up on his feet. He waived his knife menacingly in Gorski's direction. "Last time we fought, you really hurt me! This time, I am going to eat your heart!"

Gorski could see the larger man's face clearly as they faced one another. He remembered him as one of the men that had tried to rape Elektra and cut Dray's throat. "I remember you." Gorski told him. "You have a lot of things to answer for."

"I am going to cut out your heart while it is still beating!" Jackson screamed and began running at Gorski once again.

Harrison jumped from out behind his metal barricade and drop kicked Cleon Alexander in the chest. Alexander fell backwards and dropped his laser rifle to the ground. As Alexander struggled to regain his balance, Harrison was on him again, kicking him in his torso and abdomen. Alexander fell head over heels, toward one of the iron pieces that the Clovis Academy cadets had placed into the trenches they had made. Alexander hit his head on the large metal and his enviro-suit helmet cracked. Letting out a hissing sound as his oxygen levels began to decrease.

Alexander drew a flame dart and jumped at Harrison. "I will burn you alive!"

Harrison moved to his left and karate chopped Alexander's arm, knocking the flame dart out of his hand. Alexander made a move to attempt to retrieve the dart from the sand. Harrison kicked Alexander's protective glass covering on his helmet and the glass cracked some more as Alexander was sent flying backwards.

Harrison attempted to press his advantage when a hand grabbed him on the back of his neck. Harrison felt himself being lifted up off the ground from behind. His feet were dangling in the air. Harrison grabbed the hand around his throat.

"Try picking on someone your own size!" David Rosenburg hissed. He threw Harrison in the air about fifteen feet high and watched as the cadet landed face first onto the lunar surface.

Harrison pushed himself up to his feet in time to see David Rosenburg was swinging a large wooden club at his face. Harrison attempted to dodge the weapon and was hit on his left shoulder with enough force to break the wooden club and send Harrison rolling to the ground in agony. David began kicking

Harrison in the abdomen and in the ribs. The metallic bones of David Rosenburg were too much for Harrison's normal bones. Harrison screamed as two of his ribs on his left side fractured under the assault.

Jurgen Doernitz kept calling out to the person walking toward him. Doernitz warned that he would open fire if he did not stop and identify himself. The figure kept approaching without answering. Doernitz watched as the person stopped about eight to ten feet from him. Doernitz could see the figure more clearly as the sun was rising. The person was wearing an orange enviro-suit with a black helmet. The uniform was old, one that Doernitz recalled was similar to a space suit that engineers or miners would wear in deep space to dig deep tunnels or seek out minerals or silver and gold on asteroids. The uniforms had been out of service for about twenty years. The person in the uniform took off the helmet.

Jurgen Doernitz dropped his hand laser to the surface, his mouth wide open. It was impossible.

"Jeez, kid. You're hurt!" Marco Andolini said as he ran to Doernitz. He quickly looked over his leg. "Your leg is definitely broken."

"Marco? How? We thought you were dead!" Doernitz exclaimed.

"So did I," Marco said softly. "I am going to pick you up and carry you to the Lunar Transport. We'll set your leg when we get inside."

"What Lunar Transport?" Doernitz remembered some rough terrain vehicles that carried that name, manufactured by the Allen Corporation. They had been discontinued at least a decade or two ago. They had been used in terra-forming projects, similar to old style tanks or large military trucks. Doernitz groaned in pain as Marco picked him up in his arms

"I tried to get back to all of you sooner," Marco explained as he carried Doernitz. "My enviro-suit was damaged when my ship exploded. I had no way to communicate with any of you. I was lucky that my ejection seat worked just seconds before the rockets hit me. My gliding mechanism was damaged and I crashed on the surface really hard. I broke a few ribs."

"No one saw you," Doernitz told him. "They scanned for life forms, and we could not locate you."

"I made it to one of the terra-forming buildings," Marco said as Doernitz saw the Lunar Transport in the distance. It was orange, just like Marco's space suit, and had eight large tires on either side of the vehicle. Each tire was about six feet in radius. The transport was thirty-nine feet high and forty-seven feet long. It had a huge window in the front and the rest was metal.

Marco carried Doernitz to the back of the vehicle and Doernitz saw that the back ramp was open. Inside the vehicle were the unconscious Ellen Benson and Hal Palmer. They were lying on the floor.

"I found them first," Marco set Doernitz next to Palmer. "I followed the explosions in the sky and drove as fast as I could to where I thought each of you fell. I was lucky to find all three of you."

Doernitz was startled when he heard a loud noise behind him that sounded like: "Reeooor!" He turned his head to see an Akarzdamedian in one of the orange suits inside the ship.

"Jurgen, this is Cla Cuchullain. He was one of the Akarzdamedian pilots we fought," Marco introduced them. "Cla Res ju Jurgen Doernitz."

The alien extended his hand to Doernitz. The young man extended his and watched as the Akarzdamedian shook his hand. "Nice to meet you."

The Akarzdamedian shook his head and was tending to Ellen Benson' wounds, placing gauze on her forehead and injected her with a sedative.

"How?" Doernitz asked.

"We both were on the surface together," Marco explained. "When Cla ejected, the microchip in his head was damaged somehow so the Rosenburg's lost control over him. He and I helped each other to survive. I convinced him to help me come find you. Mary and the others? How are they?"

Doernitz shook his head, "We gotta get to them. They are under attack. Porfirio is dead and some of the Newton cadets were killed also. Mary. Mary, she lost her left leg. That is all I know. Please, can we get back to the others?"

Marco nodded. At least Mary was alive. The leg could be replaced by a metal substitute. Marco asked Cla Cuchullain to tend to Jurgen's leg. The Italian climbed into the driver's seat and closed the rear ramps of the vehicle. He started up the engines and began driving toward the Tyr Academy building.

Julia Steiner heard the doors to the building slide open behind her. She had been prepared to receive any injured from the fight for some time so she picked up a hyper dermic needle filled with pain killer drugs and walked over to the front entrance. She stopped in her tracks when she saw a man in a purple colored enviro-suit. He had a hand laser trained on her.

"Yuri? Les?" Steiner asked, confused as to why he her friends would aim a weapon at her.

The lone figure removed his helmet. It was not Yuri Gorski or Les Gillis. It was a man Steiner had never seen before. He smiled at her. Steiner watched as he looked her over. She felt as if he were undressing her with his eyes.

"You are very beautiful," Caine Rosenburg remarked, staring at Steiner's body and face. "I am going to enjoy this."

Steiner began backing up, holding her hands up in the form of surrender. "Who are you?"

"My name is Caine," he responded as he began walking toward her and slapped the hyper dermic needle out of her hand.

Steiner backed into the hospital bed that Sara Barnes was sleeping on. She watched as the man continued toward her, his laser pistol still trained on her.

"Where are the others?"

"Dead. Dying. Who gives a shit where they are?" Caine

laughed. He glanced down at the face of Sara Barnes. "Ah, how sweet, you saved the bitch. She was a fantastic piece of ass. After I finish you I am going to take her again. This time I will make sure that she does not survive the experience."

Steiner slowly ran her hand under Barnes' hospital bed, feeling for the knife she had taped to the bottom of it. "You did this to her?"

"Yes I did," Caine told her as if he was proud of himself. "I raped her and beat her. And she was not the first. I have raped many women. I enjoy raping and then torturing and killing them. I tried to do it to your classmates, Elektra and April? I think about them from time to time, and wonder how much fun it would have been to violate both of them and then cut them up while they were still alive, to hear their screams. Ah, when we finish each of you here I am going to get those two girls and rape them repeatedly. Just like I am going to do to you right now."

"You were on the space station, Cy-7? You were there when Dray was stabbed?"

Caine began laughing, "That stupid fuck. Why did he stick his nose in my business? Of course we cut him. Now, strip your clothes off. Do it!"

Steiner shuddered as she listened to his confession. Caine saw her nose wrinkle and her lips pull back showing her perfect teeth. He grinned.

"You will never hurt another woman again," she said to him.

Caine dropped his helmet to the floor and then dropped his hand laser. "You women are all alike. I don't need any weapons to take you. I will beat you with my bare hands and strip you myself."

Steiner waited for him to get closer. He was moving toward her slowly, as if he savored the chase more than the kill.

"Aren't you going to run? Aren't you going to beg me to stop? Plead for your life?" Caine asked her with each step toward her.

"No," Steiner said calmly. Caine was now two feet away from her. Steiner pulled the knife out and buried the entire ten inch blade into Caine's abdomen.

He screamed as he felt the blade rip into him. His eyes were wide with shock and the sting of the cold metal inside of him. He felt Steiner pull the knife out of his stomach and she kicked him to the floor. He was screaming, trying to crawl away from her. Steiner kicked him in the side and rolled him over on his back. Caine was holding his stomach, attempting to stop the loss of blood.

"David! Avery! Help me!" Caine pleaded.

Steiner pounced on his chest, driving her knee into the knife wound. He screamed again. She put the blade of the knife to his throat.

"No, please!" He begged. "My family is wealthy. I will pay you! I can pay all of your student loans! I can give you more money than you ever dreamed of seeing!"

Steiner snarled and looked him in the eyes. "I never negotiate with weasels. This is for the sister-hood you little bastard!"

She cut his throat open, slicing his jugular. She stood up and watched as he made gurgling sounds as he slowly bled out on the floor.

As Caine Rosenburg died, Julia Steiner heard a weak plea for help. She ran to the entrance and saw Alan Anderson crawling on the floor, his shoulder bleeding.

Steiner ran to him, "Alan, what happened?"

"Saharakaree got me," Anderson said. "I need anti-venom."

Steiner carried him over to one of the empty beds and helped him on top of it. She ran to her medicine cabinet and found one of the prepared hyper dermic needles. She rushed back to Anderson's side and pulled off his enviro-suit helmet and injected him in the neck.

She watched as Alan Anderson passed out on the bed. Steiner realized things might not be going well for them men outside. She grabbed the hand laser that Caine Rosenburg had trained on her and a handful of stun darts. Time to end the battle she thought to herself.

CHAPTER EIGHTEEN

Les Gillis and Kai Chin ended their mutual stalking motion and began throwing leg kicks at one another. Chin narrowly missed Gillis' head and Gillis was able to connect with a crescent kick to Chin on his shoulder. The two men began slashing their weapons at each other. Chin's knives clanging against the metal weapons Gillis had made out of the pieces of the blown up Raumschiff. Each man parried the other's slashes.

Gillis felt he found an advantage. Chin was favoring one of his arms. Gillis concluded that Chin must have injured the arm or shoulder at some point during the last few days. Gillis moved in toward Chin on the side of the weaker arm. Chin kicked out at Gillis causing him to lean back to avoid the kick. Chin then slashed at Gillis and seeing the Irishman avoid that, Chin spun quickly behind him. Gillis tried to turn but was a second late. Chin slashed Gillis in the back with one of his knives. Gillis felt the blade cut him. His enviro-suit was now split opened just at his shoulder blades. The knife cut went across Gillis' back about five inches across.

Gillis continued his turn and saw the same droop of the

arm as before. Gillis charged in and this time he was successful. Chin could not lift his injured arm in time to parry the blow. Gillis stabbed the sharp metal rod into Chin with enough force that it was buried six inches in his chest. Gillis then used his other makeshift weapon and stabbed Chin repeatedly in the stomach and then stopped.

Kai Chin stumbled around and dropped his knives. Blood began to form at his lower lip as he fell to his knees and coughed a few times before collapsing face first to the planet surface.

Gillis had little time to celebrate his victory as he heard a cry of anger from behind him. Cleon Alexander was running at him, his face contorted with rage over the death of his friend. Gillis rolled toward a discarded hand laser and snatched it with his left hand, set it on stun and fired. Alexander screamed as he felt the laser energy engulf him. He fell; his forward progress caused him to land in Les Gillis' lap.

While Gillis and Steiner were engaged in their personal conflicts, Yuri Gorski continued with his fight with Avery Jackson. The two men were grappling, punching each other in the sides. Gorski punched upward and caught Jackson on the bottom of his chin. Jackson released Gorski and staggered backward from him. Jackson began cursing and spit out pieces of his teeth. Gorski ran and jumped, feet first, into Jackson's chest. The larger man groaned and fell on his back.

Gorski leaped in the air again and landed on top of the

prone Jackson. Gorski pinned his opponent's arms with his knees and began to remove Jackson's enviro-suit helmet. Jackson protested to no avail as Gorski pulled the helmet off and he threw it high into the air so that Jackson would not be able to recover it without disengaging the battle. Gorski began smashing his balled fists into Jackson's exposed face. Gorski broke the man's nose and bottom lip as he kept hitting the man. He then gave Jackson some more punches in the stomach and side, knocking the breath out his opponent.

Jackson was breathing in the deadly chlorine gas. He could feel his lungs burning from the deadly gas which caused him to beg for mercy.

Ignoring the pleas from Jackson, Gorski delivered the final punch to the side of Jackson's face. The man fell unconscious. Gorski stood and surveyed the scene and saw that his friend Drew Harrison was being beaten badly by David Rosenburg.

Gorski screamed and began running at the Rosenburg giant. Gorski noticed that Les Gillis was doing the same thing.

David Rosenburg was kicking Drew Harrison over and over again. He saw Les Gillis running at him from the front and heard Yuri Gorski screaming from the rear. David lifted Harrison up with his right hand and threw him like a football at Les Gillis. Gillis was unable to avoid the flying Harrison. He fell to the ground when Harrison collided with him. Gorski was about to try and slide and undercut David Rosenburg's legs out from under him when the nearly seven foot tall Rosenburg jumped into the air. His mechanical legs propelled him about fifteen feet high. He came falling down, aiming to land on Gorski' torso. Gorski stopped his momentum and tried to run the opposite way. As David Rosenburg landed, he slammed his balled left fist on top of Gorski's helmet. The helmet cracked like an egg shell and Gorski collapsed.

Gillis had rolled Harrison off of him and he charged in. David Rosenburg was laughing at the three men.

"You are ants to me!" David backhanded Gillis, sending him sprawling to the ground. Gillis was certain that his cheek bone was broken from the impact. He struggled to even get back on his hands and knees and spit some of his own blood out onto the lunar surface.

"I will kill all of you!" David promised them, turning in circles and glaring at the three injured cadets. "Which one should die first? The Russian, the Irishman or the black man?"

Harrison stood to his feet, "I volunteer you son of a bitch."

"Ah, the black man!" David smiled to Harrison. "Very well. I will reward you for being the only smart one here. At least you are astute enough to recognize that I cannot be beaten. I will give you the quickest death. Your two friends are going to suffer."

"Let's do this," Harrison said as he struggled to breath. His broken ribs were causing him substantial pain.

David Rosenburg walked over to Harrison, a gloating smile on his face. "No need to hurry, all three of you are injured so I can take my time."

Gorski had ripped off his enviro-suit helmet, or at least what was left of it. He stood up to see David Rosenburg walking toward Harrison.

"Drew! Run!" Gorski admonished as he ran at David Rosenburg's back.

Rosenburg must have realized Gorski would attempt to continue the fight. As if he had radar, David turned slightly to his left and swung his right arm at the charging Gorski. His fist connected with Gorski, on the side of his face. Gorski was sent flying backwards about five feet into the air. The metal in David Rosenburg's hand left Gorski seeing stars. Gorski found it was getting more difficult to stand up. This last opponent had to go down quickly; otherwise Gorski, Harrison and Gillis would not be able to continue.

With Gorski dispatched once again, David Rosenburg smiled and continued to walk toward Harrison, who stood silently, holding his rib cage and breathing with difficulty. Harrison did start to run, not away from David Rosenburg, but directly at him. David thought that Harrison must be in a hurry to die. Concealed in Harrison's left fist was a discarded and unused flame dart. As David laughed and slapped Harrison to the ground, just as he had done to Gillis and Gorski, Harrison was able to stab the flame dart into the giant's left arm.

Harrison rolled as far as he could from Rosenburg. "Fire in the hole!"

David Rosenburg looked puzzled at Harrison's statement. He looked over his body and at his left arm and saw the flame dart stuck in his wrist. Harrison had stabbed the dart in the giant's arm as he was hit by him which David had not expected it.

"No!" David Rosenburg screamed as he attempted to grab the dart. He was too late. The protective bubble formed around his body just seconds before the dart let loose its' deadly function. David Rosenburg was incinerated to death when the dart exploded. His screams were loud and shrill for a few seconds. Soon, the flames were gone and the metallic skeleton of David Rosenburg fell to the ground, smoking and glowing red with heat.

Gillis was coughing and somewhat laughing, "Fire in the hole? That was my line."

Harrison smiled at him, "I'll pay you royalties."

Gorski walked over to his two friends and the three men embraced in a tight hug. They had done it. They beat the Rosenburgs and they had survived the impossible.

In the distance they saw the Lunar Transport coming their way.

"Now what?" Gillis was breathing heavily, his oxygen supply almost diminished.

Gorski walked over and picked up one of the laser rifles

on the ground. "Get ready."

Julia Steiner was now next to them, holding the hand laser she took from Caine Rosenburg. She looked over the other three men and shook her head. "You boys look like poggie dung."

"Nice to see you, too," Gillis laughed and then winced in pain.

"Who is in that Lunar Transport?" Steiner asked.

"Don't know," Gorski responded with effort. He had taken in several breaths of chlorine gas. He felt as if his lungs were on fire.

The transport stopped at the outer wall. By now, Harrison and Gillis had armed themselves. All three men were bleeding and needed treatment.

Steiner suddenly turned to her right and aimed her laser pistol and fired two shots. Gorski, Harrison and Gillis watched as the two surviving Ragnarsson clones crumpled to the ground. "I thought you boys got them all? Do I have to do everything around here?"

"Good shooting there, Julia." Gillis complimented.

"Let's see what we are dealing with," Gorski pointed toward the transport. The sun was behind the massive vehicle. They all watched as the large driver's side door opened and one lone man stepped out and jumped to the lunar surface.

"By the Stars," Steiner exclaimed when she saw Marco Andolini step out of the vehicle. She ran as fast as her legs would carry. She had missed his voice and his hugs. Steiner and Marco embraced. The Italian then ran to his three friends.

"How in the name of Mother Russia are you alive?" Gorski began as Marco hugged him.

"Long story, my friend." Marco said as he hugged Gillis and Harrison.

"Then you can tell your story while I give these boys medical attention," Steiner informed them.

"I have three other patients," Marco pointed back to the lunar transport. "I found your three heroic pilots on the way in. Doernitz has a broken leg. The woman was bruised up pretty badly. The other kid had some cuts and bruises."

"Let's get everyone inside to my growing hospital unit," Steiner suggested.

"I also have medical assistant who is also a pilot," Marco motioned with his arm.

The others watched as Cla Cuchullain was walking toward them, carrying Ellen Benson.

"Is he one of them?" Gorski asked.

"He was," Marco responded. "Now, he is one of us."

Steiner led the men inside the quarters. As they walked, Gorski explained there were a few men that would need to be restrained. Marco volunteered to take care of that task, once Doernitz and Palmer were inside.

Steiner and Cla Cuchullain began taking care of the injured. Everyone had suffered some harm, Gorski had a split lip and gash on his forehead, Gillis had some knife wounds, Harrison suffered some broken ribs, Doernitz had a broken leg, Anderson had been poisoned, Benson had a concussion, Palmer had bruised ribs and cuts and bruises. Steiner was busy for almost a full day treating the wounded. By the time all of the cadets were given the medical attention they needed, Steiner decided she deserved a vacation.

Two days later, after the survivors played chess and poker, told tales of their respective schools and grew closer, Dirk Fenster arrived, landing his Raumschiff near their building. Steiner was happy that Patel, Blundell and Windfohr were a part of Fenster's rescue operation as they lent some valuable assistance with tending to the wounded.

The cadets waited for about another day before the rescue Battle Cruiser *Cortez* arrived. Although they had wanted to go home with Fenster and the others, Colonel Jamal Lincoln ordered them to wait.

They spent the time enjoying each other's company. They talked, laughed and shared tears for those that did not survive. Steiner noticed that Dirk Fenster and Lupita Calderon seemed intimate and later learned that the two had started sleeping together on the trip to the moon.

Marco Andolini took the Lunar Transport with Les Gillis and Jurgen Doernitz to recover Porfirio Cardenas' body. On the long drive there, Marco told Gillis and Doernitz that God had spoken to him. He swore that when he was about to die, when his ejection lever jammed, he heard a voice that told him, "Not yet." After he heard the voice, Marco was flung from the ship, just seconds before it was destroyed. Marco had become a believer as Porfirio Cardenas had always hoped, that there was a higher power out there and that nothing happened by chance.

Gillis speculated that the voice Marco heard, or thought he heard, could have been his own subconscious.

Doernitz disagreed, believing that Marco had been touched by something more powerful than any of them could comprehend. It was the only explanation as to how Marco was still alive.

Andolini and Cla Cuchullain also told the survivors a story that caused them all to doubt their history as they had been taught in school. The alien sat in the center of all of the humans and gave them a completely different version of the Racial Wars.

"My race never attacked humanity," Cla Cuchullain told them. "We came in peace. Your leader, Vladimir Sikorsky, used us and framed us. It was Sikorsky that had dropped weapons of mass destruction on Africa. He was the one that murdered almost fifteen percent of the human population of Earth. We did not do it."

Gillis grunted at the story, "My ancestor fought in that war. She was one of the leaders that took the war to your home world. Why would humans wipe out so many humans in such a manner? It makes no sense."

Cla Cuchullain pointed at Benson and Harrison.

"Sikorsky did it because he hated people like you two. He hated those with the dark skin. He used us to commit genocide against the dark skinned humans."

"How do you know this?" Harrison demanded.

"Because I was there," Cla Cuchullain said simply. "I am over four hundred of your years old. My ancestors visited Earth thousands of years ago." He turned to Gillis, "Your people made stories about one of them and called him Cuchullain. Our leader was what you would call a Princess. Her name was Danu. You named a river after her. Her sisters and brothers all had legends written about them. Mannanan Mac Lir was one of our people; he was a commander of undersea explorations. That is why he was associated by your legends as a sea God. Other names from early humanity were from my race. Drimios, Odin, Tyr, Zues and Hera were some of my people. We visited your planet many times and we always came in peace. Your Sikorsky betrayed us and you for his own gain. My people were never your enemy."

"But you fought us," Gorski said.

"We defended ourselves," Cla Cuchullain responded.

Gillis and Doernitz looked at each other and nodded as they believed Cla Cuchullain story.

"So you were tricked into destroying the Earth defenses?" Katarina Strahovski asked with disbelief in her voice. "You came to Earth with superior intellect and technology and you were tricked into doing something so vile and wicked? How did that happen?"

Cla nodded as she spoke. He pointed to the sky, "Sikorsky and some other humans told Danu and some of the others that there were other humans that were planning to use the weapons on your African Continent to be a first strike against our home world. Sikorsky promised that he would side with my people if we destroyed the weapons there. We only did as we were asked to do by Sikorsky."

"Sorry, I do not buy it." Rolf Rhinehard pointed at him. "For starters, Odin and Tyr are real. I pray to them every day. When I die, I will go to Valhalla as a celebrated warrior. Besides, Kat is correct, there is no way an advanced race like you would not commit such an act unless you were predisposed to violence in the first place."

Cuchullain shook his head, "Believe as you will."

CHAPTER NINETEEN

On the seventh day the rescue arrived on the Blood Moon.   Colonel Jamal Lincoln directed that five Raumschiff's immediately land on the moon at the location of the surviving cadets. Most of the crew on the five ships were military intelligence and medical personnel. Gorski had suffered several bruises and a minor concussion. He met with Colonel Lincoln first.   Gorski informed the highly decorated Colonel that his daughter, Mary, was in stable condition.

Mary Lincoln was taken back to the Battle Cruiser *Cortez* to receive her new leg. Transported along with Lincoln were Sara Barnes, Alan Anderson, Eamon O'Grady, Hal Palmer, Ellen Benson, Laurence Thompson, Angelique LeClair, Drew Harrison and Jurgen Doernitz. Colonel Lincoln ordered that each of the surviving cadets receive the best medical attention that the Empire could provide.

Gorski, Steiner, Andolini and Gillis were the last four to leave. They made certain the bodies of the fallen were taken as well for a proper burial. Gorski secured the infant Saharakaree. They had grown close to the survivors, but not as pets. They were like their own children.

Cla Cuchullain was also taken to go back to Clovis City for a hero's welcome. Due to his advanced talents as a pilot, he was able to secure employment back on his home planet, Sikorsky's Planet, which he always referred to as Akarzdamedia, and began to search endlessly for any of his surviving relatives and Princess Danu.

The four cadets met Lieutenant Commander Marywood and Lieutenant Shigeta as they began to recover evidence to be used against the surviving attackers.

The Captain of Military Intelligence of the *Cortez*, Mara Sowa, also met the four cadets. She, like the others, was very impressed.

"You fight like mad dogs," Captain Sowa said to them. "The Glorious Leader proclaimed that each of you will get to choose your first duty station upon graduation. I really could use men and women like you."

"Military Intelligence is the way to go," Shigeta told them. He hugged his soon to be brother-in-law, Marco Andolini. "I am so happy you are alive."

"Thank you sir," Marco responded.

The two green skinned Ragnarsson duplicates, Avery Jackson, Burton Stapler and Cleon Alexander were taken into custody. Each man was charged with thirty-four counts of conspiracy to commit murder, twenty-four counts of felony murder, one hundred thirty-nine counts of aggravated assault and assault with a deadly weapon and one count each of rape. There were also charges of destruction of United Nations property, conspiracy to transport slaves and many more.

As they were being taken aboard a prison transport Avery Jackson looked over his shoulder at Yuri Gorski. "You should have killed me! I'll be back!"

The Blood Moon was scanned for more dead or living. None were found. The universal assassin named Dell Ragnarsson had disappeared without a trace.

Although they were not yet Space Command soldiers, all of the cadet survivors were awarded a special Red Cross medal for the injuries they received. They were each awarded the Medal of Valor, for demonstrating bravery against all odds. Those that had died received that medal posthumously.

Julia Steiner was awarded the Medal from The Order of the Humanitarians to signify her efforts to save others. Although Steiner was not a Doctor, the Order made an exception for Steiner due to her tireless efforts for the injured cadets. She was the first person without a medical degree to receive the Award.

Cadet Sara Barnes would fully recover from her wounds. But the psychological impact of the brutal treatment was deep. She attended hundreds of hours of therapy to no avail. She would suffer depression and post-traumatic stress disorder for the rest of her life. She left her Academy and did not finish her senior year. None of the other survivors ever heard from her again.

Dirk Fenster and Arch Frazier were each given one

demerit from Dean Harvard for leaving campus without authorization. The other cadets that had taken the risk with them were cussed at by a few professors, but that was the extent of their punishment.

Fenster found that the Calderon brothers and the rest of the extended family did not object to his involvement with Lupita. Fenster continued to see her and at some point was sleeping with her exclusively. Dino Black, Fara Kiesbye, Katarina Strahovski, Rolf Rhinehard and the other members of the cadet rescue mission found that their reputations among the other cadets had risen in popularity. Although they did not attain the status of the actual Blood Moon survivors, they were all admired by their fellow students for the risk they took.

Hal Palmer returned to Newton Academy as a junior and had achieved the rock star status that he deserved. Palmer had been deeply moved by the manner the cadets from the other schools were able to come together and fight a common enemy. He maintained contact with all of the cadets from Clovis Academy that he had met on the Blood Moon, never forgetting their fellowship during that trying time.

In May, Alan Anderson graduated as a Doctor in Search and Rescue and was commissioned an officer in the armed forces as a Lieutenant in Search and Rescue. He was assigned to a Battle Cruiser that was to be sent to the farthest reaches of space in search of the lost ship known as the *Bismark*. Anderson remained good friends with Gorski, Steiner and the others.

Mary Johnson Lincoln received a new leg and graduated in May at Clovis Academy. She decided she would not serve as a pilot on her father's ship as he had requested of her. The mission to find the *Bismark* resonated with her due to her desire to see the farthest reaches of outer space. The *Bismark* had disappeared while on a mission to a planet that seemed to be just like Earth. Lincoln signed up to serve as a pilot on the Fleet that was being dispatched to find the lost ship. She also knew that Anderson had signed up for the mission as well. Lincoln had other friends that were volunteering to serve on the historic mission. Dr. Mozgov, the psychiatric doctor in Clovis City joined as well as Eamon O'Grady and his wife Ginger. Lincoln also knew of some of the officers already serving on the assigned Fleet.

But, one of the reasons Mary Lincoln wanted to go to the outer reaches was to put a long distance between herself and the two men in her life. When her ship had been damaged and she was going to crash, she believed death was coming to take her. As her ship spun out of control, Lincoln had called out Yuri's name, not Marco's. Lincoln knew she would always love Yuri Gorski. He was the love of her life. That realization caused her much emotional turmoil as Marco Andolini had been a wonderful lover to her. Marco was warm, kind, loyal, handsome, dynamic, smart, talented, athletic and heroic. But given all of his wonderful qualities, her heart would always belong to Gorski. So Lincoln decided to do what she believed to be the right thing. She had to set Marco Andolini free to find a woman that could love him as he deserved to be loved. Before graduation, Lincoln ended her relationship with Marco. He was hurt, but in time, Lincoln was certain that Marco would find the love of his life.

Although Lincoln hoped she would be far enough away from Yuri Gorski so that her heart would heal, a dramatic and miraculous event would soon put her back in Gorski's life. But that is another story.

Lawyer Sean Collins was appointed by the Glorious Leader to handle the prosecution of the Rosenburg conspirators. Collins took his staff and investigators to bring each defendant to justice. The jury trials were called the "Trials of the Century." Collins became a celebrity and his fame grew with each finding of guilt against the defendants.

The evil of the Rosenburg family was finally broken. Alfred Rosenburg, II, was dead and the majority of his family in prison. Alfred's older brother, John, took over the Rosenburg Ranch on New Edinburgh. John Rosenburg promised Collins and Colonel Nikolai Gorski that they had nothing to fear from him. John Rosenburg took control of the Rosenburg Corporation, which continued to manufacture weapons for the Space Command.

Just before the graduation day at Clovis Academy, the student body was treated to several happy endings. The wedding of Dominic Andolini and Harumi Shigeta was attended by hundreds. Drayton Love-Easter and Yesenia Guevara were honored to re-affirm their vows in a double wedding with their best friends, Les Gillis and Sophia DuBravac, also committing to each other for life. The two couples were happy to be reunited. Klaus Rhinehard and April Mejia were also married, both agreeing they wanted to have their wedding so that all of the Gorski Gang could be in attendance. Arch Frazier and Elektra Papanikolaou had a beautiful ceremony, thanks to Dirk Fenster footing the bill. Jurgen Doernitz and Lila Zapata were the last couple to make their vows to each other before their friends and family.

Freya Doernitz Cardenas remained in Clovis City as a medical doctor and worked hard as a single mother. She was one of the first to receive a monetary settlement from the Rosenburg Corporation for the damages associated with the loss of her husband. She put the money into investments for her children. Freya would always be a moral compass for her younger brother.

Cara Perez Guerrero also received a monetary award from the Rosenburg Corporation for the benefit of her unborn child. She later learned that she was actually pregnant with twins. Perez Guerrero would continue her education at the Academy with the hopes that she would graduate two years later as a fighter pilot in the Space Command. She vowed that the posthumous Medal of Valor would be available for her children, so that they would know that their father had been a brave man that stood by his friends.

Everyone had mourned the fallen. Colonel Jamal Lincoln allowed Les Gillis to take a Raumschiff to the gas giant

Osiris and jettison Pierre Zerbe's body in a very public ceremony. Marco Andolini and Jurgen Doernitz flew the Raumschiff that transported Zerbe to his final resting place. Gillis told one and all it was Zerbe's wish, to be buried on the beautiful planet.

The burial of Porfirio Cardenas was held at the cadet graveyard at Clovis Academy. His children were brave, but the tears flowed when his widow, Freya, was presented with his Medal of Valor. It was to be the largest attendance at a funeral held on the young colony. Porfirio had shown bravery and selflessness in serving his fellow man and woman. The United Nations Space Command created a new medal that was given his name to be awarded each year to astronauts that exhibited the highest marks in their day to day service.

Michel Evart graduated as a pilot and given the rank of Lieutenant Junior Grade. He was assigned to a Battle Cruiser called the *Azteca* in Admiral Yamamoto's fleet. He left New Edinburgh after graduation, saying good bye to all. His sister, Flora, who would start her sophomore year at the Academy, was very proud of her older brother.

Eamon O'Grady graduated as a doctorate and was assigned to the Military Intelligence branch as a Lieutenant. He volunteered to serve on the mission to find the lost *Bismark*. His wife, Ginger Collins O'Grady, transferred her civil service position to join her husband on the mission. Her talents as a computer technician were among the best and the commanders were happy to have her on the assignment.

Several of the graduates went on to study for their doctorates. Les Gillis, Julia Steiner, Siobhan Collins, Clark Blundell and Robert Windfohr joined Laurence Thompson and Angelique LeClair on Sikorsky' Planet to study at the prestigious university there.

Marco Andolini, who was heartbroken over his break up from Mary Lincoln, agreed to serve under the famous Admiral Khan on the U.N.S.C. Battle Cruiser *Amistad*. Marco Andolini was commissioned as a Lieutenant Junior Grade. He was surprised on the day he arrived on the *Amistad* to find a familiar face, Ellen Benson, who was also assigned to the ship as a pilot.

Drayton Love-Easter #2 and Yesenia Guevara also were commissioned as officers and were assigned together on a science colony on planet New Berlin. They would stay in constant contact with Les Gillis and Sophia DuBravac. They would remain best of friends. The only near argument they had was over who got to keep the cat, Cosmos. The decision was made for Sophia to house Cosmos as she stayed behind on New Edinburgh to finish her education.

Les Gillis went on to study for his doctorate at Sikorsky's Planet. After he graduated a year later, he and his wife, Sophia, would share many adventures as officers in the Space Command. No matter the odds, they stuck it out together. Gillis would, many years later, be destined to have a command of his own on a planet that desperately needed his leadership and compassion. But that is another story.

Domini Andolini and Marco Andolini said their good byes. The twins were to be separated due to each man receiving different orders for assignment. Marco was sent to the *Amistad* while Dominic was assigned as a Second Lieutenant in Military Intelligence on board the *Cortez*. Dominic was elated with his orders in that he would join Drew Harrison and Yuri Gorski on his first assignment. Dominic, inspired by Sean Collins, decided to study law while serving as an officer. Dominic registered for computer classes to begin that dream.

Dominic was deeply saddened that he would be separated from his wife for at least one year before she would graduate. But as fate would have it, that one year would pass quickly due to a political crisis that would involve all of the planets of the eight solar systems.

Drew Harrison did as Yuri Gorski had and accepted the invitation of Colonel Lincoln to serve on the *Cortez*. Harrison also received a commission of Second Lieutenant in the Military Intelligence branch. LaShondra Lewis requested and was granted a transfer to the Cortez so that she and Harrison could be together.

Yuri Gorski decided to serve on the *Cortez*. He was impressed with Colonel Lincoln and the officers that he met when they were transported from the Blood Moon back to New Edinburgh. It was exactly the type of crew that he had hoped for and he concluded that the officers could teach him and help him grow as an officer. Gorski was given the rank of Second Lieutenant in Military Intelligence and assigned under Lieutenant Shigeta and Captain Sowa. Gorski said his farewells to his father and brother.

One of Gorski's last acts as leader of Gorski's Gang, was to turn the leadership over to Klaus Rhinehard, Jack Harcourt and Jen Staszko. He elected to have them run the gang as a triumvirate mainly due to Gorski's inability to decide which of the three would be the best leader. All three had excellent qualities that gave Gorski all the confidence that they could keep the gang together and carefully select new members over the year to come. The gang members that were juniors and sophomores were sad to see the seniors leave. But the gang would continue, as Piotr Gorski would be a freshman at the Clovis Academy the following year. So, at least for another four years, they could still be called "Gorski's Gang." There would also be an Evart, with Flora added as a new member and there would be the addition of five new Andolini members. Jurgen Doernitz and Lila Zapata joined the gang as well.

Jen Staszko and Yuri Gorski loved each other more than words could describe. On the date of graduation, Staszko revealed her past to Gorski. She told him everything. She confessed that her name had been changed, her papers forged, all because she had killed a man on Earth. They agreed that for the next year that they should see other people. Staszko had to finish her senior year. Gorski would be serving on a Battle Cruiser going God knows where. They split as close confidants, friends and perhaps one day as lovers again.

Gorski joined Harrison, Dominic and LaShondra Lewis on a transport ship. They had packed all of their belongings. They had said good bye to their friends and Professors. The time had come for them to begin their new chapter in their lives. Jen Staskzo and Harumi Shigeta waved from the crowd of well-wishers. Gorski blew a kiss to Staszko as the doors to the Transport slid shut. Gorski fought back the tears, knowing he had loved his University and the friends he had made. Leaving Jen, his brother and father were emotional moments for him.

Yuri Gorski watched from the observation window of the Transport as they flew through space. He was silent as he watched New Edinburgh grow smaller as the ship traveled further from the planet. Drew Harrison and Dominic Andolini were standing next to Gorski, watching the view of their former home fade from sight. In the distance was the Battle Cruiser *Cortez*.

"From this distance, the Cortez looks pretty small." Harrison commented.

"You lived on Battle Cruisers before, didn't you?" Lewis asked him.

"Almost my entire life," Harrison smiled at her. "The sole reason I went to the Academy was to get back on one of them and see more of the universe."

"At least the four of us will be serving together,"

Dominic said. "I will really miss all of our classmates and my family. I suppose this is what life is all about, moving on from our parents and becoming men and women, building our careers and hopefully making a difference in the world. What do you think, Yuri?"

Gorski smiled at Dominic, Harrison and Lewis. Like all of them, he was elated that they were all together and he would likewise miss all of their friends that were receiving different assignments.

"I think that we already made a difference, Dominic. We beat the Ragnarsson assassins and helped bring an end to the terror on New Edinburgh. Quite a start for each of us, don't you think? I wonder how the rest of the eight solar systems will react to us if and when we are in the satellite broadcasts again?" Gorski mused over the thought.

"We are heroes," Harrison laughed. "Enjoy it while you can. Fame is fleeting."

Gorski pondered that last comment by Harrison. At one time, the Rosenburg family had been treated like Gods and now they were disgraced, had no influence at all on New Edinburgh and those that were not dead were either incarcerated or wanted.

"We all need to be mindful of the lessons we learned from all of this. Never grow arrogant like the Rosenburg's did. We must always be humble and treat everyone like we would like to be treated. What was it that Les said? That we are burdened with morality? I think that burden is one I will gladly shoulder all the way to my grave."

"You being a philosopher now, Yuri?" Dominic asked his friend.

"No, just hoping that we all remember what we went through to get to where we are. Besides, I never studied philosophy. I wanted to be an astronaut and discover new worlds, so I doubt I would have time to consider the ethics of things."

"As Porfirio would have said, A-men to that brother." Harrison put his arm around Gorski.

A new life awaited Yuri Gorski and his friends.

And a new adventure.

CHAPTER TWENTY

Captain Ruiz of the United Nations Space Command Science Cruiser Colorado was one that believed in keeping oneself physically fit. She would spend an hour a day in the ship's large gymnasium, lifting weights and working on cardiovascular exercises. Her ship had now been in the deep reaches of space, photographing the void, utilizing telescopes to see farther than man had ever seen. The photographic images were astounding. Her scientists were rapidly inspecting the images and then sending the photographs as attachments to the Space Command officers on Sikorsky's Planet. Ruiz commanded a crew of eight hundred men and women. There were about forty children on board, offspring of crew members. Most of the crew of the *Colorado* were scientists. There were about sixty pilots on board and she had not received replacements for Ilyasova, Griffin or Jahn. Ruiz had selected several new pilots from the graduating classes to fill her empty slots.

But the *Colorado* was not the only ship that had been ordered to inspect the deep reaches of space in that quadrant. There were three other Science Cruisers that were performing similar scientific analysis. There was the Science Cruisers *London*, the *Theodore DeMartino* and the *Qian Woo*.

As Ruiz continued her weight lifting, she heard over the ship's communication system that she was wanted on the command station. Ruiz told the computer to inform the command she was on her way. Ruiz walked rapidly out of the gymnasium, grabbing a white towel as she left to wipe the sweat from her brow. Ruiz showered in the locker room and then changed into her dark blue, one piece Space Command uniform. The standard issue clothing was long sleeved, zipped up at the front from the midriff to the neck line. Her rank of Captain was evidenced by the gold patch on each sleeve, just below her shoulder line. The dark blue color of her uniform signified that she was from the Flight Command Section.

The Science Vessel *Colorado* was constructed as per specifications for all Cruiser Class space ships. There were six levels to the massive craft. Level Six, the lower level, had the Docking Bays for the numerous Raumschiff's and small fighter ships. Most of the extra enviro-suits were stored on that level as well as the extra parts for the engineering technicians to effectuate repairs when needed. Level Five was the Engine Room and the Life Sciences Section. Level Four was reserved for scientific research and testing. Level Four held the living quarters, Cryo-Sleep Chambers, Restaurants, Bars and the gymnasium. Level Three was reserved for the medical staff, computer section, the Stellar Cartography section and more living quarters. Level Two was the section where the defense of the ship would occur. Weapons Section, the Marines barracks, more of the computer sections, military intelligence and the Executive Meeting Rooms. The top Level, or Level One, held the Command Station, Executive Quarters, more computer banks, more Executive Meeting Rooms, a private gymnasium for officers only and the Officer's Club (a private restaurant for officers).

Captain Carol Ruiz took the elevators to the top level of her six level Science Ship. As she walked in, all of her officers stood to attention. Present were eight officers and two Marine Corps guards. Both of the Marines were wearing one piece uniforms colored in a camouflage pattern of several greens, black and brown. The two Marines held the rank of Lance Corporal. They had laser rifles slung over their right shoulders by a strap. Their web belts displayed a hand laser and stun darts.

Ruiz saw her First officer, Commander Marvin Sikorsky, approach her, "Marvin, what is the emergency?"

Marvin Sikorsky had risen up the ranks from the Military Intelligence section. His uniform was similar to Ruiz, with the exception that his uniform was solid black. His gold Commander rank was on each sleeve, just below his shoulders. Marvin Sikorsky was the great grand-child of the Glorious Leader, Vladimir Sikorsky. He and Captain Ruiz had been lovers for the last year. They kept their relationship secret from the rest of the crew. "Carol, we have a distress call from the

London. There is an officer on the Command Station named Michael Green. He is a Lieutenant Commander and is the chief of the London's Computer section. He says it is urgent."

"Put him on three dimensional view," Ruiz ordered and sat in her Captain's chair.

The image of Lieutenant Commander Michael Green appeared before Ruiz and her officers. "Ah, Captain, thank the Stars!" His uniform was completely gold color, other than the spatters of blood that Ruiz and Sikorsky immediately noticed.

"Mister Green, what seems to be the emergency?" Ruiz asked.

"Captain, I do not know how to tell you this." Green began. "It is horrible."

"Just start from the beginning." Ruiz told him.

Green nodded, "About three hours ago we were attacked."

Ruiz looked to her First Officer, "Any evidence of hull damage?"

Sikorsky shook his head as he performed a scan on the opposite Science vessel. "None. The London looks fit for service."

"No, that is not what I meant," Green continued. "We were not attacked in the conventional manner. Three hours ago we were all knocked out, the entire crew, by some high frequency sound wave. It is a weapon we have never faced before."

"But you are okay now?" Ruiz stood up; Green's story now had her full attention.

"No ma'am, we are not okay," Green said sadly. "Doctor Rose Scola-Danforth, our lead doctor has the bodies in the medical level."

"Bodies?" Ruiz shot back. "There are casualties? How many?"

"Seven dead," Green told her. "All seven were in the top ranking positions. I am now the ranking officer on the London."

"Seven? How?" Ruiz demanded and was pacing back and forth. She was stunned by the news. The Captain of the London had been a personal friend to Ruiz; they had attended the Academy together and had remained good friends over the many years.

"They were, I mean it seems like the seven were stabbed in the heart with a short sword and then decapitated." Green reported with disgust in his voice.

"Decapitated?" Ruiz stopped pacing. "Who were the seven victims?"

"Captain, Sierra Sikorsky, the First Officer, Commander Michael Murdock, Commander and chief of security, Patricia Welker, our chief pilot, Lieutenant Commander Garvin Urbanczyk, our Engineering Commander, Curtis Tsukifuji, our weapons commander, Lieutenant Commander Lea Ming, and our commander of Explorations and Geology, Lieutenant Alfredrick Goodman. All dead and all decapitated."

"An inside job?" Ruiz suggested out loud. She looked at her officers. "Any clues as to why those seven and not the rest of you?"

"The seven victims only had two things in common," Green told her. "All seven are officers on the London and all seven are descendants of the Glorious Leader, Vladimir Sikorsky."

"Are there any other descendants of the Glorious Leader on the London other than the seven dead?" Ruiz asked quickly.

"No ma'am," Green responded. "They were the only seven Royal Family members we had on our ship."

"Damn," Ruiz said under her breath. It was an outright attack on the Royal Family, which was considered treason by Empire Law. The perpetrators, if apprehended, just bought themselves an automatic death sentence. "Mister Green, we need to rendezvous and pool our investigative resources. At best speed the Colorado can be at your location in two days. Until we rendezvous with your ship, continue to have your security investigators look into every possibility. I recommend you look at your crew members. See if any of them have a bone to pick against the Sikorsky family."

"Yes ma'am. I will see you in two hours."

The image of Green disappeared.

Ruiz turned her attention to Marvin Sikorsky, "You are part of the Royal Family."

"Yes, Carol, I am."

"How many of your cousins or siblings are on board the Colorado?" Ruiz asked.

"Thirteen of us," Sikorsky said quickly.

"I want all thirteen, you included, to have a Marine Corps guard with you at all times," Ruiz instructed.

"You don't think that is a bit excessive do you?" Marvin Sikorsky asked softly. "All of us, the thirteen that are part of the Royal Family, are officers. We hold top command positions on the Colorado. We don't need extra security."

"That is an order," Ruiz said firmly. "It sounds to me like someone on the London, or someone that boarded the London, has a serious grudge match against your family. I am not taking any chances. Get the guards on the others and for yourself. Do it now."

"Yes ma'am," Sikorsky nodded.

"Captain!"

Second Lieutenant Hillary Parsons interjected from the communication station to the left of Ruiz. Her gold uniform signified that she was a part of the Science Branch in the Space Command.

"Yes, Hillary?"

"Ma'am, I am detecting a strange noise, it is a frequency setting that I cannot compare to any form of communication that we have been exposed to in the past." Parsons told Ruiz.

"Where?"

"Inside the ship," Parsons said, her eyes narrowing as

she pressed buttons on her keyboard and she was watching her monitor at the same time. "It is on every level of the Colorado, from an unknown origin."

Ruiz and the others watched as Parsons began to run her fingers over her keyboards to find out what the source was. As Parsons worked the entire crew heard a rising noise, like a roar of a massive snow storm. The sound rose in pitch and it caused pain on each and every crew member.

Ruiz screamed and placed her hands over her ears. All of the other occupants of the Colorado had the same reaction. The entire crew of eight hundred men and women and their children on the Colorado fell to their knees, holding their ears. Mercifully, they were all unconscious within ten seconds. The shrieking sound stopped. There was silence all over the ship.

No one moved.

That is until three figures materialized out of thin air on the Command Station. The three were wearing black leather uniforms, black boots and grey hoods. The three had with them short swords and large black back packs over their shoulders. One of the three walked over to the security station and pressed several buttons, turning off all recording devices and security measures on the ship.

"It is done," Drayton Love-Easter #7 said as he removed his hood.

Penelope Rosenburg and Charles Bennington also revealed themselves, pulling their hoods away from their faces.

Penelope saw the prone figure of Marvin Sikorsky on the floor. She walked over to him and lifted the man up. She sat him in the chair designated for the executive officer.

"This is one of the thirteen," Penelope said softly. "He was a good friend of my brother David."

Bennington and Love-Easter's Replicant began propping up several other unconscious crew members. Only Hillary Parsons, Captain Carol Ruiz and the two Marines were left lying on the floor. The rest were in chairs, with their heads leaning over the back.

Penelope pulled out her short sword and stabbed the unconscious Marvin Sikorsky through the heart. She pulled the sword out with a jerk and then arched her arms back and swung her sword with all her might, severing Sikorsky's head from his body. The body was spilling blood all over the chair and the metallic floor of Level One. Penelope collected the head of Marvin Sikorsky and placed it into her large back pack.

"Kill the other twelve quickly," Penelope said without mercy. "We have two other science ships to hit within the next few hours. When the Glorious Leader hears of this, he will know that we are out here. He will stop at nothing to find us."

Using their swords, Bennington and Love-Easter #7 began stabbing the Sikorsky family members in the heart and cutting off their heads.

Bennington had never been a willing participant in cold blooded murder. But, due to the evidence that Rosenburg had shown him and the past events that he had observed, he elected to participate in the acts of treason.

A war is coming, Penelope Rosenburg had once promised Sean Collins.

Indeed it was. Soon the entire eight solar systems would be in the middle of the bloodiest Revolution in the history of mankind.